LOLA IS
MISSING

LOLA IS MISSING

Alison James

bookouture

Published by Bookouture in 2017

An imprint of StoryFire Ltd.
Carmelite House
50 Victoria Embankment
London EC4Y 0DZ

www.bookouture.com

ISBN: 978-1-78681-550-7
eBook ISBN: 978-1-78681-331-2

Previously published as *The Lying Kind* (ISBN 978-1-78681-332-9)

For my children, who inspire me every day.

PROLOGUE

She stirred and stretched as the light in the room changed. Then she opened her eyes. The shiny light from the landing made everything look a different colour, and played a shadow across the wall to her right. It was this that came into her head, waking her.

There was someone in the room.

At the exact second she opened her mouth to speak, a hand clamped down hard over it, silencing her.

'Keep still. Don't move.'

She wriggled anyway, trying to free herself.

'If you keep still, it won't hurt.'

There was a sharp stab, a pinching sensation. It was like when the nurse put the big needle in her arm at school.. It hurt more than that time, though.

'Keep still!'

She struggled. And then the world went first fuzzy, then black.

PART ONE

Not every puzzle is intended to be solved. Some are in place to test your limits. Others are, in fact, not puzzles at all…

Vera Nazarian, The Perpetual Calendar of Inspiration

CHAPTER ONE

Chirrup. Chirrup. Chirrup. Chirr—

You were supposed to sleep more lightly as you grew older, Rachel thought her hand groping to shut off the chorus of crickets on her phone's alarm, but at 6.15 a.m. most mornings she still managed to be fast asleep. Deeply asleep. She lay on her back for a few seconds, then hopped off the bed and performed some tentative stretches, switching on the TV news.

An inset picture of a small fair-haired child flashed up on the screen, zooming in on her face before cutting back to the newsreader.

'Surrey Police have released a statement in reaction to criticism about scaling back their operation into the search for missing six-year-old Lola Jade Harper. Detective Chief Inspector Clive Manners said: "We are keeping our existing lines of enquiry open, and are reaching out to other agencies with a view to establishing new leads." Lola Jade disappeared from her mother's home in Eastwell, Surrey, at the beginning of May.'

Rachel switched off the TV, pulled on her Lycra running gear and took the lift to the ground floor of the converted cotton warehouse, heading out into the still-dozing streets of Bermondsey. A misty autumn morning was unfurling with the promise of a warm late-October day to come. Rachel pounded the pavements of South East London to the strains of Arcade Fire and The Killers. The damp in the air had left the cobbles near Tower Bridge covered in a greasy film, and as she slowed to change direction, she slipped, twisting her right knee awkwardly. The pain made her wince, but with plenty of adrenaline still coursing through her veins, she decided to push on and run back to her flat.

It was only after she had she showered and her body was cooling that her kneecap started to hurt in earnest. Rachel ignored it, changing into her preferred work uniform of black trousers and a plain white shirt. Standard plain-clothes-police-woman garb. She twisted her blonde hair into a ponytail, applied some subtle make-up and viewed her reflection in the mirror. The woman looking back at her was tall, muscular but narrow-waisted (and a little too flat-chested, in her own opinion), nose a bit on the long side (but straight at least), large hazel eyes, decently shaped eyebrows. There were a few faint lines at the corners of her eyes, but otherwise she could still pass for thirty in sympathetic lighting.

'Could be worse,' she told herself, then grabbed her bag and car keys. At 8.35, she parked her car in the underground car park of the National Crime Agency's headquarters near the South Bank and limped into the office.

'All right, douchebag?' Her detective sergeant, Mark Brickall, greeted her cheerily as she reached her desk. He seemed to be in good spirits today. When it came to Brickall, you never knew what you were going to get: he was distinctly moody. And consistently rude, whether the mood was good or bad. They had first worked together for a year in Serious Organised Crime after Rachel transferred there from the Metropolitan Police, then met up again when they both joined Interpol, before it became absorbed by the National Crime Agency. She liked him and, more importantly, she trusted him, despite his occasional flakiness. He was too short to be her type – at five feet nine inches; she preferred men to be at least six feet tall – but just about attractive enough for a joshing sub-flirtation to simmer between them.

'Hold on!' he said as she lowered herself onto her chair with painful slowness. 'Don't bother sitting down. The boss wants to see us. Now.'

Deputy Chief Constable Nigel Patten was the director of Major Crime Investigative Support, referred to as MCIS. The unit existed to provide expertise and advice to other law-enforcement agencies investigating complex crimes. Both Rachel and Brickall acted as international liaison officers on MCIS, remaining stationed in London after Interpol's main UK operation had transferred to the north-west of England.

Sighing, Rachel dropped her bag, grabbed a notepad and followed Brickall to Patten's office. Although he was well into middle age, he had recently become a father again with his second wife. He was a careworn, prematurely bald man, who had two teenage children with Wife No. 1 and had recently acquired a third courtesy of the much younger Wife No. 2. Reading his screen upside down from where she stood in front of his desk, Rachel could see that he was online shopping for sporty-looking baby buggies. Danielle Patten, from what Rachel had seen of her at departmental functions, was exactly the sort to jog behind an all-terrain buggy containing a wobbling newborn, while simultaneously checking her emails. She was a sinewy, fake-tanned marketing executive with perfectly groomed nails and hair and zero sense of humour.

'DI Prince… DS Brickall… sit down, sit down.'

They sat.

'Lola Jade Harper. You are familiar?'

How could they not be? It was no coincidence that the case had been on the news that morning: Lola Jade Harper was still the UK's most high-profile missing child. A six-year-old girl who had been taken from her bedroom in a Home Counties suburb one spring night and no one had seen her since. A child at the centre of a bitter custody battle, whose father had continued to protest his innocence of any involvement. The tabloids had feasted on every detail for the first few months, but now it seemed that public interest was starting to wane.

'Surrey Police are at a bit of a dead end,' Patten affirmed. 'But they've asked for our support following a recent development, which has not yet been disclosed to the press.'

'Which is?'

'Surrey CID were working on the premise that the child was targeted and snatched to order. Neighbours' witness testimony supports this, as does the mother's – to an extent. But in the past few days, the girl's father, Gavin Harper, has completely disappeared. As you probably know, the parents are estranged, but Family Liaison Officers were in frequent touch with them both. Only now Harper's no longer at his home address, and his family are claiming not to know where he is.' Patten raised his eyebrows to indicate scepticism. 'So, given there have been some reported sightings of Lola Jade abroad, and Gavin Harper has for no apparent reason done a bunk, the hope is that a couple of support officers with international experience, such as your talented selves, might be able to help. They went to Scotland Yard, but since it's not a Met-based case, Scotland Yard pushed it our way.' He smiled, in what he clearly hoped was a disarming fashion.

'Lazy Met tossers don't want the work, as per…' Brickall caught sight of his superior officer's face and fell silent. Patten pushed the hefty case file towards them. 'I'll leave it to the two of you to get yourselves up to speed as soon as possible, and advise me on a list of actions. Obviously the media interest has been intense, so you'll have to think carefully about what information you release, and work closely with the press office. And you'll need to liaise with CEOP as well.' Patten trotted out the acronym for the NCA's Child Exploitation and Online Protection command.

'You'll enjoy that, then, Prince,' smirked Brickall as they returned to the office.

'What's that?' Rachel was lost in thought: specifically, that the last thing she wanted to get involved in was a case that was simultaneously cold and high-profile.

'Liaising' – he made quotation marks round the word – 'with CEOP. That guy you fancy works there. Deacon.'

'Giles Denton. And I don't bloody fancy him,' insisted Rachel, who absolutely did.

'Whatever…' Brickall glanced at Rachel's awkward gait. 'You're looking even more of a spaz than normal: why the gammy leg?'

He loved to draw attention to Rachel's occasional fits of clumsiness. She didn't correct his insubordinate tone; she would never hear the end of it if she did. Instead, like the parent of a recalcitrant toddler, she picked her battles and only pulled rank when it was strictly necessary.

'Twisted it running. It's no big deal.' She spoke with more confidence than she felt. The pain was building still further, and she was glad to sit down at her desk and take the weight off it. 'What's the latest update on the file?'

He flicked through the top few pages. 'Couple of muggles phoning in with alleged sightings. Same shit; different day.'

Brickall shrugged, and slid the folder in her direction.

Rachel started turning the pages, scan-reading as much of the information as she could. Case activity was cooling, and Surrey Police CID had only made two new entries in the past month: a report that Lola Jade had been sighted on Fairfield Road, Eastwell, being 'led away' by a dark-haired woman; and a child saying they'd seen Lola in the playground of their school. As Brickall had said; same old. Dozens of similar tip-offs had been followed up and still no Lola Jade. But someone knew what had happened to her. Someone out there knew. Their not-so-insignificant task was to work out who that was.

After she had finished reading, she passed the file to Brickall again, but he declined to read it. 'Sodding waste of time if you ask me. The kid'll be dead.'

'Either way, we still need to find her. So what d'you reckon we do first?' Rachel reached discreetly into her bag and fished out some painkillers, downing them with water.

Brickall shrugged.

She gave him a hard look, suppressing irritation. 'Given the golden rule of detecting is to start with the closest relationships and work outwards, then it's a no-brainer. We talk to the mother. Let's aim to go down there tomorrow.'

'Okay, boss.' He gave a mock salute.

'And while you're in subordinate mode, go and fetch me some coffee.'

Brickall opened his mouth to protest, but she pointed to her knee and he relented, trudging off in the direction of the coffee machine. While he was gone, Rachel went into the Ladies' and carefully inched up her trouser leg. Her knee was swollen and throbbing, and the pain was intense. She had little time for the medical profession and hadn't been near a doctor in years. In fact, she made a point of avoiding them at all costs. But she was not going to be able to ignore this. Damn.

'You coming to the party tonight?' Brickall enquired as he put the coffee down on her desk, slopping it over her paperwork.

'Party?'

'Hayley Snowden's leaving do. In one of the conference rooms.' Hayley was a member of the civilian Operations Support staff, about to transfer to a position in the Queen Street offices.

'Yeah, maybe.' Rachel hauled herself to her feet. 'But right now I need to go and get this bloody knee sorted out.'

A private clinic near London Bridge obligingly offered Rachel an appointment that lunchtime. Being able to flash a warrant card helped, as did the health insurance policy for serving police officers. Her right leg was X-rayed, then she was sent to a different floor for an MRI. Finally, after waiting around forty minutes, she was seen by an orthopaedic specialist.

'You say you're a runner, Ms Prince?' he asked, looking at the images on his computer screen rather than at her face.

'Yes. I was running this morning when it suddenly started hurting.'

'Did you stop abruptly, or change direction?'

Rachel nodded.

'Thought so…' He pointed to a white blur on the screen. 'You've torn your ACL. Anterior cruciate ligament. It's a very common sports injury, especially amongst women. And you're thirty-nine,' he told her, as though she didn't know her own age. 'Your joints are not as resilient as they were twenty years ago.'

Rachel ignored this. 'Can it be fixed?'

He turned from the screen and made eye contact at last. 'In severe cases, the ligament can be replaced. With a tissue graft.' He met Rachel's dismay with a professional smile. 'I don't think this is one of those cases. It should repair on its own, eventually. But you'll need to rest it as much as possible.'

'Will I be able to run?' Rachel asked, although she knew what the answer would be.

'No exercise involving running, not for at least three months.'

'Three?' Rachel was horrified. Running was like breathing to her.

'Look; I'll see you again in six weeks and we'll assess where we are then, and I'm also going to refer you for some physio. In the meantime, ice it and use painkillers as needed. I'll write you a script for some tramadol. If you need me to, I'll sign you off work.'

Rachel shook her head firmly. 'Out of the question, I'm afraid.'

'We usually recommend crutches for a few days.'

'Also out of the question.'

*

By the time she had picked up her prescription from the pharmacy it was late afternoon, and there was little point returning to the office. Instead Rachel went back to her flat and changed into jeans, heels and a floaty green top, taking down her customary ponytail and amping up the make-up. An hour later, she was in the first-floor function room in the NCA's Tinworth Street headquarters, surrounded by balloons and a foil banner that read: '*Sorry You're Leaving!*'. A paper-covered trestle was laid out with boxes of cheap wine, plastic glasses and an assortment of finger foods.

'You look nice, Rache.' Margaret, another of the unit's admin staff, enveloped her in an embrace that sloshed tepid white wine down the back of Rachel's top. 'Doesn't she, Hale?'

'She does,' agreed Hayley, resplendent in false eyelashes, mini dress and skyscraper heels. 'You look fantastic when you make a bit of an effort. Ever so glam.'

'You might even pull,' added Brickall, with his mouth full of cocktail sausage. 'Though sadly there's no one from Child Protection here tonight.'

'Ooh,' breathed Margaret. 'Gossip! Do tell!'

Nigel Patten loomed into view, red wine in one hand, fun-size Scotch egg in the other. He cleared his throat and brushed breadcrumbs from his chin.

'Hayley, now might be the time for me to say a few words?'

'Might be the time for a sharp exit, more like,' muttered Brickall. Rachel, struggling to balance her injured leg in heels, staggered slightly. Brickall caught her. 'Easy tiger! Bit early for the falling-down-pissed act.'

As she leaned on his shoulder and righted herself, her phone rang. She grabbed it quickly and held it at eye level to cut off the call before it interrupted Patten's speech.

The call was followed within seconds by a text from the same unrecognised number.

This is Stuart Ritchie.

Rachel jumped so violently in shock that she dropped the phone at Brickall's feet. He bent to pick it up, just as it stopped ringing, squinting at the text message.

'You all right, DI Prince? You look like you've seen a fucking ghost.'

'I'm fine.' She shoved the phone to the bottom of her bag. 'My knee's killing me, that's all. See you tomorrow.'

Before he could say anything else, she grabbed her coat from the chair where she'd left it and hurried out of the room and down the stairs, the four words still jangling in her brain.

This is Stuart Ritchie…

Outside the building, she leaned against the wall for a few minutes, catching her breath and waiting for the shock wave to subside.

CHAPTER TWO

There was no going for a run this morning, Rachel reflected miserably when she woke up. Her knee was still swollen, and so stiff that she hobbled around her stylish kitchen – all exposed brick and brushed-steel finishes – like a pensioner. Yet she managed to jump every time her phone buzzed.

Exercise. She needed exercise to settle her jangling brain; if not running, then something else. She grabbed a swimsuit and a towel and drove to the nearest municipal sports centre to join the early-morning lap swim in the chlorine tank that posed as a swimming pool. I'll just do ten lengths and then get out, she told herself. She ended up doing forty, and her head felt better for it. The mindlessness of it was soothing, but her knee joint was now screaming, and she'd probably done even more damage to it.

On her way out of the building, she stopped and peered through the glass panel in the gym door, even though she was emphatically not the gym-going type. Everyone looked so busy and at the same time so vacuous, churning the pedals on their static bikes. The gym bunnies seemed universally bored, with the exception of the ones using the boxing punchbag hanging from a bracket in the far corner of the room. Now that *did* look like fun. A lot more fun than the physio her consultant had suggested. Rachel watched them for a couple of minutes before heading back to the car park.

*

As she sat down at her desk, wincing with the effort, her phone pinged. Hesitating, she checked the screen, wondering if it would be Stuart again. But it was a message from Mark Brickall.

Sorry, got hauled into Bogdhani case conference. Will have to do the Harper mother thing tomorrow.

The Bogdhani case was an Albanian drug-trafficking ring he had been investigating for the past three months. Sighing, Rachel composed a reply. Normally she would carry out an initial interview alone, but she was fairly confident that her knee would not permit her to drive to Surrey and back in heavy stop-start traffic.

Any excuse, you lazy git. ☺ I'll get reading, and see what my Spidey sense tells me.

She hobbled to fetch coffee, then picked up the Lola Jade Harper file and started to read through it again. Looking for detail this time, and for whatever lay between the lines. Details were her detective lifeblood: the stuff that spoke to her instincts. Things other people didn't even notice.

She began with the initial missing person's report, filled out on a standard pro forma dated 10 May 2016. It gave the complainant's details as Michelle Harper, 57 Willow Way, Eastwell. Lola Jade was described as being 48 inches tall and weighing 58 pounds. Her hair was blonde, her eyes hazel and her skin fair. She had no distinguishing marks, but her ears were pierced. There were no significant medical conditions, and her blood group was O positive. She was left-handed. When last seen, at 9.15 p.m. on 9 May, she had been wearing lilac pyjama bottoms and a pyjama top printed with pink and purple butterflies. A photocopy of her birth certificate had been appended to the report, along with a copy of her registration as a pupil at St Mary's C of E Primary, Eastwell.

The 'Further Remarks' box stated that Michelle Harper had phoned the emergency services at 6.47 a.m. on Thursday 10 May. She had gone into the child's bedroom to wake her for school and found the room empty. Lola Jade had no siblings, and her mother was currently living apart from her estranged husband.

Rachel put in her headphones and listened to the 999 call.

'Operator: which service do you require?'
'Police, please.'
'Hello, you're through to the police.'
'My name's Michelle Harper. My daughter's gone… she's been abducted.'
'And how old is your daughter?'
'She's six, nearly seven.'
'Okay, can you tell me exactly what's happened?'
'Right, I put her to bed as normal last night, but when I went in to wake her this morning, she wasn't there. The bed was empty and the French window downstairs was open.'
'And you're sure she's not in the house: you've looked for her?'
'Of course I have, I've looked everywhere. Inside and outside.'
'Are you at the property now, Michelle?'
'Yes: where else would I be?'
'Okay, I want you to give me the address, and an officer will be with you as soon as possible.'
'How long?'
'As soon as we can get a unit there; I'm contacting dispatch now.'
'Can't you give me a rough idea?'
'I don't have an exact time, but it should be less than half an hour.'

Rachel listened again, then a third time. It was unusual, she thought, that Michelle had stated straight away that Lola Jade had been abducted. Not that she couldn't locate her, or that she had disappeared, but that she had been abducted. Past publicity surrounding missing child cases had probably put that word into her mouth. That and watching too many TV crime shows. Her tone was tense rather than hysterical. But then Rachel knew from her years as a beat officer that there was a huge spectrum of reactions to grief and trauma.

She looked at the photo of Lola Jade that Michelle Harper had supplied when the missing person's report was filed. It was a standard school headshot, and showed a plain, stolid child with long, mousy-blonde hair, staring down the lens with a blank expression.

In a more detailed statement given after Lola Jade had been missing for two days, Michelle outlined how she had put Lola to bed as usual the evening before she disappeared, and checked on her once after she had fallen asleep and before Michelle herself went to bed, sometime around 9 p.m. There was no one in the house but Michelle, her daughter, and the family Pomeranian, the unfortunately named Diva.

'I went to bed at 10.30 p.m. At around 3 a.m. I was woken by a loud banging noise followed by a scuffle coming from outside somewhere. I opened my curtains and looked out of the window. I saw a man standing there a few yards from the front of the house. He was average height and build and wearing a hoodie pulled up. I couldn't see his face. I got back into bed for around ten minutes, then looked out of the window a second time. The man that I had seen was gone. It was quiet, so I got back into bed and fell asleep until 6.30.'

Elsewhere in the file, among the statements taken from neighbours during the door-to-door, a Mr Steven Arnold had said that he had seen two men, one of whom was short and of slight build, the other bigger, hanging around the close earlier on the 9th. He described their demeanour as 'shifty'. Another neighbour, Anna Wozniak, reported seeing a white Transit van with its engine idling, parked around the corner from Willow Way. It was too dark for her to read the number plate.

Michelle's husband, a self-employed builder called Gavin Harper, had been cooperative when police first spoke to him, but adamant he knew nothing about his daughter's disappearance. But fast-forward a few months and he had vanished, with no one – including his own family – apparently knowing where he was. If they were telling the truth. The behaviour seemed too unusual to be mere coincidence. Yes, after such a stressful period anyone might want to take off for a while; gain some distance, clear their head. But not without telling their nearest and dearest where they were going.

Questioned further, Michelle had admitted that Gavin could be aggressive, although he had no criminal record other than petty motoring offences. There was a statement from Sonia Kenny, Michelle's mother, corroborating her daughter's claims but being vague about the detail; only able to offer that Gavin had shouted and thrown stuff on a few occasions, and after one argument – she couldn't remember exactly when – he had pulled Michelle's hair so hard that some of it had come out in his hand. From the look of Michelle's elaborate extensions and hairpieces, that could easily happen, Rachel concluded.

After standing up and limping around the perimeter of the office to ease the stiffness in her right leg, Rachel read through the forensic report and looked at photos the SOC officer had taken at Michelle's house. Lola Jade's bedroom was an explosion of sugar pink and stuffed toys, exactly as you would expect for a girl her age. There were DVDs on a shelf on the wall, a small TV and a CD player, but no books in evidence. The bed was slightly rumpled, the duvet in its *Frozen*-themed cover folded back. On the rug next to the bed was a white stuffed bear wearing a garish pink Lurex dress that Michelle had said was Lola Jade's favourite. Apparently she'd never go anywhere without her Katy Bear – named after Katy Perry. Tiny spots of blood were found on the pillowcase, and this was confirmed to be Lola's when compared with the DNA from her toothbrush, although puzzlingly the amount was not enough to be consistent with a significant injury.

There was also a trace amount of blood found on the rug and, significantly, DNA that was a familial match to Lola Jade but did not belong to Michelle. Following a search of the property where Gavin Harper had been living, detailed in a statement by a DS Rajavi, a second forensic report confirmed that the DNA in Lola Jade's bedroom belonged to her father. This made Rachel's hackles rise, and she highlighted the relevant paragraph in the file.

Without reading further, she put in her headphones and played the video file of the original press conference held by Surrey Police. Michelle Harper sat between a heavy-set woman with dyed pink hair and DCI Clive Manners, Katy Bear clutched on her lap, shifting in her seat. Shock had finally set in, and her demeanour was quite different to that of the assertive woman on the 999 call. She seemed shrunken, cowed. But not pale, thanks to the copious fake tan and bronzer she was wearing. Her fingers were tipped with acrylic talons, and her eyelashes were as heavy as a pantomime cow's. She dabbed at her eyes with a tissue and turned frequently to glance at the pink-haired woman for reassurance. Checking through the transcript and some of the press cuttings, Rachel discerned that Pink Hair was Michelle's older sister, Lisa Urquhart, who lived in the Eastwell area.

DCI Manners had emphasised how his force were doing everything in their power to find Lola Jade, and appealed to people in the local area to come forward with information. 'No matter how unimportant it may seem to you, it could help the investigation.' The usual guff.

Then Michelle herself spoke. She did not make eye contact with the camera, choosing instead to hang her head and look down at her lap. 'Whoever's got Lola Jade… please, please, just bring her back. That's all I want. I just want her brought back safe.' She rubbed her eyes with the tissue, then Clive Manners shepherded her away with his hand on the small of her back.

There was also footage of an interview with Michelle filmed in her home a few days later by the local independent news channel. Her make-up was freshly done, her extensions artfully arranged, and she seemed calmer. Rachel paused the VT and scrutinised the living room. Michelle was seated on a squashy cream leather sofa and there was a matching cream armchair to her right. In between the two was a gilt side table with an ashtray containing a few lipstick-stained butts and the ash from the cigarette that Michelle was smoking during the interview. The wall behind her was covered with a montage of family photographs – mostly babies and toddlers – and its centrepiece was a huge gilt-framed studio portrait of Lola Jade aged about three or four, wearing a shiny white dress that wouldn't have looked out of place at a gypsy wedding, and leaning awkwardly on a plastic Doric column in a white satin landscape.

Rachel pressed play.

'… Lola's my absolute world. She means everything to me.'

She's going to use the P word, thought Rachel. Women like her couldn't help themselves.

'She's just my little princess. My angel. Princess Angel, that's what I call her.' Michelle dragged greedily on her cigarette, her fingers trembling. In only a few days, she had lost some weight. The not-quite-pretty face was drawn, and her clothes were loose.

'I know this must be terribly hard for you,' the interviewer said, dropping her voice to the hush of professional concern.

Michelle dropped her face into her hands to cover her sobs, sending a flutter of ash onto the carpet. 'I just want things back to how they were, you know? No one can be expected to cope with this, it's literally like being in a nightmare.'

She gathered herself, and went on to talk about how a group of friends and neighbours had been organising their own search efforts locally, working through brownfield sites and open heathland. Someone else had started a 'Find Lola Jade' page on Facebook. Rachel booted up her desktop monitor and immediately found the page online. The profile picture was the same studio shot of Lola in the white satin dress. The most recent post was by someone called Tanya Dickerson.

Our Lola Jade still missing, even though Surrey Police have randomly decided to downgrade the case!!!!

So wrong, babes! a Stacey Fisher had commented.

There was a link to a JustGiving page. Rachel clicked on it. The total raised stood at £47,963.

Returning to the paper file, she flicked through the sheaf of witness statements taken during the investigation. They represented a lot of footwork on the part of uniformed officers, but had thrown up precisely zero new lines of enquiry. Nobody had seen or heard anything unusual at 57 Willow Way the night that Lola Jade disappeared, and family, friends and neighbours all claimed they knew nothing. A brick wall of silence, despite the substantial reward offered by one of the tabloid newspapers.

Rachel flicked back to the description of the hoodie man that Michelle claimed to have seen, and sat staring at that paragraph for a few seconds. Then she phoned the main switchboard for Surrey Police and asked to speak to DS Leila Rajavi.

'Did you ever meet Gavin Harper?' Rachel asked, once she had introduced herself and the professional niceties had been dealt with.

'Yes. I did the first interview with him.'

'And his alibi for the night Lola Jade went missing?'

'Said he was at home in his flat all night. There was no one who could corroborate either way. Also…'

'Go on.'

'Well, Gavin Harper does have form. He once failed to return his daughter after a routine access visit. Couldn't be contacted for around twenty-four hours.'

'A bit of a dry run, perhaps? Testing the waters?'

'In retrospect, it does look significant, yes.'

Rachel absorbed this. 'And how would you describe him? Physically.'

'Hmm, hard to say. Ordinary-looking… average height, average build.'

In other words, exactly like the man on the street the night Lola Jade was taken.

The second she had hung up, Rachel's mobile rang in her hand. An unknown number. The same unknown number. Stuart's.

She snatched it off her desk, switched it off and hurled it into her bag as though it was a grenade. Then, for a few moments, she sat with her head dropped and her face buried in her hands, telling herself that if she didn't look, it wasn't happening.

CHAPTER THREE

'So who is he?'

Brickall hit the horn of the pool car hard as he negotiated one of London's overused A roads, attempting to head south. It was morning rush hour, and the lanes were snarled with buses, vans, bikes and jaywalking pedestrian commuters.

Rachel, right leg propped awkwardly in the angle of the seat well, pretended she hadn't heard him. Instead she reached into her bag and pulled out a blister pack of tramadol, swallowing a couple with the cooling takeout coffee in the cup holder.

Brickall persisted. 'Whoever phoned you at the party – who is he? Or she. I mean, your face! You went white as a sheet.'

'No one.'

'Must be someone if you were that freaked out.'

Rachel gave a wry smile. 'What are you – a detective?'

He cruised to a stop at another of the interminable traffic lights and turned to face her. 'So?'

She kept her head turned away. 'Just an ex, that's all.'

Brickall raised his eyebrows slightly, but before he could ask any more questions, Rachel had inserted her headphones and closed her eyes.

Willow Way was one of a handful of roads on a private estate to the south-west of the dormitory suburb of Eastwell. They were all named after trees – Birch Close, Ash Crescent, Sycamore Drive – and when construction had taken place in the early nineties an abundance of trees had been planted to reinforce the point. The buildings now looked dated, but the trees had matured to give an air of suburban comfort. They were modest houses in linked pairs and small terraces – blocks of three or four homes aimed at young families and junior executives. Tidy, but not aspirational. Brickall parked outside number 57, and they both took in the property before getting out of the car. The front garden was laid to lawn, and it looked as though it could do with the attentions of a mower. Most of the neighbours had added hanging baskets and large pot plants; Michelle had none. There were no children's bicycles and toys as there were in front of the other houses. But the house seemed well maintained, and the windows were clean. They walked up the path and rang the bell.

Silence. No dog barking, no footsteps, no sound of a radio or television. Rachel rang again, then peered through the window into the open-plan living and dining room. No signs of life, no lights on. In the kitchen, which she could just glimpse through the arch at the back of the room, the countertops were clear of any of the detritus of daily life.

'What d'you reckon?' asked Brickall.

'Looks like she's gone away. Given what's happened, I can't really blame her.'

'Would've been nice to know that before sitting in traffic for over an hour…' Brickall vaulted over the side gate and disappeared towards the back of the house, re-emerging a couple of minutes later shaking his head. 'Nada. Not a fucking sausage.'

'Good job I brought the file with me, then. Her number will be on the contact sheet: I'll phone her.'

As soon as the call was picked up, she recognised the defensive tone from the emergency call.

'Who is this?'

'Michelle, this is DI Prince, from Investigation Support at the National Crime Agency in London. I'm at your address, hoping to have a quick word. Are you around?'

There was a brief pause.

'I'm out shopping.'

'When will you be back?'

'No idea. An hour maybe?'

After telling Michelle that they would wait, Rachel and Brickall parked at the nearest parade of shops and found a café. Brickall ordered his usual: a full English with the works. Rachel took the file out of her bag and continued reading it.

'Just double-checking for more info on the father,' she told Brickall as he dipped a sausage into egg yolk. 'Want to get the facts before we ask Michelle about him.'

Gavin Harper had been named as a person of interest at the start of the enquiry into Lola Jade's disappearance. After her phone call to Leila, Rachel had checked the PNC nominals file, and sure enough, earlier that year he had been cautioned for violating a court order relating to shared custody, following an allegation made by Michelle Harper.

'He's got to be the most likely culprit,' she told Brickall. 'Gavin Harper. He tried to snatch her before, apparently.'

'Divorced dad syndrome,' Brickall observed through his mouthful of fried food. 'Using the kid to get at the ex. It's classic stuff.'

Other than that, there were just a few traffic offences and a very minor Public Order Offence when Gavin Harper was a teenager. According to the file, a blue notice had been issued on Interpol's database, requesting any information about his whereabouts, along with the statutory yellow notice aimed at locating missing minors. If he had left the country after the notice had been issued, then his name would automatically have been flagged up at border crossings, airports and anywhere else where passports would have been checked. The notices had been issued on the morning of 20 October after local officers had attempted to re-interview Gavin Harper and been unable to find him. If he had been travelling with his daughter, the chances of no one spotting them and reporting it were virtually zero. Not now that Lola's face had been on the front page of the papers for months.

Among the raft of paper statements was an alleged sighting of Lola Jade in Brussels, and another in Portugal, both around a week after her disappearance. Officers from the Surrey force had flown to Belgium and to the Algarve to investigate these claims, but had drawn a blank. A few more such sightings were reported in the weeks that followed, but it had been decided that they would only be actively pursued if substantial evidence came to light. It did not.

Local sightings had also failed to throw up any concrete leads. Sniffer dogs and divers in the local quarries and reservoirs had drawn a blank. After twenty days with no sightings of the child, a cadaver dog had been through Lola Jade's home, but found no evidence that she had died there. Inevitably, as weeks had turned into months, Lola was demoted from front-page headlines to the inside pages as the fickle public started to move on.

When Brickall had finished his breakfast and they had both drunk their coffee, they returned to Willow Way. This time, there was a white BMW hatchback parked outside the house. The front door opened after the first ring. When Brickall held up his warrant card, the woman pulled the door fully open and stepped aside, indicating that they should come in. They followed her into the living room.

Michelle Harper wore tight white jeans and a T-shirt with a designer logo. Her toenails and fingernails were immaculately painted, and her hair – no longer blonde but a nut brown – looked as though it had recently been professionally blow-dried.

She did not offer tea or coffee, but indicated that the two of them should sit on the armchairs that matched the cream sofa. The room was tidy to the point of sterility, and although photos of Lola Jade still graced the wall, there were few other reminders of her in the room.

'I'm DI Rachel Prince, and this is DS Mark Brickall. As I told you over the phone, we're from the National Crime Agency. We—'

'National?' Michelle interrupted, 'So you're nothing to do with Surrey Police?'

'No. I'm… we're the investigation support team reviewing your daughter's case.'

'So Surrey Police aren't bothering with Lola any more?' Michelle blinked hard, reached for a tissue and gave her eyes a quick wipe. 'Sorry, can't help getting emotional when I talk about her.' She pulled a packet of cigarettes from her bag, lit one and then cast around for an ashtray. Unable to find one, she took the plastic saucer from under a fake orchid and used that to collect the accumulating ash. 'They've given up on her: I knew it.'

'It's not that they're not bothering. It doesn't work like that,' Brickall explained. 'They'll pass on any new leads, of course, and we'll liaise with them in return. But they haven't got officers out there looking for her at the moment, no.'

Michelle's face wore an unreadable expression. 'They reckon she's dead. It's obvious. And I keep telling them: how can she be when it's Gavin that's done this. He's organised it somehow. I don't know how, but he's done it. It would be absolutely typical of him.'

Rachel attempted what she hoped was a reassuring smile. 'Nobody's suggesting Lola Jade's dead; we're very much working around the possibility of finding her alive. We wouldn't be getting involved if that possibility didn't exist. And obviously we will be looking very closely at your ex-husband.'

Michelle nodded, and even managed a brief smile, as she pushed out a stream of smoke through collagen-plumped lips.

'That's all well and good but – no offence – Surrey Police have been telling me the same thing, and five months down the line we're no closer.'

Brickall leaned to one side to avoid the plume of smoke. 'What makes you so sure it was your ex-husband?'

'Because she didn't cry out. If she'd woken up and there was a stranger in her room, she'd have screamed the place down. She made a racket even if she had a bad dream. But there was nothing. Whoever took her, she went with them willingly. So it has to be Gavin. Who else?' She flicked a tube of ash from her cigarette. 'And by the way: he's not my ex, we're still married. That's the point: he was afraid of losing custody of Lola Jade in the divorce.'

'Can you think of anyone else who might know where Gavin's gone?'

Michelle pursed her lips. 'Well, his family – his dad and his brother – they say they don't know, but…'

She let this hang for a while, then stubbed out her cigarette and pressed her hand to her forehead. 'I'm afraid I'm going to have to ask you to go. I'm getting a migraine. Talking about Lola Jade brings them on: it's the stress.'

Rachel started to speak, but Michelle buried her face in her hands, drooping like a flower. 'Sorry: I can't. I just can't.'

'Talk to the hand!' sniggered Brickall as they headed back down the drive. 'Bloody Nora, she's a fragile little thing, our Michelle, isn't she?'

'Hardly,' scoffed Rachel. 'But there's no point badgering her at this point: we need to try and find Gavin Harper. Who sounds a right piece of work.'

'So: you're up to speed on the file,' said Brickall as he swung out of the housing estate and rejoined the London Road. 'D'you think he did it?'

'I'm going to go back and reread his statement, that's for sure.' Rachel's tone was careful, but Brickall knew she was forming a hunch. 'Think about it: he's the one with a motive for taking Lola. Plus, he previously violated a custody agreement, in effect abducting his own child, however briefly.'

'But?' Brickall persisted.

'If he managed to take her out of the country with him when he left, then where has she been since May? And would they not have been spotted, given her face has been on the front page of every paper?'

'He could have managed it if he snatched her and handed her straight over to someone else before Michelle raised the alarm. Someone who took her abroad for him and kept her hidden there until he could join her. Or what if Gavin Harper's taken her but hasn't gone abroad? They could be hiding somewhere in this country.'

'Assuming she's alive,' pointed out Rachel. 'But you know the statistics. Ninety per cent of missing kids are found within seventy-two hours. Of the remaining ten per cent, the vast majority turn up within three weeks, most of them in body bags.'

'Either way, we'll need to speak to Michelle again at some point,' said Brickall firmly. 'We were only just getting warmed up.'

'Agreed.' Rachel nodded. 'We're definitely not done with the lovely Michelle.'

CHAPTER FOUR

Howard Davison lived boxing.

When he wasn't hitting a punchbag, he was teaching other people to hit it, and when he was at home, he watched boxing on TV as often as his wife would allow it. It showed in his body, which was top-heavy, with a thickly muscled neck and shoulders. Sweat was gathering on his sun-bed-browned face, and soaking through the back of his vest.

'Stand with your legs apart like this; arms at shoulder height. Then shoot out your right arm…' he thwacked the punchbag, '…like this.'

He stepped off the mat. 'Your turn,' he told Rachel.

She shuffled forward on her injured knee, twisted awkwardly and landed a feeble punch on the bag, losing her balance as she did so.

'You have to get the stance right, or you're not going to have enough power. Legs apart, with right leg back. Keep the tension in those legs, like you're about to kick a football.'

Rachel grimaced at him. 'Difficult when one of your legs isn't working. And comparing stuff to football is never going to help. My sergeant's obsessed with it; I know nothing.'

Howard grinned, creasing the corners of his piercing ice-blue eyes. His buzz-cut hair was an indeterminate mousy colour not quite short enough to hide the beginnings of grey round the temples. Rachel had signed up for some personal training with him when she realised that swimming was making her knee worse. She calculated that a sport where you kept your lower body largely still and moved your upper body would work for someone with a torn ligament, but it wasn't proving that easy. She still needed to move her feet. And she'd had to sweet-talk Howard into taking her on at all in her current condition.

'Okay, Rachel, keep your chin down. Chin up is just begging to be hit.'

'By a punchbag?'

'The stance should be the same even with no live opponent. Now try a double jab – one, two.'

Rachel flailed ineffectively at the bag.

'Problem is what you're wearing.' Howard indicated the baggy sweatshirt, hanging loosely over equally baggy tracksuit bottoms. 'It's getting in your way. Next time try wearing a vest and shorts: it'll be much better.'

Rachel raised an eyebrow. 'Really. You want me in school PE kit?'

Howard laughed. 'Hey, it doesn't matter what you look like. I train people of all shapes and sizes, and I'd say you're in better shape than most of them… Now try it again. I know your right knee's an issue, but try keeping the tension in those legs, both arms shoulder height. That's it!'

Rachel landed a couple of more convincing punches on the bag. Then again. Adrenaline coursed through her body, just as it used to years ago when she was a cop on the beat. It felt good.

'When you mentioned your sergeant…' Howard said, as she eventually collapsed breathless on a weights bench. 'Does that mean you're in the military?'

'Police. I'm a detective.'

Howard raised his eyebrows a fraction. 'The boxing will come in handy then. When you come up against a villain.'

Rachel was about to explain that the NCA's role was mainly one of oversight and intelligence-gathering, and that she spent the majority of her time driving a desk, but thought better of it and buried her sweaty face in her towel. After all, she was a trained firearms officer and very occasionally took part in tactical operations. 'I think we ought to stop now: I don't want to overdo it and make my leg worse.'

Howard smiled. 'To be honest, I'm still not sure you should be doing this at all. But if you build up strength in your quads and your abs, it will help your injury in the long run.'

'That's the plan.' Rachel gave him a sweaty high-five. 'You don't get rid of me that easily.'

Back in the office, she flicked a rubber band at Brickall, who was engrossed in checking Premier League results on his computer terminal.

'Oi, deadbeat! I've been thinking.'

'Careful: you know how dangerous thinking is.' He didn't look away from the screen, but flicked the rubber band back at her.

'I think I should go and talk to Michelle Harper on my own. Maybe I'll get more out of her woman to woman.'

Brickall made a scoffing noise. 'Whatever.' He pointed at her knee. 'What about your gammy leg? Thought you couldn't drive that far?'

'I'll get a bobby to drive me. But ask the questions on my own.'

Brickall shrugged. 'Worth a try, I suppose. Only make sure she's in: save wasting everyone's time.'

Two hours later, WPC Wendy Nicholls parked outside number 57 Willow Way and cut the engine. A council refuse truck was lumbering its way round the street, with the bin men snatching and tipping the contents of wheelie bins. Michelle's bin wasn't out, Rachel noted.

'You want me to wait here, ma'am?'

Rachel nodded. 'Shouldn't be too long: I phoned to say I was coming.' Once she'd struggled out of the passenger seat, she stuck her head back into the car and said, 'And while I'm inside, go into the back garden and see what's happened to the bins. Take some photos. Oh, and hold on a sec…' She took Wendy's empty paper coffee cup. 'I'm going to need this.'

Michelle Harper opened the door wearing a grey velour tracksuit and sheepskin boots studded with diamanté.

'Come in, Rebecca.'

'Rachel.'

'Yes. Sorry.' She hovered as Rachel lowered herself into an armchair, placing the takeout cup next to her on the side table as though she was still drinking from it. Michelle perched herself on the very edge of the cream sofa, not acknowledging Rachel's injury, so that she felt she had to.

'Running accident.'

Michelle ignored this. 'Look, I'm obviously going to do all I can to help you.' She hesitated, checking her own attitude, and added: 'But I'm going out of my bloody mind with the stress. It's still literally giving me migraines. I've already told Manners and the Asian girl everything I can remember. Multiple times.'

Rachel gave her best professional smile. 'Just a few more questions if you don't mind. We didn't exactly have a proper chat last time.'

'Sorry, but like I said… the migraines. I can't help it.' Michelle adopted a self-pitying expression, as she reached into her bag for her cigarettes and lit one.

'We'll take it slowly…' Rachel decided the best approach was to ignore the histrionics. 'Let's start by talking about your life before this happened. How long was it since you and your husband had split up?'

'A year and a half, roughly. Bit longer maybe.'

'And what was your relationship like during that time?'

'Things were okay, to start with. But he started bringing Lola back late on his access days. And then he abducted her.' Michelle's tone was oddly impassive.

Rachel nodded. 'I've been wanting to talk to you about that… What happened exactly?'

'He was supposed to bring her back one Saturday evening and he didn't. Wouldn't answer his phone. Kept her all day Sunday, without a word. I was going out of my mind: literally losing it. I ended up calling the police.' Michelle puffed smoke at the ceiling.

'And how about when you were together? How were things between you then?'

'Well. You know.'

'No, I don't know. That's why I'm asking.'

The self-pitying look appeared again. 'He used to knock me about.'

'And this was reported to the police?' Rachel had read the whole file, so she already knew the answer to this question.

Michelle shook her head. 'No, it wasn't. No point. You know how it is: you lot aren't interested in domestics.'

'And what did he used to do exactly?'

Michelle picked up her phone, opened her photos app and started scrolling through the pictures. When she found what she was looking for, she thrust the phone in Rachel's face. 'Look!'

The photo was of the inside of a forearm – or wrist; it was hard to tell – swirled with bruising in shades of vivid magenta and lemon yellow. She flicked to another close-up of what looked like a neck and shoulder, smeared with livid scratch marks.

'Can I see?'

Rachel reached for the phone to get a closer look, but Michelle snatched it away and put it back on the side table.

Rachel let this go. For now. 'And how was he with Lola Jade?'

'Pretty good, on the whole. She was a real daddy's girl. Adored her dad. Like I said last time, that's why she'd always have gone with him without question. She'd have thought the whole thing was a bit of a game.'

'So where do *you* think Gavin could be now?'

There was a pause while Michelle subjected her cigarette to a long, intense drag. There was a clean ashtray on the table this time. Rachel was longing for a drink, but no offer was made, presumably because of the empty coffee cup.

'Come on… you must have a theory. Your daughter vanishes and then so does your ex, five months later? After – you say – he'd previously attempted to take her.'

'Oh, don't worry: I know exactly where he'd go. He'll have gone back to Spain. He worked in a bar in Torrevieja for a while when he was younger, as a package holiday rep for a bit, then at the Asturias Bar – and he was always banging on about how he wanted go back. Wanted me and Lola to move out there too… said it would be a great childhood for her, growing up in the Mediterranean sun.' She sucked on her cigarette savagely. 'But I said no.'

'Have the police followed that up?'

Michelle curled her lip. 'They just said they were looking into all relevant lines of enquiry. But they never found anything…' Smoke escaped from her mouth as she spoke. '… Apparently.'

'But you think Torrevieja could be a good starting point?'

'Definitely. He'd have taken her there. If it is him that's done this, and I can't see who else it would be.'

Rachel waited for Michelle to elaborate, but she simply flicked at her cigarette and stared vacantly ahead.

'And what about other people who came into close contact with Lola Jade? Other adults in her life – relatives, her friends' parents, babysitters?'

Michelle shook her head firmly. 'I never used babysitters. I didn't like leaving my princess with strangers; I liked her with me. The odd time she needed minding, she'd go to my sister Lisa's...' Michelle thought for a moment. 'I know when she was with Gav, if he needed to go out somewhere he'd leave her with his cousin Tony. Tony and his wife Joyce.'

'Their surname?' asked Rachel, pen poised over her notebook.

'Ingram. They didn't have kids of their own and they adored Lola. Every time she went to theirs she'd come back with a present. Usually just cheap rubbish.' Michelle screwed up her nose to indicate distaste.

'Any chance of a cup of tea?'

'Sure. Sorry.' Michelle gave a non-sorry smile as she ground the butt into the ashtray and headed into the kitchen.

'Okay if I have a look around?' Rachel called after her.

Michelle was filling the kettle and taking mugs from the cupboard. 'Course. Go ahead.'

'Let me just get rid of this.' Rachel indicated the paper coffee cup, reaching past Michelle to throw it into the kitchen swing bin, before heading back into the sitting room. While her back was turned, she grabbed Michelle's phone from the table. It was unlocked, so she scrolled quickly through the photos app, taking screenshots of a few with her own phone before heading for the stairs.

Immediately in front of her was Lola Jade's room, all too familiar from the crime-scene photos. It was bleakly tidy, with toys displayed in regimented rows and her clothes – mostly pink dresses – hanging in the wardrobe on small satin hangers. From the top of the stairs, the landing made an L-shape, with the bathroom immediately to the right of Lola Jade's room and Michelle's room at the front, occupying the space over the living room and taking up the entire width of the house. This too was extremely tidy, the frilly cream duvet and pillows neatly arranged, the bedside tables bare of clutter, and dresses and tops ordered by descending length in the wardrobe, shoes arranged by heel height below them.

The landing itself was freshly decorated with a garish wallpaper featuring oversized purple poppies, the sort that was designed with a single feature wall in mind. Looking at it gave Rachel a headache. There was a fourth door, identical to the doors of the two bedrooms and the bathroom. Rachel opened it, releasing a pungent chemical gust of air freshener and detergent, and revealing a shallow storage cupboard stuffed with loo roll, multiple cleaning products and spare carrier bags. There were scented oil plug-ins in the landing sockets, releasing a sickly perfume. She used her own phone to take pictures of everything.

As she came downstairs, Michelle was carrying two mugs of tea back into the living room. 'I've got biscuits, if you want them?'

'Trying to avoid them.'

Michelle looked Rachel up and down.

'The knee injury. I'm not burning up as many calories as usual.'

'Fair enough.' This was said without any genuine interest.

'Do you have any other pictures I could see? Anything that might help?'

Michelle took a photo album from the sparsely-filled book-shelves and handed it to her. Inside were pictures dating back to the early days of Gavin and Michelle's marriage. The wedding shots themselves showed a tanned, good-looking man with a receding hairline, awkward in a cravat, and the bride with a wet-look perm and a shiny white toilet-roll cover of a dress. There were pictures from what looked like a stag weekend, and some of a bare-chested Gavin on a beach next to another tanned and good-looking man.

'Who's this?' asked Rachel, although the two men were so alike she was pretty sure she knew the answer. The dolphin tattoo on Gavin's left forearm was the only way she could be sure which was him.

'That's Gav and his brother Andy. They used to go on lads' holidays together.'

'So they're close?'

'Yeah. Thick as thieves.'

Then there were pictures of a pregnant Michelle, and Lola Jade's baby pictures. A few of the three of them on family holidays, all looking miserable despite the sunshine.

'Actually, I think I'll have that biscuit after all. It's been a while since breakfast.'

While Michelle was in the kitchen again, Rachel took out her phone and snapped images of the pages that featured Gavin and Andy.

'I can't find the biscuits, sorry.'

Michelle was back in the room, snatching the photo album from Rachel and holding it defensively against her chest.

'I just needed a picture of Gavin. So I can show people who we're looking for.'

She relaxed her grip a fraction. 'Oh. Okay. Only he doesn't look like that now. He's got less hair.'

'Well. If you could send me an up-to-date photo, that would be helpful.'

Michelle narrowed her eyes. 'You said you were from the NCA. Does that cover other countries?'

Rachel inclined her head. 'There are a few of us that used to be Interpol, before the NCA took it over. I happen to be one of them. But we cover cases on the mainland UK too. Wherever our expertise is needed, really.'

'So you're going to go to Spain, right?'

'It's something we'll be looking into, certainly. Anyway, thanks for your time today – it was helpful.'

Rachel stood up, giving Michelle her cue to stub out the cigarette and walk her to the front door. Outside, WPC Nicholls was sitting bolt upright in the patrol car, munching on a ham sandwich.

'Find anything?' Rachel enquired as she climbed back into the passenger seat.

WPC Nicholls handed her phone to Rachel and she examined the shots of the inside of Michelle's bin. 'Interesting.'

'Is it?'

'It certainly is. Do me a favour and send them to me, please.'

'How d'you get on?' Brickall enquired when she was back at the NCA building.

'Not sure.' Rachel gave a cursory debrief of the visit, then uploaded the photos she and WPC Nicholls had taken to her Ikena Forensic software and examined them in greater detail. Every picture tells a story: wasn't that what they always said? Whoever 'they' were.

She washed down some tramadol with a can of Coke and turned back to the Lola Jade file. She flicked through it until she found the original MG11 form recording Gavin Harper's witness statement.

My name is Gavin Harper. I live at Flat B, 209 Carlisle Road, Eastwell, Surrey. On the afternoon of 10 May, I received a phone call from my brother asking if I knew about Lola Jade, who's my six-year-old daughter. I said I didn't know what he was talking about, and he told me that he'd heard on the local news that she was missing. I tried to phone my wife, Michelle Harper, but I couldn't get through. I drove over to the family home, 57 Willow Way, but I wasn't allowed to see or talk to Michelle. Her sister, Lisa Urquhart was there and said she was too upset. I wanted to join in the search for Lola Jade, but I was told it was best to let the experts get on with it. I was told I should go home and wait there until the police could come and speak to me.

It's true that relations between my wife and I had broken down and that we were arguing over custody and my access to Lola Jade. I know nothing at all about her disappearance.

Signed by: Gavin Thomas Harper
Witnessed by: DS 2394 Rajavi

With the photos the CSO had taken of Lola's bedroom spread out in front of her, Rachel then reread the entire forensic report, including the lab results that were stapled to it.

And then stopped in her tracks with a sharp intake of breath.

She had assumed the DNA found belonging to Gavin Harper was hair or skin; something not unusual for a parent frequently in their child's bedroom. But it wasn't. A brief typed sentence confirmed something she'd missed. The sample found was seminal fluid.

CHAPTER FIVE

At 6.15 the next morning, Rachel was out of bed and climbing into a sports bra, a vest and a pair of loose athletics shorts that she used for running in hot weather.

Howard was waiting for her at the gym, standing next to the pull-up bars.

'Up you jump, Rachel,' he said, nodding in their direction.

'Howard, I *can't*. I don't have enough upper-body strength.'

'Exactly why you need to work on it.'

Inhaling hard and holding her breath, Rachel bent her knees and mustered as much aerial projection as she could, but only succeeded in banging her wrist on the bar. Howard gripped her round the waist and lifted her up as though she weighed no more than a child. She hesitated, savouring the moment of weightlessness, then grabbed hold. He let go, and she dangled awkwardly.

'All right, now pull! Pull hard!'

Rachel managed to hoist herself a couple of inches higher, but then lost her grip and fell, landing awkwardly at Howard's feet and sending a painful shock through her damaged knee joint. She grimaced.

'Come on: again! You need to keep trying.'

'I want to box.' She was aware that she sounded whiny.

'Do this, then you can box. You need to work on your dead hang. Literally hang like a dead man. Person,' he corrected himself.

'If your lats and chest are tight, you're going to damage your shoulders and spine when you're boxing. Hang! Like you're dead!'

Thirty sweaty minutes and ten pull-ups later, Howard allowed her to give the punch ball a good beating. She headed to work with aching arms and shoulders but a glow of satisfaction.

'Your face is as red as a beetroot,' observed Brickall. 'Early-morning shag, was it?'

Rachel shot him a warning glance.

'Okay! How did you get on with the lovely Michelle then?'

Rachel shook her head slowly. 'Not sure. She's definitely buying into the possibility that Gavin Harper's disappearance and Lola's are related. And I did find out that he's very close to his brother, Andy, so I reckon we talk to him next.'

'Wasn't he interviewed?'

Rachel shook her head. 'They almost certainly spoke to him informally, but there's no MG11 on the file. See if you can track him down.'

Half an hour later, Brickall slapped his desk in frustration. 'I'm getting fuck-all here. According to the electoral roll, the only Andy Harper in the Eastwell area is sixty-eight. So he can't be Gavin Harper's brother.'

'Then we widen the search.'

Rachel scoured local newspaper reports and social media but drew a blank, apart from the Facebook account of a fourteen-year-old Andy Harper.

'See!' said Brickall triumphantly. 'The man doesn't exist.'

'Perhaps he's moved out of the area. Try the General Register Office.'

Brickall frowned. 'That's only going to provide a record of his birth, not where he lives now.'

'Right now, it's all we've got.'

After an hour and a half of trawling the General Register database, Brickall found a handful of Andrew Harpers born between 1970 and 1990, but none of the family details matched Gavin Harper's. 'Waste of bloody time,' he grumbled, and went off to find lunch.

Rachel went back to the drawing board, searching online articles about the case. There was an interview, in one of the many hysterical Lola Jade pieces, with Gavin Harper's father.

LOLA GRANDAD SPEAKS OUT: 'My son is no killer.'

The photo was of an overweight man with iron-grey hair and a jowly face that would once have been handsome. The gutter journalist writing the piece mentioned Terry Harper agreeing to meet him in his local pub, and the photo showed him standing outside it. Rachel googled it. The Hand and Flowers, Whiteley. She then checked the electoral register and found Terry's address on a housing estate in Whiteley, a few miles from Eastwell.

Brickall wandered back into the office with a slice of pizza and a can of Coke.

Rachel shook her head vigorously as he went to sit down. 'You can eat that in the car. We're off to talk to Lola Jade's grandfather.'

Terry Harper was wary, which she had expected. He was a short man, so short that even Brickall loomed over him. The three of them filled the cramped hallway of his modest bungalow.

'How much will I get paid?' he asked, when she told him they wanted to talk about Lola's disappearance.

'Paid?'

'By your paper?'

'We're not journalists,' she corrected him. 'We're police officers. Working in crime investigation support.'

Terry tutted at this, but led them through into a small, over-furnished living room. There were family photos on display, including one of Gavin and Michelle's wedding; the bride resplendent in her shiny meringue.

Rachel poised herself gingerly on a Dralon armchair, decked out with an antimacassar, that reminded her of her mother's house. Brickall took the sofa.

'I'm going to come straight to the point, Mr Harper,' he said. 'Do you know where Gavin is? Or why he's disappeared?'

He shook his head vehemently. 'Honest to God, I don't. I mean, I've tried phoning him, obviously, but his mobile's disconnected. All I'm hoping—'

'Do you think he has Lola Jade with him?' Rachel leaned forward and engaged eye contact.

Terry hunched his shoulders in a helpless gesture. 'I mean, he must have, mustn't he?'

Rachel looked at him sharply. 'Why do you say that, Terry?'

He shrugged. 'It's just the obvious explanation. Why else would he do a runner like that? But he wouldn't hurt her, I know that. He wouldn't hurt a hair on that precious kiddie's head.'

Rachel thought back to the DNA sample found in Lola's room. 'How was her relationship with her dad? Did she enjoy spending time with him?'

'She adored him. Adores him,' he corrected himself.

'So there were no… issues between them?' Rachel was aware that she was pussyfooting, but she couldn't quite bring herself to ask if he thought his son was abusing his own daughter.

Terry shook his head. 'To be fair, there was that time when Michelle reported him to the police for not taking her back on time. But he had his reasons,' he added darkly.

Rachel raised her eyebrows.

'Husband-and-wife stuff, you know. She likes playing games, does our Michelle.'

Brickall shot Rachel a look.

'Go on,' Rachel said to Terry.

'Their relationship was what you might call volatile.'

'Michelle seems to think Gavin could be in Spain,' Brickall interjected. 'Do you think that's true?'

'Could be. He's spent time over there, you know, speaks some Spanish, so I suppose it would be relatively easy for him.'

'And your other son – where is he?' demanded Brickall.

Terry looked confused. 'My other son? I've only got the one. Gavin.'

It was Rachel's turn to look confused. 'What about Andy?'

The penny dropped, and Terry's face relaxed into a smile. 'Ah, Andy! Andy's not mine, he's my ex-wife's kid. He and Gav are half-brothers, you know? Pat and I split when Gavin was a nipper, and she remarried soon after and had a couple more kids: Andy and Karen.'

'Ah, I see.' Rachel smiled back. That would explain their singular failure to track down Andy Harper. 'Michelle showed me photos and they were so alike, I just assumed…'

'They both look like their mother.'

'So Andy's surname?' asked Brickall.

'Whittier. Andy Whittier.'

'Easy to find someone in 2017 when you've got the name right,' mused Rachel as Brickall drove them back along the main road that led back towards London. 'I've just gone into Facebook and found him right away.' She held up her phone. 'If this is correct, then Andy Whittier's still living in the Eastwell area.'

'Bloody hell, does that mean you want me to turn round?'

Rachel shook her head. 'We could get his home address from the PNC, but right now he's probably going to be at work, not at home.'

'His employment status will be on Facebook too, dummy!'

Rachel checked, and sure enough it was. 'According to his profile, Andy works at JBH Distribution Ltd,' she read out to Brickall, then broke into a grin. 'It supplies building and construction materials. And conveniently, the address is London Road, Whiteley. We just passed it about quarter of a mile back.'

Swearing under his breath, Brickall executed a sharp U-turn.

The receptionist at JBH explained that there were two shifts: early, from 7.30 until 4.00, and late, from 11 till 7.30. Andy Whittier was on an early that day. It was now 3.30, so they parked outside and waited.

'One thing…' Rachel said, washing down painkillers with a bottle of water. 'Did you read the forensic report from Lola's room?'

Brickall shook his head.

'The paternal DNA sample found on the carpet. It was semen, for fuck's sake. What's that all about?'

'I'm pretty sure Surrey CID will have asked him that. Funny old thing, though: we can't question him ourselves because he's done a bunk.'

Rachel sighed. 'Mind you, I can't find anything that suggests he's a paedo.'

'That doesn't rule it out. But then the presence of the DNA doesn't rule it in either. Any number of reasons you might get your jiz smeared in your kid's room.'

Rachel looked askance at him. 'Seriously, Detective Sergeant? And Harper wasn't living there either. Bit bloody weird.'

Brickall exhaled hard, making a whistling sound through his teeth. 'The whole case is weird, if you ask me.' Workers from the early shift had started streaming out of a side entrance. 'Okay, who are we looking for?'

Rachel took out her phone and flicked back through the images she had captured from Michelle's photo album until she reached the one of Gavin Harper with his brother, holding it up to Brickall. The two men were sitting under a coconut-palm pergola at a beachside bar, shades on the top of their heads, a strip of cobalt-blue sea in the background.

At 4.05, a man strode into the car park, rucksack slung over his shoulder, car keys in hand, and Brickall said, 'Bingo!'

'Andy!' Rachel climbed out of the car and placed herself between Whittier and his own vehicle. 'Andy, hi. My name's DI Rachel Prince. Could we have a word?'

He tilted his shoulder down and attempted to barge past her. 'Sorry, I don't want to talk to you. We've all had enough hassle.'

'Just an informal chat.' Rachel used her recent boxing training to block him. 'Otherwise we'll be bringing you into London with us for a formal interview.'

He hesitated, looking her up and down again. He had an attractive face, Rachel thought, with regular features and warm brown eyes. 'Okay,' he sighed. 'But not here. There's a place a couple of hundred yards up the road, towards the bypass. Sid's Caff.'

CHAPTER SIX

Sid's Caff was a greasy spoon favoured by the lorry-driving fraternity, all Formica and strip lighting. The three of them had mugs of stewed tea and Andy ordered a full English, which he set about with the gusto of the condemned man at his last supper, Brickall looking on enviously.

'Sorry, bloody starving,' he said through a mouthful of baked beans and sausage.

'That's fine.' Rachel stirred sugar slowly round her creosote-coloured tea. 'Take your time. I expect you know what we're going to ask you anyway.'

'If I know where Gav's gone.' He dabbed bread and butter in the baked bean juice and wolfed it down.

'Spot on,' Brickall confirmed. 'That deduction hardly takes a criminal genius.'

Andy shrugged, starting to relax a little now that his blood sugar was on the rise. 'Sorry, you're wasting your time. I have no bloody idea where Gav is.'

'Your father – sorry, Gavin's father; your mum's ex – thinks he's taken Lola Jade and gone abroad.'

Andy returned to looking down at his plate. 'Like I said, I wouldn't know anything about that.'

Rachel nodded, reaching into her bag and groping reflexively for the blister pack of painkillers. The two she took earlier didn't seem to be working. Andy watched her pop out another one and swallow it with her tea.

'Bad knee,' she said hurriedly.

He nodded sympathetically. 'Loads of the guys at work have knackered their backs and knee joints loading the rigs.'

'Can we get back to your niece,' said Brickall sharply. 'You and your brother are very close: you must have an idea where he is.'

Andy laid down his knife and fork. 'And I've just told you I don't.'

'Look, our main objective at this point is to talk to Gavin. You have to agree he has some questions to answer. If he didn't take Lola, then why did he up and vanish. *How* did he up and vanish?' Rachel levelled her gaze at Andy, who was mopping his plate in a studied fashion. 'What's your theory when it comes to Lola Jade?'

'If she was dead, then I reckon you lot would have found her by now. But on the other hand, in my opinion you've been pretty bloody useless, so who knows?'

Brickall scowled at him.

'I'm not sure that's fair.' Rachel drained what was left of her tea. 'Surrey Police threw a hell of a lot of resources at the investigation. Every single bit of available manpower was used in the search.'

Andy leaned back in the chair, giving her a sceptical look.

'And the case has now been passed from Surrey police to us at the National Crime Agency. You know: fresh eyes.'

'We've already talked at length to your sister-in-law,' Brickall chipped in. 'She's the one who told us you and Gavin are close.'

Andy gave a mirthless laugh. 'Michelle? Jesus Christ!'

'You don't have a very high opinion of her, I take it?'

He pulled a face. 'Well, you've met her, right? She made Gav's life hell when they were together. Never happy; never satisfied. One minute she wants them to split up, the next she wants him back, then she chucks him out. Blowing hot and cold: demanding his attention one minute, ignoring him the next. Poor sod never knew where he was with her. And then she goes and makes up stories about him abducting Lola, as well as… other stuff.'

Rachel looked straight into the brown eyes that now flashed with indignation. 'What do you mean by that?'

'Implying things about Gav that were a load of crap… He'd never have done the things she was talking about.' His voice trailed off.

'You're talking about sexual abuse?' Rachel thought it was time to dispense with euphemism.

Andy nodded. 'Never, not Gav. Not in a million years.'

'So Michelle made up a story that her husband was interfering with his own daughter?'

'Let's just say, of the two of them I know who was the better parent.'

'I got the impression that she's devoted to her daughter,' Rachel countered.

He shrugged. 'You could say that. But at least Lola knew where she was with her dad.' Andy buttered the last piece of bread left on his side plate. 'Well, good luck anyway, starting from scratch, months down the line. Your chances of finding her must be slim to none.'

Brickall scowled again.

The clock over the counter said quarter to five, and the crowd of truck drivers was starting to thin. Andy threw his paper napkin onto his plate and pushed it away. 'Sorry, but I'm going to have to get off. The wife'll be wondering what's happened to me.'

Brickall held up a hand. 'Hold on a minute: can we get back to where we started. Gavin's whereabouts. I understand he'd spent time in Spain?'

Andy shrugged. 'When we were young, before we both married, we used to spend time repping in the resorts in the Med. But that was over ten years ago.'

'Michelle said something about Torrevieja.'

Andy reached for his wallet, ducking his head to avoid eye contact as he counted out coins. 'I don't know anything about that.'

'Please, Andy.' Rachel tried to reinstate eye contact. 'It's in everyone's interest for us to find Gavin.'

He nodded briefly, still avoiding her gaze. 'Look, as far as I'm concerned, he could be anywhere. He might not even be abroad.'

He had stood up to leave, but Brickall was quickly on his feet, blocking his path.

'Got to go, okay?' Andy said firmly, whacking Brickall with his rucksack as he pushed past. 'Sorry, but I can't help you.'

'Is there an address he might go to? A contact who might be helping him?' Rachel called as she limped after him, but Andy strode straight outside to his car, jumped in and drove off without looking back in their direction.

Rachel was already googling flights as Brickall drove them back to London. 'Alicante or Murcia: the airports for Torrevieja. Michelle's given us a lot more to go on than Andy has.'

'He gave us fuck-all,' Brickall pointed out.

'So we might as well get on with it and head out there as soon as possible, I reckon. I'll sort it with Patten tomorrow.'

It was now rush hour, and they were crawling with painful slowness through the outer suburbs. By the time they reached the centre of the city it was 7 p.m.

'Makes sense if I drop you at home,' Brickall suggested. 'It's a bit late to go back into the office.'

Rachel was about to agree when her phone rang. The same number as before. Stuart's number. Her whole body tensed.

'You okay?' Brickall eyed her sharply. He missed nothing, unfortunately. They were pulling up outside her block of flats when Rachel suddenly gripped his forearm. 'Don't stop!' she barked.

A familiar figure was standing on the pavement outside the door to her building. Stuart.

'Keep driving! Drive!'

Brickall changed up through the gears and hurtled to the end of the street, yanking the steering wheel left round the corner. Then he pulled over abruptly, stalling the engine and making the driver behind them hit the horn and flick a V-sign in their direction. Brickall waved his warrant card in response, then turned to face Rachel.

'What the fuck's going on, Prince?'

'I thought I saw my ex. Or it might not have been him. I'm not sure. Fuck!' She slammed the heel of her hand against her forehead.

'Jesus, you're so fucking jumpy! What exactly is the problem?'

'I just don't want to see him, that's all.'

'Is this the same one that was phoning you?'

Rachel nodded.

'Want me to come with you and check if it's him?'

She shook her head. 'No, it's fine. Just wait here with me for a bit until he's gone. If it is him: I'm not even sure. But thanks, Mark.'

They waited in awkward silence for a few minutes, then Rachel reached for the door handle. 'No wait!' Brickall started the engine. 'Let me drop you at the front door; then we'll both know you were imagining things.'

There was no one waiting outside the building when they got there. Rachel patted Brickall's arm as she got out of the car. 'Thanks. We'll sort the Spain trip in the morning, okay? Make sure you pack plenty of sunblock.'

He grinned at her. 'Like I've said before: you're such a weirdo, Prince.'

*

'I think we can agree I'm never going to bloody win Olympic gold.'

Rachel stepped back from the punchbag, shoulders heaving from the effort, sweat trickling from her temples, cheeks flushed bright pink. It felt good. Her anxiety levels had plummeted and for a while, at least, she hadn't given any thought to Stuart Ritchie.

'Don't be so hard on yourself. You're doing well.' Howard went to pat her shoulder, then, seeing the slick of perspiration, hung back, his hand hovering. 'I'm seeing real progress.'

Rachel's right knee was still sore, but after only a few sessions she could feel that she was toning up, gaining muscle. She went to grab her towel from the bench and reflexively reached into her kitbag for a couple of pills, sloshing them down with water from her sports drink.

Howard's silhouette loomed over her, biceps bulging in his corporate gym T-shirt, and of course his eyes zeroed in on the tramadol. Before she could escape, he pulled the blister pack from her hand and studied them.

'You want to be very careful with these things, they're extremely addictive.'

Rachel snatched the pills back and shoved them into her bag.

'Maybe you should, you know, go and speak to your GP about an alternative?'

Rachel stomped past him, swung the gym door open and headed for the car park. 'Maybe you should mind your own fucking business!' she shouted over her shoulder.

Sitting in her car, she rested her head on the steering wheel for a few seconds, waiting for her breathing to steady. *Shit*, she thought, *that was a stupid thing to do*. She'd had a terrible night's sleep, between the pain in her leg, her paranoia about Stuart having discovered where she lived, and her mind churning over the details of the Lola Jade Harper case. She'd mentally revisited Michelle's house, replaying every detail of what she'd seen and heard. And there was Andy Whittier. He had been evasive, and her experience left her in no doubt he was hiding something. They should interview him again, in a more formal setting. But first: Spain.

As she trudged into the office, one glance at Brickall let her know that he was in a foul mood.

'What?' she asked as she lowered herself carefully onto her desk chair.

'What d'you mean: what?'

'You've got a face that looks like a wet bank holiday weekend in Scunthorpe. Only less fun.'

'Bloody Patten won't let me go with you to Spain. The Bogdhani case is going to court this week and I'm needed to give evidence.'

'Oh Christ.' Rachel rolled her eyes. 'I was counting on you to do the driving.'

'Thanks a bleeding bunch. Good to know where my skills lie.'

'And I was relying on you for feedback and insight too, obviously.' Rachel leaned back in her chair, closing her eyes. She usually enjoyed the international element of the job, but this morning she was too tired to summon any enthusiasm for the trip. Especially now that she would be going alone. 'We'll have to do our video conference calls, okay? I'll still need to run stuff by you, and have you run data checks for me… Detective Sergeant?'

Brickall sighed, and nodded reluctantly.

'Good. I guess I'd better go and see Janette about a flight. And schedule a case conference with those lovely people at Child Protection for when I get back.'

'By lovely people, you mean lovely person: our Mills and Boon hero.'

Rachel flushed slightly, which seemed to be a reflexive response whenever she thought about the dark, handsome and faintly mysterious Giles Denton.

'Whatever. Just do it, douchebag.'

CHAPTER SEVEN

The first thing she noticed was the bright sunlight streaming in through slatted blinds. The second was the thrumming pain and stiffness in her right leg.

Rachel had arrived at Murcia airport at eight the previous evening and driven a rental car for an hour to the Costa Blanca resort of Torrevieja, a magnet for British tourists. Now, hobbling out of bed, she pushed back the blinds and stepped out onto the balcony, squinting into a cloudless sky. A pristine aquamarine hotel pool twinkled below her, and she longed to go for a morning swim but knew it would only make her leg worse. She would allow herself a poolside lounging session later, but first there was work to be done.

The Asturias Bar was on the promenade, a paved, pedestrianised thoroughfare fringed with towering palms. On one edge was the beach, dotted with colourful umbrellas, and on the other a strip of bars, ice cream parlours, restaurants and 'Irish' pubs. Inside the bar there was restaurant service, and a large awning at the front gave shade to more tables and chairs. A couple of hardened Brits were sitting outside, already downing pints of lager when Rachel arrived at 10 a.m. She showed her warrant card and was taken to the manager in the back office, a small, wiry man with a comedy moustache, called Jorge.

He nodded vigorously when Rachel showed him the photo of Gavin Harper.

'Yes, I remember. He work here.'

'When?'

Jorge shrugged. 'Long time ago. Maybe ten years?'

'Have you seen him recently? More recently than that?'

This was met with blank incomprehension, but Jorge summoned one of the waiters, a young Latvian called Andris, who spoke near-perfect English and stood in as a translator. Yes, Jorge remembered Gavin but hadn't seen him since he worked there. No, Gavin hadn't been into the bar recently, and he hadn't seen him anywhere in Torrevieja in recent months.

'Ask him if he can think of anyone else who knows Gavin Harper, anyone he was friends with.'

Andris relayed this, and told Rachel that yes, there was a guy called Cristian Aguado who used to be friendly with Gavin Harper and who still worked at a nightclub called Discoteca 33. He might know something, Andris said, but from Jorge's Hispanic shrug, Rachel was not so sure. She stayed and drank a coffee and ate some churros, and then worked her way methodically along the promenade, showing Gavin's photo to everyone she could find. After three hours, her leg was throbbing, her right foot puffy, and she had no leads at all. She decided to limp back to the hotel, put on her bikini and rest by the pool until it was dark and resort nightlife swung into motion.

Discoteca 33 was in a semi-residential street that led down to the Cala Cornuda beach. Now that it was nearly November, peak holiday season was over, and at 8.30 it was still early for the party crowd, so there were only a handful of other people in the club. Rachel perched herself on a bar stool, feeling conspicuous. Within twenty seconds, a portly man with greased-back hair sidled up to her.

'Buy you a drink, lovely lady?'

Lovely lady? Hard to believe men still said that. She grimaced, wishing she hadn't put on a sheer pale pink shirt, but had instead stuck to something more workmanlike. Rachel turned down the offer and bought herself a glass of sangria, using the interaction with the bartender to ask if he knew who Cristian Aguado was.

'Sure.' He pointed to his own tanned chest, which was exposed by a shirt unbuttoned almost to the waist and looked as though it had been oiled. 'I am Cristian. How can I help?'

My first piece of luck, thought Rachel. Few cold cases were solved without a certain amount of it. She added in a generous tip and explained that she was looking for Gavin Harper.

Cristian frowned. 'Of course, I know him. But he is not here.'

'Not here in Torrevieja, you mean?'

He nodded. Rachel scrutinised his face for the tells of deception, but saw none. 'When did you last see him?'

He thought for a moment, polishing a wine glass on a cloth. 'Maybe two, three summers ago. On holiday, with *la niñita*. His little girl.'

'And if he was here in Torrevieja at the moment, where would he be? Where does he stay?'

'But he's not here,' Cristian repeated stubbornly. 'If he was here, I would know this. I know everyone in this town.' He flapped his towel around the bar area to indicate that this was his kingdom, then rearranged his shirt front to display the optimum amount of pectoral muscle. 'Peoples tell me everything.'

'What if he was hiding – if he didn't want anyone to know he was here?' Rachel persisted.

Cristian gave a Hispanic shrug and went back to polishing glasses. 'When he's here, he stays in Apartamentos Playa Soleada. But he is not here; this is the truth.'

Rachel googled the apartments while she was finishing her sangria. They were just round the corner, which would explain why Gavin was a regular at Discoteca 33. She walked past on her way back to the hotel; showed her warrant card and the photo of Gavin to the building manager. He was also adamant that Gavin wasn't staying there, and even offered up all the last month's CCTV tapes from the lobby by way of confirmation.

'Maybe,' Rachel told him. 'I'll get back to you.'

Back at the hotel, she sat with her right leg raised on pillows, a makeshift ice pack on her knee, and Skyped Brickall. On a plate in front of him was his evening dietary staple – pizza laden with hot sauce – and his mood was buoyant.

'Turns out the trial's actually quite good craic.'

'Really?'

'Of course it doesn't hurt that the junior barrister on the prosecution side is a stunning brunette.'

Rachel grinned. 'Asked her out yet?'

He tapped the side of his nose. 'Let's just say I'm working on it… How's your jammy little skive on the Costa?'

Rachel sighed. 'I'm pretty sure Harper's not here in Torrevieja. I've got a load of CCTV tape to go through tomorrow.' She added: 'It could prove useful, I suppose.'

Brickall inhaled from a can of lager. 'What's your gut telling you, Prince?'

'That we're wide of the mark. I've been looking at the photo of Gavin and Andy together at some beach bar every time I made enquiries, and something was bugging me. I've remembered what it was. The same building they're in front of appeared in most of the photos of them in Michelle's albums. Hold on a second…'

She reached for her phone and sent the image to Brickall so that they could look at it together. The bar in the background had a tin roof, a coconut-palm pergola, and the exterior walls were painted bright turquoise, daubed with blocks of bright red and green. Over the entrance hung a driftwood sign with lettering burned into it by hand. Rachel zoomed in as far as she could and could just about make out the name: *Tiago's*.

'Hang about,' said Brickall suddenly. 'It's obvious, you plank. The red and green rectangles are the Portuguese flag. They're in Portugal.'

Before Rachel had a chance to reply, he consulted his phone and held it up triumphantly to his laptop screen. 'Here you go: Tiago's Bar in Albufeira. It's the Algarve.'

Rachel shook her head slowly. 'Shit. Andy did say they'd travelled all over the Med. So d'you reckon he could be in Portugal?'

'Only one way to find out.'

The next morning, Rachel phoned Nigel Patten's assistant, Janette, and enlisted her help in getting to the Algarve.

It was not straightforward. If she flew, she would have to change planes in Lisbon, but there were no available seats that day anyway. Or the next day. If she drove all the way, she wouldn't be able to return her Spanish-registered car in Portugal. A train would take eleven hours, which she couldn't face. The resourceful Janette suggested she drive to Seville, leave the car, and take one of the very frequent buses from there to Faro.

'I definitely think that's your best option. You'll be able to get to Albufeira by early evening, no problem. It's a longish taxi ride from Faro, or there's a train that only takes twenty minutes.'

'Thank you.' Rachel didn't point out that this route would still mean at least five hours behind the wheel. Her gammy leg was hardly Janette's problem. She downed a couple of painkillers and hit the road, reaching a hot, dusty, traffic-clogged Seville in the middle of the afternoon. A woman at the car rental office saw her limping pathetically with her luggage and offered the services of one of their pickup drivers to drop her at the bus station.

Brickall texted her as she was climbing onto the coach for the two-hour trip to Faro.

You on your way to the Algarve?

I'm now on leg two of the journey. It's a remake of Planes, Trains and Automobiles.

Her own leg was very painful after nearly six hours in the car, but she kept thinking of Howard's warning about opioid abuse and avoided taking more painkillers. Instead she gratefully accepted a plastic tumbler of wine from one of her fellow travellers, and slept most of the way over the border.

At 9 p.m., Tiago's Bar was about half full. No doubt revellers were thinner on the ground in October than during the summer season, but it had been a hot day and people were lingering at the beach for one last cold beer, and to watch the informal volleyball match that was taking place.

Rachel sat at one of the plastic tables and ordered a glass of *vinho verde* and – because she hadn't eaten all day and was ravenous – a paper plate of chips. There was only one waitress serving, and Rachel beckoned her over and showed her the photo of Gavin Harper sitting outside this very bar.

'Do you know him?'

She shook her head. 'Sorry, I no English.' But there was something there in her eyes: a flicker of recognition. After she had wolfed the chips, Rachel took her glass of wine and wandered a few yards away to a rocky outcrop, where she sat down. And waited.

At about eleven, the sound system was switched on, complete with flashing strobe lights, and gradually more people started to arrive, spilling out onto the sand in a rowdy gaggle. Cigarette tips lit the night sky like fireflies, and there was a heady whiff of marijuana. Suddenly, Rachel spotted a familiar figure strolling along the fairy-light-bedecked path that led from street to beach.

She had been looking at him for the past two days, so there was no doubt in her mind.

Gavin Harper.

She waited until he was a few feet from the front of the bar, then walked over. 'Excuse me.'

He froze.

'Gavin Harper? I need to talk to you.'

He thrust his chin down, spun on his heel and started sprinting back towards the road. Rachel dropped her beer bottle and took off after him, but her sandals gave her no purchase on the uneven sand and she stumbled. Once she was on the path, she steadied herself, but the torn ligament made it impossible to pick up any pace, and Gavin had vanished into the maze of darkened streets.

'Fuck!'

Wincing with pain, Rachel bent double to catch her breath, then limped back to the sanctuary of her hotel.

CHAPTER EIGHT

If Rachel Prince had a temperamental default setting, then it was 'stubborn'.

But on this occasion, she was forced to accept that she needed backup. Waking up the next morning in her basic hotel bedroom, she decided she would phone Patten and discuss the possibility of more personnel being sent from London. He wasn't available, but she was at least able to ask Janette to email a copy of the reported sighting of Lola Jade in Portugal.

A British holidaymaker had phoned the police information line while they were on holiday in Albufeira.

'My wife and I were on the way to the beach and we saw a youngish man with brown hair leading a blonde girl along Rua da Bateria. We agreed that it looked a bit like Lola Jade Harper, and she was around the right age. She didn't appear upset or distressed.'

But the date was 3 August, and Gavin Harper disappeared from Eastwell in late October. Perhaps someone else took Lola to Portugal and kept her there for a while until Gavin could slip away without suspicion. His brother Andy?

She texted Brickall.

Try and find out if Andy Whittier left the country during July or August.

Before she could do anything else, she needed caffeine. She wandered into the old town, with its pretty mosaic-tiled streets, and sat outside a tiny *pastelaria* with a coffee and a pastry.

It was still early, and the narrow street fairly empty, so Rachel had a good view of the people who were strolling past. Her heart lurched in her chest when she spotted him. He was wearing sunglasses and had a baseball cap pulled down low, but the dolphin tattoo on his arm gave him away. Gavin Harper.

Rachel leapt to her feet, almost knocking over her table, and walked briskly but unobtrusively down the street after him, gaining on him before he had the chance to spot her. He sensed rather than saw her, and broke into a run, but shoppers and gossiping locals disrupted his sprint, allowing Rachel to get close enough to grab his T-shirt.

'Hey! Stop! I need to talk to you.'

A gaggle of people gathered, attracting the attention of a uniformed national guard. Thinking Rachel was being mugged, he drew his baton and pinioned a resistant Gavin by the wrist.

'Get the fuck off me!' he snarled, trying to struggle free from the guard's grip, lashing out with his free arm.

Rachel wrestled her Interpol warrant card from her jeans pocket and showed it to the guard. He nodded and muttered a few words into his airwave set, and within seconds a police van arrived and Gavin Harper was bundled unceremoniously inside.

'Where's Lola Jade?'

Rachel sat opposite Gavin Harper in an interview room at the local headquarters of the Guarda Nacional Republicana. She had been at pains to explain that he wasn't yet under arrest, but that it was in his best interest to talk to her.

'I don't know.' He spoke angrily, 'You can't keep me here, Constable…'

'Detective Inspector. Prince.'

'Detective Inspector, I've done nothing wrong. I haven't done anything to Lola. I swear on my life.'

She looked into his eyes. He looked straight back, unflinching.

'So why on earth did you leave the UK and go on the run?'

'Because everyone was pointing the finger at me and I couldn't deal with it. I needed to get away.'

Rachel was sceptical. 'Without even telling anyone? Not even your brother?'

His face clouded slightly. 'I didn't want any hassle for them. I didn't want them being asked about where I was.'

'But if you'd done nothing wrong, why would they be hassled? And why were people "pointing the finger at you"' – she made quote marks – 'in the first place?'

Gavin shrugged. 'Because me and Michelle were getting divorced. And it was getting very messy.'

Rachel made a mental note to revisit the divorce proceedings. 'Okay, forget the why for a second – *how* did you do it? You were on an international watch list, but there's no record of you leaving the UK.'

He spoke coldly this time. 'I'm not going to answer any more questions. Not without a lawyer.'

Rachel ignored this.

'So the semen traces found on the floor of Lola's room, containing your DNA?' She folded her arms, but kept her voice level and unemotional.

'I just told you: I'm not answering questions.'

Rachel sighed, suddenly overwhelmed with tiredness and the longing for Brickall's infuriating yet reassuring presence. Double-handed interviews worked so much better. 'If you want an English-speaking lawyer, that's going to take a while to organise. In the meantime, you're going to be the guest of these nice Portuguese gentlemen.'

*

The body search conducted during Gavin's booking revealed a labelled set of keys for an apartment block on the Rua Cel Aguas. With him locked in a police cell, Rachel and a young Guarda called Bruno drove there, gloved up and began a fingertip search of the third-floor one-bedroom apartment.

There wasn't much to examine: just a rucksack with a few clothes in it, a charger in a box that had held a cheap disposable mobile phone, and an iPod plugged into a portable speaker. There was milk and beer in the kitchen fridge; a half-eaten box of breakfast cereal and some tea bags in the cupboard. One toothbrush, some deodorant and a disposable razor in the bathroom. A couple of towels had been used, and both sides of the bed appeared to have been slept in. Bruno bagged the towel, the toothbrush and the bed linen for DNA sampling.

The nightstand's drawer revealed a passport and credit card in the name of Andy Whittier. So that was how he had done it: exploiting the resemblance between himself and his brother. Rachel handed them to Bruno to bag.

'We finish now?'

'Hold on. One second.'

Something made Rachel go back to the rucksack and re-examine it, turning it inside out. There was a padded interior pocket, which she unzipped, pulling out a small child's nightgown: white jersey material scattered with red, yellow and blue stars. The label said 'Ages 5–7'. She held it up.

'*Meu Deus!*' breathed Bruno.

'Quite.'

She bagged it up and, once they had retrieved the building's CCTV recordings from the management office, they drove fast back to the Guarda Nacional building, with Bruno pressing the heel of his palm frequently on the car horn.

Rachel spent the next two and a half hours reviewing the CCTV footage from the apartment block, but the only images of

Gavin were of him alone. She asked for him to be released from the cell and brought back into the interview room, where she laid the nightdress on the table between them.

'Recognise this?'

He looked surprised. 'Where did you find that?'

'In your rucksack. It's about to go to our forensic lab to be tested. My bet is that it's going to have two sets of DNA on it. Yours and Lola's.'

'It must have been in there for ages. I used that rucksack when Lola and I went to a campsite in Rhyl last summer. My cousin has a place down there.'

Rachel kept her expression neutral. 'We'll corroborate that. Obviously. Right… I've requested a lawyer and a translator, who are going to come and speak to you.'

'How long will that take?'

'A few hours. But the GNR here are going to remand you in custody anyway while I get a European arrest warrant issued.'

'You can't fucking arrest me: I haven't done anything.' His body language was pure aggression, and Rachel thought back to the photos of Michelle's bruised arms.

'I'm afraid you have,' she said coolly. 'Use of a false identity document happens to be an indictable offence. That means extradition rules apply. In other words, the Portuguese authorities now have to send you back to face trial. And I get the undoubted pleasure of escorting you back to the UK.'

'Fuck's sake. You can't do this!' He slammed the flat of his hand on the table.

She paused in the doorway, as Bruno and one of his friends pulled Gavin to his feet. 'Carry on like this and you're going to be travelling home in a pair of steel bracelets.'

*

The flight from Faro landed at Gatwick the following evening. As soon as Rachel had handed over Gavin Harper and the exhibits to a uniformed team from Surrey Police, she texted Brickall.

Found Harper. He's got some explaining to do.

He replied straight away.

We're all at the Pin, loser.

Succinct, she thought. And also insolent. Par for the course. She went back to her flat, showered and changed out of her grimy travelling clothes, applied some make-up, then headed to their work local, the Pin and Needle.

'Look what the cat dragged in,' crowed Brickall, but he gave her a comradely slap on the shoulder and bought her a glass of red wine. The place was crowded, but they carved out a couple of feet of space at the bar.

'Still in a good mood, I see,' Rachel observed. 'Oh, crap!'

She had just spotted a familiar figure on the far side of the bar. Howard. 'My personal trainer,' she explained to Brickall. 'I wasn't expecting to see him here.'

'Ooh – a personal trainer now, is it? Get you.'

Brickall was tipsy, but not too tipsy to notice the faint pinkness in Rachel's cheeks, or the way she kept glancing over in Howard's direction. 'Oh, I get it,' he said with satisfaction.

'Get what?'

'You fancy him, don't you? It's obvious.'

Rachel shook her head rather too vigorously. 'Fuck off, Brickall, it's not that. We had an argument, and I was rude to him.'

'That never stopped you before.'

She gave him the finger before jostling herself out of the corner she was penned into and limping in Howard's direction. He did a comedy double-take when he saw her, and she realised it was because he hadn't immediately recognised her, with her freshly styled hair, tailored shirt and red lipstick complementing her newly acquired Mediterranean glow. He was used to seeing her bare-faced and in sweaty disarray at the gym.

'Hi,' she said. 'Can I get you a drink?'

He shook his head. 'I'm with my wife.' He pointed at a table at the far side of the room, where an attractive red-headed woman was sitting with that awkward air of the pub-goer who doesn't yet have a drink.

'Oh, I see.' She collected herself. 'Sorry, I didn't realise you were married.'

He held up his left hand, displaying a gold band. 'Not a good idea to wear a wedding ring while you're boxing.'

'Okay, well… I just wanted to say sorry. I was rude to you. About the tramadol.'

He smiled, showing she was forgiven. 'How is the knee?'

Rachel had to stop and consider her answer, which in turn made her realise she hadn't thought about it for a while.

'A bit better, I think. Yes, definitely better. And you were right about the pills: I should be careful with them.'

There was an awkward pause. 'Well, I guess I'll see you at the gym, now I'm back.'

'Sure.'

Howard gave her a brief smile, then wove his way to the table where his wife was sitting. She was staring in Rachel's direction, and the displeasure on her face was unsettling.

Rachel used what limited space she had to pivot through one hundred and eighty degrees and squeezed back through the crush to Brickall.

'Trial over, then, is it?' she asked him.

He nodded.

'So no more hot lawyer then?'

He grinned. '*Au contraire*, Prince, I fully intend there will be plenty more of the hot lawyer. Any day now, she and I are going to be going on a date.'

'Have you asked her?'

He shook his head. 'But I'm going to, don't you worry… And how about you? Amazing that you arrested Gavin Harper. Good work.'

Rachel inclined her head over her glass, acknowledging this rare praise, then took a deep gulp of her wine. Her eyes flicked involuntarily in the direction of Howard and his wife, who was still looking daggers at her.

'But obviously he didn't have the kid, or we'd all know about it by now.'

'No, he didn't. But I'm pretty certain he's involved in her disappearance somehow. And as soon as he's got a brief, I'm going to get to the bottom of it.'

'Certain? That's a dirty word round here, Prince.'

'Okay, not certain then. There's some evidence to suggest he might be.'

Despite his teasing tone, she was confident that Brickall would trust her hunch.

'I checked on Whittier's movements,' he added. 'He did go to the Med in August, but it was Majorca, not Portugal. So what next?'

'Gavin's currently in a custody suite at Eastwell nick. I'll need to interview him again, with a lawyer present this time. And then we need to make some follow-up enquiries.' She drained her wine glass, 'Which will probably start with us going back to visit Michelle Harper.'

CHAPTER NINE

Gavin Harper was now represented by an experienced criminal solicitor called Robert Neeley, but for Rachel's purposes, this made little difference. He still wasn't saying very much.

'I've got nothing to tell you,' he insisted. 'Not above what I've already told you. I was freaking out from all the attention and I legged it to Portugal. To get away for a bit. There's nothing wrong with that.'

'Apart from the tiny matter of using a false passport,' Rachel said drily.

'Because I knew if I used my own there'd be hassle. After stuff that Michelle said about me.'

'Why didn't you tell anyone?'

'I did though, didn't I? I told Andy.'

'Why didn't you tell anyone else?'

'Why should I? Not like I was on bail, or house arrest.'

'All right. So what about the night when Lola was taken?'

Robert Neeley leaned across. 'My client has already made a statement to police about that.'

They went round in circles like this for a while, with Gavin alternately mulish and aggressive, until Neeley said that he wouldn't be answering any further questions but would instead provide a prepared statement definitively setting out his position. It was a classic stall from the criminal-law playbook. Reluctantly Rachel left them to it and went to join Brickall in Willow Way.

*

'Why am I not surprised? No one here.'

Rachel and Brickall were seated in an unmarked car outside number 57, and once again there was no one answering the door, despite Rachel having left a voicemail for Michelle Harper telling her they'd like to speak to her again.

'You never know, she may have just popped out to the shops,' suggested Brickall. 'Give her a minute or two.'

But Rachel was shaking her head. She reached for her phone and pulled up the photos that WPC Nicholls had taken.

'What am I looking at?'

'The wheelie bin. Completely empty apart from a few bits of junk mail.'

'So? The bin men had probably just been.'

She shook her head again. 'No. The bin men were just about to arrive.'

'Come off it, Prince; she might not have got round to taking stuff out to the dustbin. We've all done it.'

'Ah, but…' Rachel grinned, 'I made sure I chucked a takeaway cup into the kitchen bin so I could get a good look inside it. It was empty.'

Brickall's expression was still blank.

'Come on, Detective Sergeant. If you're living somewhere, the kitchen bin is full of tea bags, eggshells, kitchen towel, food packaging… there was nothing. And what about the dog?'

'The dog?'

'She's supposed to have a dog, but there's been no sign of it on any of my visits.'

'If she's not here, it's hardly surprising in the circumstances,' Brickall said mulishly. 'She could have been staying with a relative or friend for a few weeks. God knows it must be hard enough for her being alone in that house.'

'Maybe. Either way, we haven't got all day to sit about. We've got the CEOP case conference this afternoon.'

'You can't wait to get back up to Pimlico to see your hunky Denton.'

Rachel flicked her seat-belt buckle at him, as though swatting a fly. 'You're a cock, Brickall.'

Just as he was about to retaliate by balling up a sweet wrapper and flicking it at her, the familiar white BMW drove up and Michelle Harper climbed out.

'So how are we going to play this?' Brickall asked, before they got out of the car. 'We don't want to get her hopes up, nor do we want to spook her.'

'Keep it low key. It's not like we can say we know for sure what's happened to Lola Jade. Not yet.'

'Better do the same at this afternoon's case conference,' affirmed Brickall, with a wry grin. 'Can't swagger in there claiming we've cracked it when the kid's still missing.'

Michelle's body language had changed, Rachel thought.

She'd dropped the bravado and the thinly veiled passive aggression, seeming listless, flat. The black leggings and plain top were unassuming, the make-up low key.

'She's not dead, is she?' was the first thing out of her mouth, even though Rachel had given no indication on the phone that this was the case.

'No.' Rachel shook her head. 'Not as far as we know. But I did find your husband.'

Michelle's eyes widened. 'He was in Spain?'

'No,' said Rachel. 'Not in Spain, in Portugal.'

'*Portugal?*'

Brickall glanced at Rachel, and she knew what that particular look of his meant. That the shock seemed a little overdone.

'He doesn't have Lola Jade with him.'

'He's lying.' The grieving-mum mask slipped a little as she spat the words.

Rachel shook her head. 'I don't think so. But he's now back in the UK, so we'll be able to keep a close eye on him. For now, I wanted to ask you about this.'

She showed Michelle a photo of the nightie with stars on.

'It's Lola's.' She corrected herself. 'It could be hers, I mean. She had one just like it.'

'Did your husband take Lola on holiday last summer?'

Michelle nodded. 'Yes, he took her to Wales. His cousin – the one I told you about – has a static caravan in Rhyl.'

'So this nightie was among the things you packed for her? Only he says that's why it was still in his possession when he went to Portugal: that he forgot to unpack it.'

Michelle shook her head firmly. 'No. Definitely not. I'd have remembered, because Lola Jade prefers pyjamas.'

Rachel and Brickall exchanged a glance. 'And is there anyone else, anyone at all you can think of, who might have had reason to take your daughter? Anyone with a grudge against you?'

Michelle appeared to be thinking about this. 'There was someone I fell out with once: Joanne Keen.'

Rachel took out her notebook. 'Go on.'

'Her husband, Danny, put in the kitchen for us. Only he made a right mess of it, so we refused to pay him all the money. We paid around half, I think…' Michelle picked at the polish on her fingernails, which was cracked and peeling. 'Anyway, there was a massive row about it: they threatened to sue and everything. Joanne got involved and picked a fight with me at the school gates.'

'A physical fight?' asked Rachel.

Michelle coloured slightly. 'I may have slapped her in the heat of the moment, but she gave as good as she got. It was mostly a screaming match, and when her friend dragged her away, she said she was going to get me. I remember that clear as day, her shouting: "I'm going to get you, you bitch!"'

While Rachel was playing good cop, Brickall had stood up and walked into the kitchen, opening cupboards and looking inside drawers. 'So,' he said, in his best-bad cop voice, pointing to the open cupboard, 'd'you mind telling us about this, Mrs Harper?'

'What d'you mean?'

'There's nothing in the cupboard apart from some sugar lumps and out-of-date instant coffee that's as hard as a rock. Are you actually living here?'

Michelle pulled out a tissue, shaking her head. 'I can't stand it,' she said simply. 'I can't stand being alone here at night, walking past the door to my princess's room.' She gulped, and blinked hard as though she was either trying to keep back tears or force them to start. 'So I'm spending most of my time over at Lisa's.'

'Your sister?'

Michelle nodded.

Rachel closed her notebook, which was a cue she knew Brickall would understand.

'Right. I think we'll leave it there. It might be helpful if you let us know where you are next time we get in touch.'

When they reached the car, Brickall asked, 'Are you thinking what I'm thinking?'

Rachel nodded. 'Time for a bit of vehicular reconnaissance.'

They pulled the car into a perpendicular tree-named close, positioned just out of sight, and waited until Michelle's BMW drove past, then followed at a discreet distance. She drove three miles due west, to the Albert Park area on the far side of Eastwell, a grid of Victorian workers' brick cottages, and parked outside an unassuming flat-fronted terrace. The door was opened by a square woman with pink hair. Lisa Urquhart. Her face remained impassive as Michelle went inside, then the door was closed.

'We'd need to cross-check her statement on the file, but I'm pretty sure that's Lisa's address.'

'So her story about staying at her sister's is true.' said Brickall. 'I told you: she just can't hack being alone.'

'Given we have to look at the entire family, I still reckon we should search the place,' Rachel said.

'Sounds like a waste of time to me.' Brickall started the engine and turned the car back towards London. He caught sight of Rachel's expression. 'Right you are, boss: I'll apply for a warrant.'

'We've passed the Harper file on to our Victim Identification team.'

Giles Denton, director of CEOP, was leading the case conference in the ground-floor meeting room of the department's offices in Vauxhall Bridge Road. He was around thirty-five, swarthily handsome in the Black Irish mould, with a face shaded with stubble and eyes so dark it was almost impossible to discern that they were blue. Rachel gazed at him admiringly whenever no one else was looking. She couldn't help herself.

'… they'll cross-check pictures of Lola Jade with images from sites frequented by online abusers, and liaise with the Victim ID community in other countries.'

His North Sea-blue eyes were directed at Rachel and she looked quickly down at the cup of tea that had just been provided from a trolley wheeled in by someone in Catering. Brickall was already on biscuit number four. 'So you think Lola Jade has been targeted by a paedophile ring?'

'I think it's a strong possibility, given that there's still no body, and evidence points to her having been removed from the home alive. She fits the "shopping list"…' He made air quotes. 'She's Caucasian, blonde, under the age of seven. Highly saleable in this market.'

Rachel screwed up her face in distaste, before debriefing the team on her trip to Spain and Portugal, keeping her eyes focused on the fire-drill instructions fixed to the wall rather than on Giles's stubbled jaw.

'We've re-interviewed Gavin Harper – without much success, I'm afraid – and we'll speak again to friends and family, but this time round try and cast the net beyond the original witness list. The hope is that a few months on, someone will remember something or mention a detail they didn't think important before. Make the passage of time work for us. Gavin had a cousin who apparently took a keen interest in Lola and holidayed with her: we'll need to speak to him and his wife.'

'And I've applied for a warrant to search the aunt's house,' Brickall chipped in through a mouthful of chocolate digestive. 'Lisa Urquhart. We know Lola's mother, Michelle, has been staying there. It's a long shot, but it could throw up some fresh forensics.'

With a consensus that they would convene for an update in a week, the meeting was adjourned, and Rachel and Brickall gathered their belongings and drove back over the Thames to the Tinworth Street site in Lambeth.

'A whole week.' Brickall's expression was suggestive. 'Sure you can wait that long, Prince? For another sighting of Boyzone.'

'Behave.'

After they had parked the pool car, they walked in through the lobby, heading up to their third-floor office. Rachel's knee was stiff from sitting and Brickall had to wait for her to catch up, with exaggerated sighs and eye-rolling.

'You go up,' she told him as they reached the lift. 'I'm going to go straight home and put my leg up for a bi— Oh, shit.'

The colour drained from her face. Brickall followed her gaze to the reception desk to where a man was standing. A tall, distinguished-looking man with thick sandy hair streaked with grey. Stuart Ritchie.

Brickall tipped his head in the same direction. 'That him?'

But Rachel had already turned on her heel and ducked through the fire-escape door. She headed back down the stairs to the underground car park, moving as fast as her injured leg would allow.

'Hold on, you plank!' Brickall ran after her. 'Let me drive you home. Jesus, what a head case! All this fuss about avoiding an ex.'

Rachel turned to face him as she reached her car door. 'He's not just an ex. He's my husband.'

'You really are a puzzle wrapped inside an enigma buried in a… however the stupid saying goes.'

Brickall spread himself over Rachel's sofa, not attempting to hide the smug smile of triumph that lit up his face. He had insisted on coming up to the flat with her, even though the coast was clear: 'Just in case your old man's beaten us to it and is waiting outside your front door.'

He wasn't, but Rachel asked Brickall in anyway, poured them both wine and opened a packet of crisps. She rarely cooked, and this was the only food she had in stock, other than salad and greens in the fridge. Brickall liked to tease her about her preoccupation with healthy eating, just as she poured scorn on his love of junk food.

'Done loads with the place since last time I was here,' he said sarcastically, indicating the bare white walls, the sterile kitchen surfaces and general absence of clutter or personal memorabilia. 'So…' he went on around a mouthful of half-chewed crisps, surprisingly still hungry after five biscuits. 'You've been married all this time and you never said a word. Quite the dark horse.'

'It's not what it looks like.'

'Said the criminal to the copper.'

Rachel reached for the pack of tramadol and swallowed one with a deep draught of wine. It was the first she'd taken all day, but after running down the steps to the basement, she needed it. 'I mean, I'm legally married, but only because I haven't got round to a divorce.'

Brickall put down his wine glass and stared at her. 'How long have you been married? Jesus, Prince. I mean, I've known you at least five years and you've never once mentioned a *husband*. Why the secrecy? Not like I haven't seen an endless line of men traipsing in and out of your bedroom.'

She ignored this last remark. Her dysfunctional yet eventful love life was an endless source of entertainment to her detective sergeant, but she knew better than to rise to the bait. Besides, this was a subject she did not want treated with jocularity or subjected to scrutiny. 'It was a long time ago. I was twenty-two, and it only lasted around a year.'

'He in the force?'

She shook her head. 'Pathologist. Dr Stuart Ritchie. Actually, he could even be Professor Ritchie now.'

Brickall calculated on his fingers. 'So if it was… about seventeen years ago, why the need to avoid him? Water under the bridge. You've moved on, and presumably so has he.'

Rachel flushed slightly. 'Because… I didn't behave very well.'

'Go on.'

'I was very unhappy. I suppose I was still pretty immature, and I couldn't cope with being married. So one day, without saying anything, I went home, packed up all my stuff and ran away. Disappeared. This was before social media and online footprints, so he had no idea where I was.'

Brickall squinted at her as he drank his wine. 'What a little cow! But surely, after the dust had settled, he'd have been able to track you down. Clearly he has, finally.'

Rachel sighed. 'That's what I'm afraid of. I really hurt him.' She looked at her fingernails 'Badly. He was distraught, I know for a fact he was, because he went to my family: pleaded with them to intervene on his behalf. But I forbade them to tell him where I was. It caused a lot of bad feeling… particularly with my sister, Lindsay…' Rachel sighed again. Bad feeling between Lindsay and herself had become the norm. 'But they did what I asked and kept silent. I hid from him for so long that eventually he gave up. And I pretended it had never happened.'

'But you're a big girl now, Prince. Time to come clean. Well…' He shovelled in more crisps. 'Arguably that time has been and gone.'

She sighed. 'I'd buried it. All of that period in my life. And I don't want to rake over it now.'

Brickall was grinning. 'Whoever would have thought the cool, always-in-control DI Prince could do something so deviant?'

'And you're the only one I've ever talked to about it, so for Christ's sake keep it zipped.' Rachel helped herself to more wine, then stuck her right leg up on the coffee table. 'How are things going with the lady barrister?'

He pulled a face. 'I asked her out, but she wasn't too keen. Said maybe coffee some time, blah, blah… usual kiss-off.'

'But she'd given you her number when you were on the trial together?'

Brickall shook his head. 'Not exactly. In fact, since we're having a confessional session, I've got one to make.'

'Go on.'

'I used our access to DVLA records to check where she lives. Then I contrived to bump into her on her street.'

Rachel froze, slopping her wine. 'Mark! You know how risky that is.' Using a police database to access someone's information for personal reasons was a disciplinary offence.

He shrugged. 'No one's ever going to find out. And I know I can trust you, just like you can trust me: *Mrs* Ritchie.'

'I'm not Mrs Ritchie; never was. I've only ever called myself Rachel Prince.'

He paused with his head tipped back to swallow another fistful of crisps. 'Let's face it: you're just not wife material.'

CHAPTER TEN

'Not a happy bunny, is she?'

Brickall jerked his head in the direction of Lisa Urquhart, who was scowling fiercely in their direction, arms across her ample chest. If her sister embodied passive aggression, then Lisa was just plain aggression.

'I don't get why you need to do this,' she snarled as a team of forensics officers went through the house, examining the contents of drawers, peering under furniture, climbing up into the roof space, with one of their number snapping photos of everything. 'It's not like Lola Jade would be here. That's ridiculous.' Michelle herself was at work, apparently, but her lapdog Diva made her presence felt with a volley of yapping.

Lisa had a husband, Kevin, and two children, Chelsea and Connor, who had been temporarily moved into a shared room so that Michelle could use the third bedroom. Rachel waited until the forensics team had finished before snapping on latex gloves and going in there herself. The single bed had a Disney cover on it, and looked recently slept in; the child's dressing table was strewn with make-up and hair products and what looked like a dead tabby cat but turned out to be a nest of stripy blonde and brown hair extensions. The wardrobe contained some of Michelle's clothes and shoes, neatly arranged, and there were several skimpy lace thongs in a drawer that would have been far too small for Lisa.

'So what do we think?' asked Brickall, as the search was concluded and the forensic team stripped off their paper suits. Diva the dog darted forwards and nipped him on the ankle. He aimed a kick in its direction. 'Fuck off, you little rodent!'

'Well, we'll have to see what the DNA samples show up, but my gut's telling me Lola definitely hasn't been here recently.'

'Did we look at the husband?' Brickall asked.

'You mean Kevin Urquhart? Couple of minor disorder offences, brawling in a pub, that kind of thing.'

'Our favourite.'

'Nothing to suggest he'd be involved in snatching his own niece, but it might be worth talking to neighbours or colleagues in case.'

Rachel turned back and looked at the Urquharts' house. 'I don't know. There's something… a bell going off in the depths of my brain, but I can't think what it is.'

'It'll come to you, Prince: it always does.' Brickall unlocked the car. 'So who's next on the hit list? Gavin Harper again? Is he remanded?'

Rachel climbed into the driver's seat, wedging her right leg awkwardly into the footwell. It still hurt intermittently, but she was learning to ignore the pain. To distract herself, she looked at her phone. 'Not any more he's not.' She looked up at Brickall. 'There's a message here from Surrey Police saying that after his lawyer provided a prepared statement, they charged him with the passport fraud and bailed him. I don't think we're going to get anything else out of him by questioning him, but let's keep a check on his movements, and talk to people who might be able to tell us more. Which means you're going to find out what you can about his cousin, Tony Ingram, and I'm going to go and talk to his divorce lawyer.'

Howard had coaxed Rachel into practising her dead hang again, and while she was suspended in space, he was taking a long hard look at her body. His scrutiny made her feel self-conscious, but the warmth in her cheeks was fortunately disguised by her general sweatiness.

'Your knee looks a bit better,' he observed when she eventually relinquished her grip. 'Less swollen.'

'I think it's improved a bit,' Rachel agreed. 'And before you say anything, I have been very moderate with the drugs. I'm only taking them when I'm desperate.'

Howard grinned. 'Glad to hear it.'

He had such a nice smile, Rachel thought. And she was starting to look forward to him smiling at her, and experiencing a little flip at the base of her stomach when he did. A telltale sign.

But he was married, and she had sworn off married men. Off men in general. It was a couple of years since she'd dated anyone semi-seriously – a solicitor called Simon – and even longer since she'd dated anyone seriously, although there had been a smattering of one-, two- and even three-night stands. Nobody who had held her interest for longer than that. But with Howard there was definitely interest. Curiosity even.

'What does your wife do?' she asked.

'She's a manager in a department store.'

'And how long have you been married?'

'Six years.'

'Kids?'

He shook his head, sadly. 'I want them, she doesn't. Before we were married, she was all over the idea. She'd chosen the names and everything. Now she's done a complete U-turn; says she can't see how they'd fit into our lives.'

'There'll be time for her to change her mind, though?'

'Maybe. She's already thirty-six. We've been having rows about it, non-stop. That's why we went to the pub: to try and talk properly, on neutral territory.' He gave a rueful look. 'Didn't work, though. I still ended up spending the night in the spare room.'

Get out, Rachel wanted to tell him. *You're far too nice to be in a lousy marriage.*

'Have you got time for a drink?' Howard said suddenly. 'A couple of the swimming coaches are heading down to the pub in a bit.'

Rachel hesitated a fraction too long. 'No,' she said eventually. 'Thanks, but I'd better get going. I've got a couple of things I need to follow up on.'

She went home via the local wholefood store, picking up the makings of a salad and a bottle of organic Zinfandel. After she'd eaten, she took her glass of wine out onto her tiny balcony, enjoying the late-autumn dusk. The air was cool but ripe, much like the wine. She picked up her phone and composed a text.

Hi, Stuart.

What on earth should she say? What *could* she say, after seventeen years of silence and effectively ruining his life? A tendency towards conflict avoidance and emotional self-sufficiency were two of the many reasons she was still single. Well, technically married, but with a single lifestyle. But on this occasion, she accepted, she was just going to have to face up to her failings, conflict or not.

Sorry I didn't take your calls. I've been busy at work.

She deleted the last five words and replaced them with: *I'll admit it, I was avoiding you.*

After she had sent the text, she flicked through her Facebook account. Danielle Patten had posted a sweet picture of Nigel with their baby, Jack, on his lap. The little boy was clutching a blue plush rabbit. Rachel stared at the photo for a few seconds, the familiar bell ringing in her brain. Then she dialled Brickall, who picked up after two rings.

'I've just thought of something, something about the Urquhart house that was bugging me.'

'Go on.'

'Did you notice—'

She was interrupted by a pinging on her phone as a text arrived. A glance confirmed it was from Stuart.

'Sorry, Mark, got to go. We can talk about it in the morning.'

'Rude!' complained Brickall, hanging up.

Rachel sat sipping her wine and looking at Stuart's text. His faintly pompous tone melted the years away, and she was once again the impressionable young WPC, fresh from Hendon Police College, working on her first murder case.

That much was obvious. Nevertheless, I'm sure you'll agree that it's important we talk. Soon.

She sighed, and typed a brief reply.

Tell me where and when.

The next morning, she tracked down Brickall in the NCA canteen. He was eating a fried breakfast, his favourite meal apart from pizza with hot sauce.

'So what was that about last night? I was all psyched up for the big reveal.' He shovelled mushrooms and sausages into his mouth with hedonistic abandon.

Rachel had the grace to look sheepish. 'My husband.'

'Demanding his conjugal rights, was he?' Brickall winked as he squirted brown sauce over his fried eggs, then proceeded to puncture the yolks with his fork.

'Don't be ridiculous.' snapped Rachel. 'He thinks we should talk, and let's face it, he's probably right.' She drank some of her mug of canteen coffee, wincing at the acrid taste. 'Listen, what I was about to say was this: the early footage of the house in Willow Way shows a hideous big studio portrait of Lola on the living room wall, and her favourite Katy Bear teddy in her bedroom. Michelle then takes it to the press conference, uses it as a prop to demonstrate how devoted she is.'

'So?' Brickall slathered butter on some toast.

'So when I visited her on my own, I checked, and neither of those items – those very important items – are still in 57 Willow Way. Michelle's decamped to her sister's in Jubilee Terrace, so you might expect her to take them with her. But they weren't there yesterday during the search. Not in her room, not in the loft, not in the garage.'

Brickall thought about this for a moment. 'Maybe she's packed up some stuff and put it in storage. Or taken it to her mum's place. Doesn't want to be reminded.'

'My brain says maybe.' Rachel ventured another sip of the bitter coffee. 'But my gut doesn't necessarily agree.'

'I've got something much juicier than that anyway.' Brickall dipped the toast into the egg yolk, then swirled it through the brown sauce.

'What are you talking about?'

'You know the cousin, Tony Ingram? The one who's so devoted to little Lola Jade?'

Rachel could tell from his tone that he was excited, even though he appeared to be concentrating on his breakfast. 'Go on.'

'Old Tony's on the sex offenders' register. For molesting a little girl.'

CHAPTER ELEVEN

'Not what I'd planned to do this morning – I was going to speak to Gavin Harper's divorce lawyers. They're in the City.'

Rachel checked her phone as Brickall negotiated the South Circular, heading for Ruislip Gardens. No further communication from Stuart, which was a relief. Until she was actually face to face with him, she wanted no interaction at all; just to blank him from her mind. She looked out of the windscreen at the almost stationary queue of traffic. 'So I'm now on completely the wrong side of London.'

'Stop bloody whining,' muttered Brickall. 'You know that information like this needs looking into as soon as possible. An actual paedophile, connected to the missing child. Even if he did only get community service.'

'You're right.' Rachel forced a smile. 'Game face on.'

The Ingrams lived in an anonymous pebble-dashed end-terrace house, with net curtains and a mid-range family saloon parked on the drive. When Joyce Ingram answered the door, Rachel felt as though she'd walked onto the set of an advert for gravy, or garden furniture, with Joyce being the fifty-something mum of the family. She even wore an apron, and wiped her hands on it as she showed them into a drab but tidy living room.

'Is your husband at home?' Rachel asked, after she had introduced herself and Brickall.

'No, love. He's back at work now. He's a finance clerk at Harrow Council.' She indicated a framed photo of a harmless-looking grey-haired man in steel-framed glasses.

'Back after?'

'Sick leave.'

'So how long was he away from his employment?' asked Rachel, counting back rapidly.

'About five months.' Joyce flushed slightly. 'I know what you're probably thinking, but that… unpleasant business was years ago. It's over with now.'

'So how are you and your husband related to the Harpers?'

'Gavin's mum Pat – Lola Jade's gran – is Tony's first cousin. We used to look after Gavin, Andy and Karen quite a bit when they were little.' She gave an awkward smile. 'We couldn't have our own. We tried. Even did the IVF, when it was quite a new thing.'

'And you also saw a fair bit of Lola Jade?'

'A bit,' conceded Joyce. 'We're not exactly local, so it's only now and then. But we have a caravan in Rhyl, and Gavin used to bring Lola out there for a few days in the summer.' She screwed up her mouth. 'Not this year, obviously. It's just so dreadful.'

'You probably understand why we need to talk to your husband,' said Brickall, happily slipping into bad cop. 'With him being on the sex offenders' register.'

'Well he shouldn't be on it,' said Joyce firmly, bright red patches appearing at the centre of her cheeks. 'It was all a big misunderstanding. He was just trying to be civic-minded, helping out with the girl scouts' camp, and look what he gets for his efforts.'

Rachel and Brickall exchanged a familiar look. The well-worn wives' defence: it was all a big mistake.

Joyce saw it, jutting out her chin. 'And if you're going to ask about his whereabouts when Lola went missing, that's very easy. He was in Northwick Park Hospital having a quadruple heart bypass. He came out of hospital at the end of May, and he's been here, and in Rhyl, recuperating until he was fit enough to go back to work a week ago.' She looked defiantly at them. 'I suppose that would be easy enough for you to verify.'

'Indeed.' Rachel stood up. 'Thanks for your time, Mrs Ingram.'

As she headed for the door, she caught sight of a large photo in a frame. It was the prized caravan, awning out, against a vivid blue sky. Joyce and Tony sat on deckchairs, both wearing shorts, and Lola Jade Harper stood on the caravan steps. Rachel picked it up.

'That was last summer. Gavin took it,' said Joyce. 'It's a nice one of Lola, even if she is still in her nightclothes at ten in the morning. Gavin tended to be a bit relaxed with the rules when he was on holiday with her.'

Rachel looked at the photo. For once, little Lola Jade was smiling and it transformed her otherwise plain face. And the nightdress she was wearing was white, with coloured stars.

'Did Michelle pack Lola's clothes when she went away with her dad?' she asked, handing the photo to Brickall.

'Always,' said Joyce firmly. 'She was very organised about things like that. Always very inappropriate stuff too: frilly this and sparkly that. No rainwear or sensible shoes.'

'And when Lola went home at the end of the holiday, did you pack her stuff, or did Gavin?'

'Gavin did.' Joyce smiled fondly. 'He always left it to the last minute, then shoved everything in all jumbled up, not folded or anything. He's a bit messy, our Gavin.'

Brickall handed back the photo and they headed back to the car. 'Well, that was interesting,' said Rachel, as Brickall put the key in the ignition.

'Why? Paedo Tony's out of the frame, if the heart surgery checks out.'

'The nightdress,' said Rachel. 'Michelle said she didn't pack it for the holiday, when she clearly did.'

Brickall looked at her as the engine roared to life. 'Because her version of events makes it look as though there's something sinister about Gavin randomly having the nightie in his rucksack.'

'Exactly. She lied to us.'

Hepburn, Willis & Bell was an undeniably upmarket firm of solicitors in Blackfriars. Their offices occupied several floors of a sleek glass tower on Victoria Embankment, with a huge ground-floor reception area featuring low-level seating, state-of-the-art light fixtures and copies of *Country Life*.

Rachel was collected by a PA in an elegant black dress, and taken to see Conrad Bell, the partner who was dealing with the Harpers' divorce. He was a bony, ascetic young man with wired-framed glasses, dressed in the type of three-piece suit that Rachel's grandfather used to wear. He pointed to a chair facing his desk, revealing double cuffs and monogrammed cufflinks.

'Detective Inspector Prince,' he said smoothly. 'How may I be of assistance? And did Camilla offer you refreshments?'

Rachel began by expressing surprise that Gavin Harper wasn't using a firm of local solicitors. Bell inclined his head slightly.

'Ah yes, well, perhaps in some instances that is the most sensible thing. But this is an exceptional case that features some unusual… challenges. So Mr Harper very correctly sought representation by a firm that has expertise in children's issues.' He waved his hands in an expansive manner. 'Leave to remove overseas, child abduction, Cafcass reports, that sort of thing. And you're right in your assumption that we have done some preliminary work for Mr Harper, but he is not currently instructing us.'

'I see,' said Rachel, weighing up the plush carpet and expensive desk and concluding that this news wasn't exactly a surprise. Even if Gavin hadn't fled the country, you'd have to wonder how he would manage to pay for all of this. 'But you'll presumably be aware that his daughter, Lola Jade Harper, has been missing for five months? I'm part of the team that's investigating her disappearance, and I need access to Gavin Harper's divorce file.'

Bell leaned, back, shooting his cuffs. 'I am aware, yes: most unfortunate. But as a law-enforcement officer, *you* will be aware of my duty of confidentiality to my client. Unless records are subpoenaed by a judge, or a government body that has the statutory power to request them.'

Rachel parried with her blandest professional smile. 'Though of course under the 1989 Children Act, you are under a duty to reveal any experts' reports commissioned for the purposes of proceedings involving a child.' *Touché*, she thought.

Bell looked annoyed, but returned to the bland, professional geniality. 'There is, of course, the possibility of voluntary disclosure. I could ask Mr Harper if he's willing to let you view the papers.'

'Do you have a number for him?' Rachel thought of the disconnected UK mobile and the burner phone in Portugal, now in an evidence store.

'Indeed,' he parried smoothly. 'My client has recently returned from a trip overseas…'

That's one way of putting it, thought Rachel, picturing Gavin Harper handcuffed to her over a plane armrest.

'… and our office has recently been in touch with him, so if you'd care to wait, I could speak to him.'

Rachel did care to wait, and was led into a conference room with a huge glossy table at its centre. Camilla glided in as if on wheels, bearing a tray with a cafetière of freshly brewed coffee, a porcelain cup and saucer and a tray of Belgian biscuits. She reappeared about thirty minutes later with a couple of thick manila folders that had *Harper, G. J.* written on their spines.

'I may need copies of some of this,' Rachel told her.

'Of course.' She nodded, and floated out.

There were dozens of documents, and Rachel quickly realised that she would not be able to read them all unless Hepburn, Willis & Bell provided a bed for the night. She poured herself some coffee, settled into her chair and began to read the story of Gavin and Michelle's marriage.

CHAPTER TWELVE

Rachel started by flicking through the correspondence and weeding out what she thought was most important. First up was a lengthy report from a Dr Marian Flugman, MB BS, MPsych. She had been commissioned to conduct a psychological examination of Mrs Michelle Leslie Harper, née Kenny.

The complainant, Mr Gavin Harper, reports that his wife seemed to have a mood disorder and to be, in his opinion 'unstable'. She made repeated false allegations of child sex abuse with regard to their daughter Lola Jade Harper, aged 6. According to Mr Harper, she catastrophised his late return of the child after a contact visit and made a complaint of spousal abduction, later withdrawn. He describes constant mood swings, alternating rage and coldness or withdrawal. Her relationship with her daughter is described as 'obsessive', with the need to have total control over the child, while at the same time treating her with emotional indifference, as though she is a trophy or a possession. Mr Harper wonders if his wife might be suffering from undiagnosed bipolar disorder, and consequently be unsuitable to have primary care of their daughter.

Mrs Harper initially refused to attend for diagnostic interview, but when it was explained to her that her refusal would be a material factor in the upcoming decision about her daughter's residence order, she complied, with marked reluctance.

Method
I employed the World Health Organisation's IPDE assessment (International Personality Disorder Examination), comprising a self-administered screening questionnaire and a semi-structured interview booklet with scoring materials.

Findings
I was able to reject the diagnosis of bipolar disorder, where manic behaviour and depression must remain consistent for at least four days at a time. In Michelle Harper's case, the fluctuations were more short-lived, and triggered by external events, particularly the perceived failings of others. This is consistent with a diagnosis of borderline personality disorder.

The clinical definition of BPD is a pervasive pattern of instability of interpersonal relationships, self-image and affects, and marked impulsivity beginning by early adulthood and present in a variety of contexts, indicated by five or more of the nine diagnostic criteria. My assessment concluded that Mrs Harper demonstrates the following:

1. *A pattern of unstable and intense interpersonal relationships characterised by alternating between extremes of idealisation and devaluation.*
2. *Identity disturbance: a markedly and persistently unstable self-image.*
3. *Inappropriate intense anger or difficulty controlling anger: e.g. frequent displays of temper, constant anger, recurrent physical fights.*
4. *Transient stress-related paranoid ideation or severe dissociative symptoms.*
5. *Affective instability due to a marked reactivity of mood: e.g. alternating irritability and anxiety.*

Conclusion
There is clearly a discussion to be had regarding Mrs Harper's ability to care for her daughter appropriately. Parents with BPD typically lack insight into their own parenting abilities and become enraged when their child does not agree with them. They also attempt to control their children's behaviours, feelings and actions to a degree that inhibits their child's ability to develop independently. Lola's father reports the child becoming increasingly withdrawn as she constantly attempts to please her mother, who in turn believes her own behaviour is that of an exemplary parent.

Rachel thought back to the photos of Lola Jade: rarely smiling and with a generally unhappy air. To Gavin's description of Michelle's parenting style. Had someone snatched Lola to get her out of her mother's clutches, or was this something else altogether?

She sipped the excellent coffee and flicked through the file again. Her eye was caught by the cream and pink paper. *Certified copy of an entry of birth: Lola Jade Harriet Harper, 13 September 2009.* Attached to it with a paper clip was a copy of a second birth certificate: *Oliver Jake Terence Harper, 7 April 2008.* And behind that was a third certificate, the stark black-and-white print stating: *Certified copy of an entry pursuant to the Births and Deaths Registration Act 1953: DEATH.* That bleak word in capitals, inside a black-framed text box. *Oliver Jake Harper, 2 July 2008. Cause of death: 1. Unascertained 2. Ear infection.* The death certificate had been signed by the Surrey county coroner, and there was a police report and a summary of the post-mortem findings, both of which were inconclusive. The baby had been a little grizzly when he had been put down for a nap, and had been found dead by Michelle two hours later.

Rachel thought back to the baby photos in Michelle's album, and on display on the wall of her house. They were all of infants in lacy dresses and pale pink. Not a single image of a boy. Odd.

At the top of the file was the bill for Conrad Bell's services and other defrayed expenses, totalling £9,875 plus VAT. Stapled to it was a red bill for the same amount, with ACCOUNT OVERDUE stamped on it. So Bell had declined to move past his preliminary investigations when it looked as though he wasn't going to be paid.

Camilla sashayed in to collect the tray, and Rachel gave her the documents she wanted copied, firing off a text to Brickall while she waited.

We definitely need a chat with Gavin Harper. Meet you at the office?

'So here's an alternative theory, based on the divorce case.'

Rachel and Brickall had repaired to the Pin and Needle, where they held a lot of their informal case conferences. And in Rachel's current predicament, it was a lot more comfortable than sitting at her desk. She could stretch out her right leg.

'Go on.' Brickall bent his head and carefully siphoned up lager from an overfilled glass, then started on a bowl of chips. Rachel had limited herself to mineral water, but stole one of the chips.

'Gavin Harper wants to get full custody of his daughter, so employs a top lawyer who finds a psychiatrist willing to say that Michelle is a dangerous nutter. But he runs out of money to retain said lawyer long before the case reaches the family court. So he takes matters into his own hands and runs off with Lola.'

Brickall squinted, his expression sceptical. 'But you said that apart from the nightdress – which we've cleared up – there was no sign he'd taken the kid to Portugal with him.'

'There wasn't. At least not in Albufeira. But what if that was just a move to take us down the wrong track? What if he's actually hidden her somewhere else?'

'According to Surrey Police, since he was bailed, he's been shacked up at his dad's. At least that's the reporting address he's given them.'

'So we should start by visiting Terry again. And possibly Andy. He obviously knew more than he was letting on. The family are certainly not fans of Michelle: it's perfectly plausible they'd want to see Lola Jade taken away from her.'

Brickall shovelled in the remaining chips and drained his lager. It never ceased to amaze Rachel that not only was he not overweight, but he never seemed to gain an ounce, despite his shocking eating habits. 'Shall we head down to Eastwell then?' He jangled his car keys in her face.

She checked the time. Nearly 5 p.m. 'Not this evening. I'm going out.'

He did a mock double-take. 'A date, Prince?'

She nodded. 'It is, as it happens.'

'Who's the lucky man? Married, is he?'

'Yes. To me.'

The restaurant Stuart had chosen was on the South Bank, and boasted a Michelin star.

It was a combination of the setting and her nervousness that made Rachel break with tradition and wear a dress. Her sole little black dress was short, made of heavy crêpe and trimmed with a pleated flounce that flared as she walked. She added red suede heels – wincing at the effect on her knee – and bright red lipstick. *Style it out*, she told herself. *Make it look as though you're in control.*

Stuart stood up when she came into the dining room, and his very physical presence made her catch her breath. She was reminded of how she had felt when she first met him, how *impressed* she had been by his self-possession. Everything he said and did was deliberate and carefully considered, in contrast to men her own age, who had seemed chaotic and immature.

He was fifty now, and had lost some of his glamorous aura, but still carried himself well. Distinguished, Rachel thought. That's what men like Stuart become. She hesitated for a long time near the maître d's station, part of her willing herself to turn and walk out.

I don't want do this. I don't want to talk to him about that time.

As she prevaricated, he turned his head and saw her, standing up and beckoning her over. He reached in for a European double-cheek kiss, as though they had last seen each other only months ago. Rachel did not return it.

'Rachel, look at you! You look magnificent. And you haven't aged at all.'

She looked askance at him as she sat down. 'That's very gallant, but not true.'

Stuart smoothly summoned a waiter and pointed to something on the wine list. 'It's making me wonder why we didn't do this a lot sooner.'

Rachel flushed slightly. 'I think we both know why we didn't. And that that's my fault.'

He smiled faintly. 'Well, you certainly made it as challenging as possible for me to get in touch with you. But I've kept track of your career: you're a high-flying member of Interpol.'

'It's part of the National Crime Agency now, but yes, I am.'

'Mind you, as soon as I met you, I knew you'd go far. You were so adorable, so fresh-faced, with all that blonde hair pinned up under your uniform hat, but there was a fire in your eyes. The only person I could look at in that courtroom was you.'

He was referring to the case of an unidentified body that Rachel had found in an alley when she was on the beat. They had both been witnesses at the subsequent coroner's inquest.

His admiring tone made Rachel uncomfortable, and she pretended to examine the menu. A waitress arrived with a bottle of Puligny-Montrachet in an ice bucket, and two glasses. 'I think you'll love this: it's the style of white you used to go for.'

'Actually I tend to drink red these days.'

Stuart looked suitably chastened. 'Yes, well, an awful lot of water – and wine – has flowed under the bridge since then.'

For a while they kept to more neutral topics: his work – he now held a prestigious chair in pathology at the University of Edinburgh – the weather, London property prices. But Rachel had no desire to prolong the encounter, so eventually she saw no option but to blunder straight in. 'So, why did you get in touch?'

She took a sip of the wine to calm her jangled nerves. He was right: it was delicious. But then Stuart being right about everything had been the root of the problem: the reason she ran away. She had felt micromanaged, suffocated.

'I want a divorce.' He softened this bald statement with a smile. 'It's silly that we're still legally married after all this time. Time to formally sever the tie.'

Rachel nodded. 'I can't argue with that.'

'I'm with someone now, in a stable relationship, and I expect she'll want to get married at some point.'

'*She* wants to… but you don't?'

The waiter was hovering. 'Shall I order for us both? Simpler that way?' And without waiting for her response, he did so, selecting dishes that Rachel had no objection to but wouldn't necessarily have chosen herself. Case resting, she thought. She'd spent much of the day reading the story of the Harpers' marriage and here, in a nutshell, was the story of hers.

Stuart gave her a rueful look. 'Obviously my view of marriage has been tainted somewhat. But Claire's never been married before, and she'd like to have children, so… I feel I should be in a position to offer her that. Do you have children?'

Rachel shook her head firmly, looking down at her lap. 'No.'

'Ever wanted them? Since we split, I mean.'

Rachel created an imaginary problem with one of her shoes, reaching under the table to fiddle with it, then launching into a treatise on the effects of wet leaves on light-coloured suede. To her relief, the waiter then arrived with the starters,

'This is delicious.' She stuck her fork into the turbot mousse, still avoiding his probing.

She should have known he would not be deterred. Not Stuart's style. He set down his own fork and gave her a long, steady look; the look of a disappointed parent. 'So what happened, Rae? Leaving me was one thing, but taking off and vanishing, with no contact at all – it's… well, it was just plain bizarre.' He hesitated, colouring slightly. 'Not to mention deeply upsetting. I had no idea what I was supposed to have done, and therefore no means of making it right.'

She gave a half-shrug and dropped her gaze to the floor, returning to scrutiny of the red suede courts. He put his fingers under her chin and tried to lift it and re-establish eye contact. She flinched.

'Don't, Stuart. Please.'

'Do you really not think I'm entitled to an explanation?'

That exasperated, paternal tone.

'Yes, I do. But…'

'So what did I do? What was it about being married to me that was so terrible you had to run off one night while I was at work?'

'It wasn't just about you. I was—'

'Rachel, please. Don't insult me with the "it's not you, it's me" excuse. You owe me better than that.'

She suppressed a sigh of exasperation. 'I don't doubt that; it's just that after so many years have elapsed, it seems futile to go over it all again.'

'But that's just the point,' Stuart said insistently, raising his voice enough to make the other diners glance in their direction. 'There is no "again" about this. How can there be when we didn't have a single conversation about what was going through your mind?'

Rachel stood up abruptly. 'I'm sorry: I just can't do this. I can't talk about it.'

She flung her starched linen napkin onto the table and hurried out of the restaurant as fast as her stilettos would allow.

CHAPTER THIRTEEN

'He's here, and he's not here.'

'What the fuck does that mean?' Brickall demanded. He and Rachel were once again in the tiny hallway of Terry Harper's house. 'We're not after riddles. We're after facts. And your son, who's given this as his bail address.'

'Gav's been staying with me, yes, but he's hardly ever indoors. He's spending most of his time with Andy.'

'Is he working?' Rachel was aware, as she asked the question, that she couldn't remember what Gavin Harper did for a living, even though it had been mentioned on the original police file.

Terry filled in the gaps for her. 'He's getting a bit of plastering work – you know, he trained as a plasterer back in the day, before he set up his own building contractor's outfit.'

'That'll explain how he managed to hire the big shiny divorce lawyer,' said Brickall as they headed out to the car after checking the small single bedroom where Gavin was sleeping and ascertaining that the contents were much the same as in the apartment in Albufeira. 'Plasterers make a bloody fortune.'

'Except that he hasn't paid the lawyer,' Rachel reminded him. 'Hence my theory about taking the law into his own hands.'

'Another little chat with young Andy next, then.' Brickall started the engine and drove back to JBH Distribution, parking at the side of the building. As he cut the ignition, Rachel made to open the passenger door, but he put a hand on her arm and restrained her.

'Hold on, Tonto. Let's try and use the element of surprise this time. We should see where he heads after he's finished at work.'

'Yes, probably.' Rachel sat back. 'The trouble is, we don't know how long it'll be before he leaves. He could be working a late shift.' The prospect of being unable to bend her knee for several more hours did not appeal.

'Come on, Prince, you know you love a good stakeout! Ninety-five per cent utter tedium; five per cent cardiac-arrest-causing stress. I'll get supplies.'

'No, I will,' said Rachel firmly. 'I need to stretch my leg.'

She trudged up to the parade of local shops and came back with Brickall's five a day: crisps, biscuits, chocolate bars, sweets and cans of fizzy drinks. He was busy on his phone when she returned.

'Just texting Amber.'

Rachel looked blank.

'Amber Crowley, the hot barrister.'

'How did you get her number?'

He tapped the side of his nose.

'Please don't tell me that was another abuse of your access to personal information… Anyway, didn't she blow you out?'

'I lifted her number from the Bogdhani case file. And no, she didn't, not entirely. She said maybe coffee, remember? So I thought I'd give her a second crack at the goods. It would be a shame for her to miss out on this.' He indicated his convention-ally good-looking features. 'Who wouldn't want to experience a law-enforcing love god?'

Rachel was about to name some people for whom this might not be an enticing prospect when she was distracted by her phone bleeping. It was a text from Stuart.

Hi, Rae, I'm in London for a couple more days, and I'd still like the chance to talk properly before I leave. It would help us both to close this chapter, I think. I wondered if you'd like to meet up again.

I have a couple of tickets for Covent Garden tonight. La Traviata. I have a box.

Rachel sighed. As if mentioning the cost of the seats would swing it.

Sorry, I'm on ops at the moment.

Well, it was true. But even if it hadn't been, she would have come up with some excuse. She had blanked out the strange and abrupt ending of their marriage for so long that it seemed impossible to make things right by discussing it further. Especially in an opera box. She just wanted to sign the divorce papers and be done.

By the time Andy Whittier appeared with the rest of the early shift, Brickall had munched his way through the crisps, the chocolate and half the biscuits, and they were both starting to get restless. Andy walked out of the warehouse waving cheerily to a couple of colleagues who were leaving at the same time, and climbed into his car. But he didn't drive off. He sat and waited.

An hour later, it was almost dark. Andy was still sitting motion-less in his car.

'What the fuck's he doing?' grumbled Brickall. 'Why hasn't he left?'

'That's kind of the point of surveillance: to find out.'

'Sod this, I need a slash.' He disappeared for ten minutes, and came back with a kebab and chips, which filled the car with the smell of fried onions.

By 7.45, the last of the late-shift workers were leaving, but Andy was still in his car. Gradually the car park emptied, and the lights in the building were extinguished one by one. A uniformed security guard arrived and positioned himself in a booth at the front of the building. At the exact moment Andy Whittier left the car, walked round to the back of the building and disappeared from view.

'He's gone back in again,' observed Brickall, through a mouth-ful of Maltesers.

'No shit, Sherlock… Oh, hold on.' Rachel pointed as discreetly as possible. 'Who's this?'

A battered estate car drove up, and a familiar figure got out.

'Bingo!' she said with satisfaction. 'It's brother Gavin.'

Gavin also disappeared around the back of the building, out of sight of the security guard. Brickall hastily tossed the bag of chocolates onto the back seat with the congealed remains of the kebab, now fully alert. A few minutes later, the men came out together, with Gavin carrying something wrapped in a bright blue plastic tarpaulin. It was several feet in length, not heavy enough to need both men but bulky enough to slow his movements.

'Oh Christ,' breathed Brickall. 'Surely not…'

Andy opened the hatchback on the estate and Gavin carefully laid the bundle down inside before climbing into the driver's seat. Andy headed back to his own car.

'My favourite,' said Brickall, starting the engine and sliding skilfully and silently forwards. 'Car chase.'

They followed the two cars at a discreet distance to a small, modern housing development not far from where Terry Harper lived. Both cars came to a stop outside a brick townhouse: Gavin's car parked on the drive in front of the integral garage, Andy's stopped at the kerb.

Rachel and Brickall watched as the package, which must have weighed fifty pounds or so from the way it was carried, was taken carefully in through the garage door. It was then closed, and both men remained inside.

'Shit,' said Brickall. 'Are you thinking what I'm thinking?'

Rachel nodded. 'Are there vests in the car? Or tasers?'

He shook his head. 'No. Didn't think we'd need them.'

'Well you should have thought about that,' said Rachel tersely. 'That's your job.'

'It's going to be a call for backup, then,' said Brickall, taking out his airwave handset. 'We need an ARV. Look on the bright side: at least Gavin and Andy have no idea we're here. That buys us some time.'

Twenty minutes later, a police support unit arrived in a van. Armed officers hammered on the front door, while others stood ready with their tubular steel Enforcer battering rams: 'red keys', the uniformed officers called them. A confused-looking young woman in an old T-shirt and pyjama bottoms opened the door, and members of the tactical unit swarmed past her, making their way to the garage.

Rachel held up her warrant card. 'Are Andy Whittier and Gavin Harper here?'

'They're watching the football, but—'

Rachel and Brickall pushed past her into the living room. Both men were already on their feet, startled by the noise, and both recognised Rachel. 'What's going on?' Gavin asked, the colour draining from his face. 'Have you found her?'

'We need to conduct a search of the premises,' Brickall said, as two heavy-booted officers thundered upstairs to prove his point.

'Hold on,' said Andy. 'My kids are asleep up there. They'll be terrified.'

Rachel held up her hand, indicating to the officers upstairs that they should wait on the landing. 'We need to have a look in your garage.'

Andy paled and exchanged a stricken look with Gavin.

Brickall had already gone through the connecting door in the utility room. Rachel followed, with the two brothers hovering in the doorway.

'Here it is.' Brickall pointed to a blue bundle against the far wall. He ripped the synthetic tarpaulin away, revealing a thick polythene bag containing what looked like small metal bricks.

'What the fuck?'

Rachel knelt down and ripped at the polythene bag with the Swiss army knife she always carried, taking out one of the metal ingots and examining it.

'It's rhodium,' said Andy, who was now standing behind her. 'Corrosion-resistant, used in catalytic converters and spark plugs.'

'And worth nearly a thousand quid an ounce,' observed Rachel. 'Mind telling us what you were doing removing this from your work premises and hiding it here?'

'It's my fault,' said Gavin. 'Andy knew I was up to my eyeballs in debt and needed to make some decent money in a hurry, so he thought we could sell it on, on the black market.'

'You do remember you're already on bail for a fraud offence? And being investigated over your daughter's disappearance?' Rachel's tone was flat, the adrenaline leaching from her body.

Andy turned on her. 'How the hell did you know about this?' he demanded.

'Followed you,' Brickall said bluntly, taking a set of handcuffs from a member of the armed unit. 'We thought you might be hiding Lola Jade.' He cuffed Gavin's wrists behind his back. 'Gavin Harper, I am arresting you on suspicion of burglary, contrary to Section 25 of the Theft Act. You do not have to say anything, but it may harm your defence if you do not mention when questioned something which you later rely on in court. Anything you do say may be given in evidence.'

'I didn't take Lola!' Gavin shouted angrily. 'I didn't take her, and I don't know who did! I thought you got that.'

Rachel cuffed Andy and cautioned him, and the two of them were loaded into the back of the armed response vehicle, along with the consignment of rhodium.

'Take them to the nearest nick and have them booked and banged up. Make sure they know Harper's already on bail,' Brickall told the unit commander. 'We'll speak to the custody sergeant and their CID in the morning.

He thumped the back door of the van, giving the driver his cue to set off. 'Well, that was fun,' he said, with evident satisfaction. 'Been a while since I've done a spot of smash-and-grab. Beats being stuck behind a desk all day.'

Rachel was shaking her head, reaching into her bag for a painkiller and washing it down with a can of Coke left over from the stakeout.

'But Lola's still missing. We're back to the drawing board.'

CHAPTER FOURTEEN

'Fancy a curry?'

Rachel stared at Brickall in disbelief.

'A curry? You've just had a kebab and chips!'

He shrugged. 'So? I'm a growing lad.'

Rachel considered for a minute. On the one hand, she was quite hungry, having only eaten a handful of Maltesers since breakfast. On the other, her widowed mother lived around fifteen minutes away, in Purley, not far off the main A road into London, and her conscience was pricking her. She hadn't visited for several months.

'I think I'm going to spend the night at my mum's,' she said firmly, programming the address into the car's sat nav. 'Drop me off there and I'll get a train in tomorrow morning. I think we're long overdue a chat with the original Surrey Police case team, so I might go there first. You never know: it could shed some light.'

Parked on the leafy street outside her mother's bijou 1930s suburban house in Purley was a familiar silver people-carrier.

Rachel grimaced. 'Oh shit. Lindsay. What perfect timing.'

'Who's Lindsay?'

'My big sister. Who never misses the opportunity to point out what a crap daughter I am.'

'Shall I come in with you? Give them something more interesting to talk about?'

Rachel smiled and patted Brickall's thigh briefly, then swiftly retracted her hand. The two of them tended to avoid physical contact, sticking to sibling-type joshing instead. 'Thanks, but I wouldn't inflict that on anyone, not even you.'

'Not too late to turn round and make a quick getaway.' He slammed down to first gear and revved the engine to illustrate his point.

'No, I'm going to do the decent thing.'

Rachel hobbled up the front pathway, with Brickall watching her. She was very stiff, and would have loved to head to the gym in Bermondsey instead. Not too late to run back to the car, jump in and order Brickall to floor it…

But the net curtains in the front room were already twitching at the sound of a car's engine, and the front door opened.

'Well, well, well, we *are* honoured.' Lindsay stood there, her arms folded. The outline of her henpecked husband Gordon loomed behind her.

Rachel leaned in and kissed her sister on her cool, dry cheek.

'I was working on a job nearby,' she offered.

'Some of us don't need an excuse to drop in,' Lindsay sniffed. 'But then some of us aren't high-flying detectives.'

'Who's that?' called Eileen Prince.

'It's me, Mum.'

'Don't worry, we're not going to stay and spoil the prodigal's visit,' Lindsay said waspishly. 'Gordon's been fixing a leak under the kitchen sink, but it's done now, so we'll be off in a minute.'

Lindsay was nine years Rachel's senior. They had not really enjoyed a shared childhood, and now, in adulthood, the same absence of closeness prevailed. Lindsay had left home when Rachel was ten, and six years later married a dull quantity surveyor called Gordon Reynolds. They had two timid teenagers called Tom and Laura, whose birthdays Rachel was perpetually forgetting, a golden Labrador and membership of the National Trust. They went on camping holidays, sang in a madrigal group, and sent round-robin letters at Christmas, with Lindsay still finding time amidst all this wholesome activity to emit disdain for Rachel's self-centred, unencumbered life.

Later, when they were alone, Rachel and her mother made beans on toast and ate them on their laps in front of a cookery show, washed down with mugs of Horlicks: a comfortable and familiar ritual. Eileen, who had noticed her daughter limping slightly in the kitchen, asked her about her leg.

'I did it when I was out for a run. It's nothing. Really.'

Eileen fussed about fetching her a footstool, cushion and ice pack.

'You and your jogging,' she sniffed.

Rachel slept like a hibernating bear in her childhood bed, under a faded candlewick bedspread, surrounded by posters of Chesney Hawkes and the Backstreet Boys. At 8.30 sharp – the orthodox time for breakfast according to Eileen Prince – she endured a fry-up so huge that she was left bloated and dyspeptic. When she arrived at Eastwell police station, she was sure they would be able to smell the lard and bacon fat seeping from her pores. It was a test of her affection for her mother – and filial guilt – that she had not pushed it away in disgust and demanded a grapefruit instead. She planned to avoid eating for the rest of the day to redress the balance.

The desk sergeant told her that the only on-duty member of CID who had covered the Harper case was currently interviewing a suspect in a burglary. Rachel elected to go off in search of coffee and on her return was met in reception by an attractive and visibly pregnant young woman with a curtain of shiny dark hair and a calm, intelligent aura.

She extended a hand. 'We've already spoken on the phone – I'm Leila Rajavi.'

Rajavi confirmed that the suspect she had just interviewed – and remanded – was none other than Gavin Harper. 'He's admitted the theft of the rhodium from his brother's workplace,' she told Rachel. 'And Andrew Whittier admitted to being an accessory. That much was straightforward. But the value of the rhodium was another matter. We're trying to work it out now, but it looks like it could be as much as half a million.'

'So a Category One offence then,' said Rachel with a sigh. 'Great.' This development added another layer of complication to their investigation of Gavin's involvement with Lola Jade's disappearance.

Rajavi's expression was half exasperated, half resigned. 'And already being on bail for the identity document fraud charge won't exactly help his case. He's looking at between three and six years, in all probability. Whittier could get one to two.'

'If the judge allows that Gavin's behaviour is down to upset caused by the disappearance of his daughter, then he might also get away with one to two years.'

'Let's hope he's got a good brief.' Rajavi gave a brisk, professional smile. 'Now, what can I do to help with Lola Jade Harper? Any solid leads?'

Rachel shook her head at the machine tea in a polystyrene cup offered by a young plain-clothes officer with pale blonde hair and protruding ears, who was introduced to her as DC Matt Coles. 'As you know, we tracked down Gavin Harper in Portugal. And of course we'll go on looking into his possible involvement in Lola Jade's abduction while he's a guest of Her Majesty.' She spoke with more confidence than she was feeling. 'Our child protection unit are also making enquiries overseas: it's still possible that she was snatched to order and taken out of the country. Obviously, in light of recent events, they're going to be focusing on Portugal.'

Rajavi was shaking her head slowly.

'You don't agree?'

'I was there at the mother's house for the original search... It was obvious that the child had been taken from her bed, but there were no signs of forced entry downstairs. Michelle said that she must have gone to bed and left the patio door unlocked. It was a warm evening, so that's possible, but…' She hesitated.

'Go on.'

'If a child's going to be abducted to order, it's got to be planned. They're not going to be able to rely on a downstairs door being conveniently left open. I don't know… We searched the place from top to bottom the day she was reported missing, and a couple of weeks later they went in with cadaver dogs, but there was nothing. No sign of a struggle, no sign she was harmed in any way. And it would have been really difficult for a stranger to get her out of the property without waking Michelle. That was the major reason for going with the theory that the father had taken her. If she woke up and saw him in her bedroom, she wouldn't have been scared. She'd have gone with him. And he could easily have had a key.'

'He'd have needed a car. Was anything picked up on CCTV?'

Rajavi shook her head. 'The council have a camera at the corner of Sycamore Drive, just where cars come in and out of the estate from the main road, but they'd been lax with their maintenance and it wasn't working that night.'

Rachel tapped her pen against her notebook. 'Okay, bit of a long shot, but do you know anything about the death of the Harpers' son, Oliver, in 2008?'

Rajavi nodded slowly. 'I'd only just joined as a WPC then, but I do vaguely remember something about that; it came up when Lola went missing… Would you like me to find the file?'

She returned a few minutes later, and Rachel glanced through it, but there were only duplicates of the reports that had been on the divorce file.

'My colleague Debbie Mount was one of the officers that went to the scene,' Rajavi offered. 'She said there was something off about it.'

'In what way?'

'Something about Michelle Harper's reaction that didn't seem right. How she kept embellishing the story. Went into minute detail about the baby's schedule for the whole of the previous twenty-four hours, as if she'd rehearsed it. Said he'd had a sore ear, then changed it to a cough. When Debbie pointed this out, she claimed he'd had both, and got quite uppity about it. And she was the same when her daughter disappeared. If anyone said something she didn't like, she became overly defensive. Almost aggressive. I distinctly remember, when we heard about Lola Jade, Debbie saying: 'Oh, she's the one with the dodgy cot death.''

'But the pathology was inconclusive. Sadly, it usually is in Sudden Infant Death.'

Rajavi shrugged. 'I'm not saying there was any evidence on which to proceed. But…'

'There was a suspicion.'

'Exactly.'

Rachel blagged a lift to Willow Way in a uniformed patrol car, asking the constable to drop her out of sight of number 57.

The precaution was redundant, however, as once again the house was empty. She rang the doorbell and peered through the living-room window, but it appeared exactly as it had been before: tidy but neglected.

The side gate was bolted, but a sharp jab with her shoulder opened it and let her into the garden. There was a plastic swing at the far end of the lawn, grimy with lack of use, and in the shed was a lilac and white child's bike that didn't look as though it had ever been ridden. The garden was backed by a ten-foot-tall brick wall, forming part of a purpose-built garage block for some of the smaller properties in the adjoining street, confirming Rachel's assumption that the only way out of the property was via the front door.

Number 57 was link-attached by the garage to its identical neighbour, and from the old-fashioned potting shed, pond and kitsch garden ornaments, Rachel guessed its residents were older than the Harpers. She approached the front porch, proudly decked with pots of dahlias, and then she saw it.

A CCTV camera.

It was almost completely obscured by a thick creeper that wound up the front of the house between the garage and the front door, and you had to look hard to see it, but nevertheless there it was, pointing towards the shared driveways, and the street.

Rachel rang the bell, and an elderly woman answered it. She was plump and rounded and rather hunched. Rachel was reminded of Beatrix Potter's Mrs Tiggywinkle. She showed her warrant card and asked if she could have a quick word.

'I expect it's about that little girl,' the woman said with satisfaction. 'Come on through, dear.'

'And you are?'

'Mrs Lewis. Marjorie.'

'Do you live alone?'

'No, dear, my husband's still in the land of the living.' She gave a throaty little chuckle. 'He's out in his shed. Norman. Shall I fetch him?'

'Yes please.'

'Drink and a biscuit for you, Detective?'

Rachel refused the biscuit, her stomach still gurgling from its intake of fried food, but accepted a glass of weak barley water. Norman Lewis came in and introduced himself, declining to shake hands on account of the soil on his. He was also rotund and rosy-cheeked, and wore a battered moleskin waistcoat. A perfect Mr Tiggywinkle.

'We used to see little Lola playing out with the other kiddies in the close,' Marjorie said without preamble. 'Didn't we, Norm?'

He grunted. 'When her mother would let her.'

'Yes, Michelle was never very keen on letting her out of her sight. Didn't seem to like her having friends.'

'Really?' asked Rachel. 'Do you know why?'

Marjorie pursed her lips. 'You don't like to talk badly about someone going through such an ordeal, but she could be a bit difficult, couldn't she, Norm, Michelle Harper?'

Norm nodded, chewing a garibaldi.

'You never quite knew where you were with her: sometimes she was nice as pie, sometimes she'd just look daggers. Wouldn't she?'

Norm affirmed that this was the case.

'And the other kids – I'm on friendly terms with Lyn at number forty-nine; she's got little ones – they never went round to next door to play, did they? They were all scared of Michelle. She used to shout at them, apparently, and—'

'I wanted to ask you about your security camera,' Rachel interjected. 'How long have you had it?'

Marjorie looked at her husband. 'Six months, is it, Norm?'

'Seven.'

'So you had it at the beginning of May?'

'Yes, definitely,' said Norman, spraying crumbs. 'Our Philip put it up when he was here for Easter lunch.'

Rachel discreetly offloaded her glass of squash behind a pot plant and leaned forward. 'Did the police ask to see footage at the time?'

'I don't think so…' Marjorie sought confirmation from Norman again. 'A young policeman came round here to talk to us the next day when they were doing their house-to-house enquiries. There were several of them out there in the close. But they didn't ask about the camera, no. And we didn't think to say anything, did we?' She looked guilty.

Rachel's heart sank slightly. Most domestic CCTV cameras automatically wiped footage within four weeks. But Marjorie suddenly perked up, having thought of something. 'Ooh, Norman, what was it Philip said about the backup thingy?' She turned to Rachel. 'Our son set it all up for us: he's the one who's a computer whizz, we know nothing at all about the things. But I do remember there was something about the recordings being saved to a computer file thingy.'

'Would I be able to speak to your son?'

'He lives in Morden, but I expect he'd be happy to talk to you. They come down for Sunday lunch sometimes, but he works ever so hard – both he and Sally work – so we don't tend to see them in the week. Sometimes we have the grandkids to stay to give them a break. Felix and Finlay. They love it because they get a bedroom each; they have to share one at home, with their parents using one for an office. But we've got the two spare rooms, so—'

Rachel interrupted Marjorie's spiel by standing up and reaching into her bag. She handed over one of her cards, which was accepted and clutched with great reverence.

'Give your son my details, and ask him to phone me as soon as he gets a minute.'

CHAPTER FIFTEEN

'Whoa, easy tiger!' Howard stepped backwards and ducked out of the way as Rachel sent flying kicks at the punch ball. 'I know your leg's improving, but I don't think you're ready to cross over into kickboxing.'

Rachel dropped her leg and slumped her shoulders. 'Sorry. I've had a bit of a day.'

It had started with a visit to Patten's office, fired up and brimming with confidence. After updating her superior officer, she had told him with utter conviction that the next step for the investigation was to put Michelle Harper under covert surveillance.

'She was adamant that if her husband was anywhere, he'd be in Spain. And yet he was in Portugal. It feels to me like a classic piece of misdirection.'

Patten had looked doubtful. 'She could just have been mistaken.'

'Perhaps. But she lied to us about why Gavin had one of Lola's nighties with him. It's as if she's trying to shift blame in his direction.'

He had thought this over before saying, 'Even supposing you're right, I'd still need something more tangible to go on, given how expensive twenty-four-hour surveillance is. Something I can give to the money men upstairs.' He'd pointed upwards to an invisible finance department. 'Otherwise I don't think I can get the requisite manpower budget signed off.'

'All right,' agreed Rachel, who had more or less expected this. 'How much do you need?'

'Come on, Detective Inspector, you know how this works! I need actual evidence that points to the mother, not just a bad feeling about her. Find me something concrete, and we'll take a closer look at her.'

Rachel's mind had been working like a hamster in a wheel ever since, which was why she had taken herself off to the gym: to try and refocus.

'Want to talk about it over a drink?' Howard asked as they headed out of the building, both still in their kit with sweaty towels draped over their shoulders.

She shook her head. 'I'd love to, but I need a shower, and then I've got some work I have to do.'

He stopped her in her tracks and turned her to face him. 'Did you mean that?'

'What?'

'That you'd love to have a drink with me.'

Rachel was not about to tell him how ridiculously pleased she had been to see him when she had arrived at the gym that evening. That she'd been low on attractive male company recently, and that in her estimation Howard was definitely attractive. Despite swearing off men, it would be fun to sit in a pub or bar with him for a couple of hours.

'Yes, I would. But you're married.'

He smiled his easy smile. 'It's just a drink, not a joint bank account.'

She shuddered, remembering Stuart, who had sent two more unanswered texts that day. 'Never planning on having one of those again. Not ever.'

He raised an eyebrow. 'Really?'

'Long story. I'll tell you about it another time. Maybe.'

She reached up on tiptoe to kiss his cheek – she was tall, but he was a giant – and hurried away before she changed her mind.

Back at her flat, she took a long hot shower, poured herself a glass of wine and started to trawl through social media. Maybe Michelle Harper had left a digital crumb trail that could lead to something concrete.

She found an early Instagram account, opened in 2012, which only had a dozen or so posts on it. One of the first was of a crying toddler Lola with her earlobes newly pierced with diamanté studs, and the caption *She hated it, but she'll thank me when she's older!* The picture had attracted 123 comments, not many of them favourable.

OMG, this is not okay! one critic had posted.

She is way too young for this: child abuse! said another. There were several others in the same vein.

Eventually Michelle had responded: *I'M the parent, she is MY CHILD. I get to make ALL decisions regarding her until she is 18 y/o. You haters need to remember: I MADE her, I OWN her.*

'Sit on the fence, why don't you.' Rachel muttered at the screen.

There were some very filtered selfies of Michelle pouting at the camera like a pantomime cow, a handful of pictures of Diva the dog, and a few more of Lola. They were posed, rather than natural action shots, and in all of them the child was staring wanly at the camera. All fairly enlightening, but it wasn't evidence. Frustrated, she Skyped Brickall. He was bare-chested above tracksuit bottoms and eating a slice of pizza. So far, so normal.

'What do you always tell me is the first rule of detecting?' he asked Rachel after she had vented her frustration.

'Go with your gut.'

'Okay then, maybe not the first rule… What's the second rule?' She shrugged.

He tapped the side of his nose. 'Follow the money. We know her old man is in all sorts of financial shit. So what's the deal with

Michelle? How's she funding herself? Who's paying for all those tacky hair extensions? Sex, revenge and money: the big three motives. So why not go with money and see where it takes us? Is there some sort of reward she could be scamming?'

He leaned back on his sofa with a look of self-satisfaction and wiped pizza crumbs from his naked torso. It wasn't a bad torso either, Rachel was forced to acknowledge. Who knew sculpted abs like that could be created solely from junk food?

An all-too-familiar spark fired in her brain. 'Hold on. You've just reminded me of something. See you in the morning.'

She hung up before he could respond, and pulled up the Find Lola Jade page on Facebook. There'd been little activity since she'd last checked it. People were losing interest. Then she clicked on the link to the JustGiving page. The donations now stood at £53,316.

Rachel phoned the NCA and asked to be put through to the on-call IT officer. It was a man called Lee Knightley, someone she had worked with before.

'Hi, Lee, it's Rachel Prince… Listen, if I send you a crowdfunding link, can you get into the account?'

'Shouldn't be a problem. Whack it over and I'll give it a go.'

An hour later, Lee phoned her back.

'Okay, I'm looking at the page now… Total raised: £53,316… Available funds: £23,316. Your withdrawals: £30,000… Raised since last withdrawal: £5,353.'

'When was that money withdrawn?'

There was a pause while Lee looked for something. 'The account was opened on the twelfth of May, and the thirty grand was taken out on the seventeenth. Pretty much as soon as the total hit the thirty K mark. Most of the donations were made within that first week, but funds have continued coming in at between one and three grand a month since the account was first opened. The total displayed on the landing page is the entire amount raised, not a current balance.'

Rachel's heart was beating a little faster. 'And the withdrawal went to Michelle Harper?'

'Yes. To her linked bank account.'

'Okay, Lee, I need you to get into that account and go through all her transactions since the tenth of May: try and work out where those funds went. Send anything you find to my work email, and call me back on this number.'

'Tonight?' Lee was doubtful. 'It might take me a couple of hours.'

'Yes, tonight. It doesn't matter how late it is.'

He eventually phoned at quarter past midnight. It turned out her detective sergeant had been right, as he so often was.

She went straight to Patten's office the next morning, only pausing long enough to print off Lee Knightley's email.

'Oi – what's going on?' grumbled Brickall as she brushed briskly past him, barely incapacitated by her right knee now.

'Tell you later.'

If she had expected Nigel Patten to become fired up by this information, she was wrong. He frowned at the email, and then back at her.

'So Michelle Harper legitimately withdrew funds from a crowdfunding account that was set up to benefit her. You'll have to forgive me, but I don't see this as significant. One of the first things any would-be detective learns, DI Prince: evidence of bad character is not evidence of a crime.'

Rachel tried to contain her exasperation. 'She funnelled the money into her own bank account, then immediately withdrew the same amount – £30,000 – in cash. Cash. She's got barely any income of her own, and is drowning in credit card debt. So where's that 30,000 gone? And how does it relate to her daughter's disappearance? I think there's a clear question to be answered.'

Patten sighed, and rested his chin on his hands, thinking. 'All right. I'll speak to Ops and get some surveillance put in place. But obviously, given that your primary role is international liaison, I want you to make that your priority. You've re-interviewed the father since he got back?'

'Yes, but he's sticking to his story. There's not going to be any more intel coming from him direct.'

'So you need to trace his movements.'

'I can't do that, sir: he's now banged up. On theft charges.'

'I meant back in Portugal. I want you to get yourself out to the Algarve, head up a team and keep looking out there until you find the girl.'

'Did Patten pull one of his classic "you're off the case" moves?' Brickall was trying to read Rachel's expression as they headed out of the building to the Pin and Needle for a much-needed liquid energy boost.

'Not exactly. He wants me to go back and poke about in Albufeira.'

'Another jolly in the sun! Cheers!' He clinked glasses with her.

Rachel scowled. 'I'd much rather be following up on ops this end.'

'Tough. So – you divorced yet?'

Rachel shook her head. 'I'm too busy avoiding my husband to divorce him.'

Brickall grinned. 'Do I smell a last-minute change of heart? Will we be hearing the patter of tiny feet before too long?'

Before she had the chance to formulate a smart comeback, Rachel's phone rang: an unfamiliar number.

'Hello? Is that Detective Prince?'

'Speaking.'

'This is Philip Lewis.'

Rachel was momentarily blank.

'You spoke to my parents, Marjorie and Norman. About their CCTV recordings.'

'Oh, yes… Thanks for calling back. I know it's a long shot, given the incident was several months ago and you probably no longer have anything from that period.'

'Oh, I do,' he said pleasantly but firmly. 'I set up a program that automatically archives all footage. We've got every bit of it.'

CHAPTER SIXTEEN

'I'm in computer programming, you see,' said Philip Lewis. 'So it was relatively simple for me to create this system.'

Looking at him, Rachel could quite easily believe it. She had expected the son of Mr and Mrs Tiggywinkle to be similarly short and rotund, but he was all bony angles, with a shaved head and Thunderbirds glasses. She had arranged to meet him in Willow Way and his parents were waiting anxiously on the patio in the garden, as if afraid to come into their own house. Their son spoke to them in a hectoring, even bullying tone, which probably explained this.

Philip led Rachel up to the smallest of the spare rooms, no bigger than a box room, which housed a child-sized single bed and a small desk with a computer monitor and an upright hard drive underneath it. He showed her the active monitoring pictures in real time, then found the relevant file in a folder on the computer's desktop.

'There was a spate of break-ins at the beginning of the year, and my parents were understandably worried about it. I told them they should sell the house and move nearer to Sally and me in Morden, but they wouldn't countenance it.' He didn't attempt to hide his disapproval of this decision. 'So I set up this security system.'

'And I'm very grateful for your expertise,' said Rachel smoothly. She'd been accused of acting cool and over-analytical in the past, but let it never be said she didn't know how to schmooze a witness.

'Yes, well…' He cleared his throat. 'My youngest is around the same age as the little girl, and you can only imagine… so, obviously, anything I can do to help find her.'

He clicked on the file labelled *9/5/17_backup* and pressed play.

The night images were black and white, but very clear, and Philip explained at tedious and self-important length why this was the case, with a lecture on image resolution and pixels. The lens of the camera picked up the shared driveway between numbers 57 and 55 and the shot also covered the front door of the Harpers' house, the pathway that led to the side gate and garden, and a section of the road in front. In short, anyone entering or leaving the house would have been picked up by the Lewises' camera.

Philip fast-forwarded through all the footage for that night, but there was no activity bar an urban fox rooting around the bins.

'Interesting, isn't it?' he observed with evident smugness. 'Mrs Harper claims someone must have come into the house via the patio door, but that's not possible, given the only access to the gardens of number 57 and 55 is through the houses themselves.'

'Hmm.' Rachel was non-committal. An intruder could potentially have climbed over the top of the garage block and jumped down into the garden. It was doable, by someone fit. To return the same way carrying a young child would be a lot harder, though; impossible for a single intruder. If indeed Lola had been stolen to order, there had to have been more than one person involved.

The next day's footage, in colour, showed the arrival of a police squad car at 7.12 a.m., then the comings and goings of Michelle's family. This pattern continued for the next few days, with Michelle only leaving the house, accompanied by Clive Manners, to attend the press conference. Then on 18 May, at 13.11 p.m., Michelle left on her own, wheeling two huge matching purple suitcases – the type with rigid polycarbonate sides – and loading them into the boot of her white car. 18 May. The day after she had withdrawn £30,000 in cash from Lola's fund. ·

Philip was observing Rachel's reaction to this. 'Do you need me to keep going?' he asked. 'I could, only it's going to take me a while to go through five months' worth of tape.'

Rachel, thinking of Marjorie and Norman hovering obediently in their garden, stood up. 'No, that won't be necessary, but obviously this constitutes evidence in the case, and as such, could be removed.'

Philip looked affronted.

'Perhaps for now you could just send me copies of all the files.'

'All of them?'

'All of them, yes. From when you first installed the camera. I'm afraid that's how this works.'

He gave a theatrical sigh. 'Of course, Detective Inspector. As I said, I'll do anything I can to help.'

Rachel drove south for another twenty miles to HMP High Down, where Gavin Harper was detained at Her Majesty's pleasure. He walked slowly into the visiting room in prison-issue sweats, his face pale and unshaven.

'I thought you'd got the message,' he said belligerently. 'I don't sodding know where my daughter is.'

Rachel ignored this. 'I'm about to head back to Albufeira,' she told him pleasantly. 'Thought I'd give you the chance to tell me where to look – save me wasting any more police time.'

He gave her a mulish look. 'I'll tell you what's wasting police time: you going back out to Portugal to look for Lola Jade. I've told you: she's not there. One hundred per cent. You're not going to find her.'

Rachel was not about to tell him that she privately agreed with him, and that the return trip to Albufeira was Patten's idea, not her own. 'Okay, then… maybe you'd like to tell me how your seminal fluid ended up on the carpet in Lola Jade's room?'

'I never touched her. I'd never do anything like that. Michelle must have set me up.'

'Set you up how?'

Gavin flushed slightly. 'Look, I'm not proud of this, but even though we weren't officially together any more, Michelle and I did still occasionally have sex. We always had a… fiery physical relationship. So I'd go round to see Lola or drop her off, we'd have a glass of wine and end up… you know…'

'Screwing?'

His face reddened further. 'Like I said, I'm not proud of it.'

Rachel leaned forward and placed her elbows on the table, getting into his space. 'Even if you did, how the hell did your ejaculate end up in your daughter's room?'

'We'd use a condom and Michelle would deal with it after. I wouldn't put it past her to tip it – the contents – onto Lola's floor.'

'And she'd do that because?'

'I tried to tell you before: she wants people to blame me. That's why I took off. She lied to some of her mates that I'd been touching Lola Jade, you know… in a sexual way. So this would be her twisted way of proving it. Now that I think about it, she was probably only up for a jump for that reason. She was always very quick to produce the rubber johnny.' He rubbed his hand wearily over his forehead, as though he had been through this explanation countless times in his mind. 'Like I said, it was because of all that that I panicked after they didn't find Lola. It was stupid; I realise that now.'

'And Michelle's allegations that you were physically violent to her?'

His eyes widened. 'Seriously? It was more the other way round. *She* was the one who would chuck things at *me*. Had a vicious temper on her.'

'So how do you explain this?'

She opened the photos she had snapped from Michelle's phone, of her bruised arms, and shoved her own phone across the table at him. He looked at the images, then something resembling a smile crept across his face.

'The date they were taken. Didn't you notice it?'

He pushed the phone back and Rachel looked. She'd snapped them hastily and the images were a bit blurred, but the date in the tag could just about be made out.

'28 October 2016. I'd been in Albufeira about a week by then. And Michelle's arms are a lot skinnier than that. These pictures aren't even of her.' He sneered. 'I mean, what kind of a person does something like that just to discredit their kid's dad. She's not fit to be a mother.'

'Is that why you were suing for custody?'

'Bloody right it is. And I want you to ask her. Ask her why she's made me out to be a child molester, and why she's given you faked pictures.'

'Oh, I intend to; don't worry.'

'And while you're at it, ask Michelle what she did to Olly. Ask her what she did to our son.'

PART TWO

You may give them your love, but not your thoughts
For they have their own thoughts
You may house their bodies, but not their souls
For their souls dwell in the house of tomorrow

Khalil Gibran, 'On Children'

CHAPTER SEVENTEEN

You see your own home through new eyes when someone visits it for the first time, Rachel thought.

Howard was at her flat for a personal training session. The consultant had not yet signed her off as fit, but the improvement in her knee was so great she wanted to try running again. The purpose of Howard's home visits was, they both agreed, to make sure she didn't undermine her progress so far.

Brickall had once categorised the decor as 'axe-murderer chic'. The walls were plain off-white, the furnishings functional, the overall look completely impersonal. True, Brickall's most recent visit had prompted her to order a few things online: a vibrant rug with green and magenta swirls on a cream background, and some framed pop art for the walls in the hallway. She had also brought back some colourful ceramic pots from Portugal and filled them with herbs. As a result, the overall result was less stark than it had been a few weeks ago. And with a concession to the approach of Christmas, she had put up some fairy lights, although she was not really a fairy-light sort of person.

'This is nice,' said Howard heartily when she let him in, though his face registered faint disappointment. 'Convenient. The location, I mean.'

Rachel laughed. 'It's okay, I know it looks a bit like a corporate rental. But hey…' she gestured round the room, 'it's now a corporate rental with fairy lights.'

Howard put her to work doing some basic stretches. She groaned at her lack of flexibility. 'I haven't had a chance to work out in weeks. I've been away on a job for most of November.'

'I thought I hadn't seen you in the gym for a while.' He knelt down beside her and grappled her left leg into a hamstring stretch. They made eye contact and he stood up abruptly. 'Right, let's try some sumo squats: see how your knee handles it.'

'I was in the Algarve,' Rachel told him.

'Fab – bit of winter sun. I thought you were looking tanned.'

'It wasn't fab at all, as it goes. It was a three-week exercise in frustration… But the less said about that, the better.'

After she had worked on stretching and warming up, Howard said, 'How about we do a test run? Just a short one: see how you get on.'

'What, now?'

He nodded. 'Why not? It may be almost December, but at least it's dry.'

'And you'll come with me?'

'Of course. All part of the personal training package.'

Rachel put on a jacket and a woollen hat, and they headed out into the darkening streets, past sparkling street decorations and festive shop windows. They jogged gently along Jamaica Road and into Southwark Park, completing a circuit of the lake before Howard said she shouldn't push her right leg too far, and insisted on her walking back. He came up to her flat with her, which struck her as strictly unnecessary.

'I really need a hot shower,' she told him, peeling off her jacket and hat. 'So let's pencil a couple more sessions in the diary now, then you can go.'

'It's okay, I can wait. I'm not in a rush.'

Rachel let her mind play out the sequence: her emerging fragrant and glowing from the shower, dressed in nothing but a towel, to find Howard waiting for her on the bed… *Okay, stop,*

stop, stop! The image had degenerated into a scene from a generic seventies porn movie. She held up the calendar app on her phone. 'No, let's do it now, then you can get going.' Their eyes met and she held his gaze just long enough to send him the message that she was tempted. Very tempted.

After she had showered and changed into clean sweats, Rachel phoned Brickall, eager to receive a debrief. For over a fortnight she and a handful of officers hand-picked from the Polícia Judiciária had combined forces with a specialist search team from Lisbon. This hastily assembled force had combed every back alley of every coastal resort, every waste tip and patch of scrubby ground, and questioned every local or tourist who had seen something suspicious or thought they had sighted Lola Jade. The press had inevitably got wind of their activity, and she had spent a lot of her time fending off a stream of calls from journalists. With no concrete news to report, the tabloids had jumped in anyway, with headlines along the lines of *UK COPS IN RESORT SEARCH FOR LOLA JADE BODY.*

On the couple of occasions she had flown back to London for the weekend, she had spent most of the time doing laundry and catching up on her sleep, and there had never been a chance to touch base properly with her sergeant.

His phone went to voicemail, but he phoned back half an hour later. 'All right, tart?'

She crooked the phone against her shoulder while she poured herself a glass of red wine, then settled herself on the sofa. 'I definitely drew the short straw, Detective Sergeant. Portugal's lovely and everything, but weeks spent combing out-of-season resorts in the rain…'

'I hear you.'

'So where are Surrey Police with Lola Jade now? Give me an update before I get stuck in again.'

'Good thing I checked up for you, eh? Seeing as I knew it would be the first bloody thing you asked me. They pulled the surveillance unit. After less than two weeks, apparently.'

'What happened?'

'Nothing: that's the whole point. They had a unit sat outside Jubilee Terrace round the clock, watching Michelle and Lisa. Michelle came and went from the house, all perfectly above board. She works in a nail salon a few hours a week, but apart from going there and to the shops occasionally, there was nothing suspicious. Before the FSU was abandoned, they got another warrant and did another full search of the Urquharts' house and Willow Way, but again: nothing. NCPA.' He quoted the acronym for 'No Cause for Police Action'. 'So, the unit was stood down. I think CEOP followed up on a couple of leads, one in France and one in North Africa somewhere: one a kid who had actually been trafficked, but both negative for the Harper kid. Patten's calling a combined team meeting soon, but I expect it will just be a formal wind-down.'

Rachel sighed heavily and pressed her hand to her forehead. 'And – as I suspected would be the case – we found nothing at all in the Algarve. This could be the end of the road.'

'Maybe. Or then again, maybe not.'

'I can't believe we're doing this. Tell me we're not doing this.'

'We're doing this.'

Rachel and Brickall were in his car, parked opposite Lisa Urquhart's house. They both wore dark hats and gloves, and were equipped with sleeping bags and a Thermos of hot coffee. Every so often Brickall would fire up the engine as discreetly as he could, and briefly fill the car with a blast of hot air from the heater. Even so, it was very cold.

They had begun their stakeout at 8.30. There were lights on in the upstairs window, and children's clamour punctuated by raised adult voices. Normal family stuff. A smell of fried food wafted from a part-open downstairs window, mingling with cigarette smoke. At 9 p.m., Kevin Urquhart returned from his shift as a baggage handler at Heathrow, parked his light blue VW Passat and went inside. There was more shouting, then the light from the upstairs room went off. Lisa emerged a few minutes later, bundled up in a fake-leopard-skin coat.

'Shall we follow her?' Brickall asked.

Rachel shook her head. 'Nah, look – she's in her slippers, and she's only got a purse with her. She'll be after fags or booze.'

Sure enough, Lisa shuffled to the corner shop at the end of Jubilee Terrace and returned a couple of minutes later with a packet of cigarettes and a six-pack of beer cans. There was no sign of Michelle Harper.

'How are we going to stay awake?' Brickall grumbled, as the digital clock ticked past midnight. 'I can feel myself nodding off.'

'We're going to have to talk.'

'As in have a conversation?'

'Afraid so.'

'Okay then…' Brickall took a swig of coffee from the neck of the flask, even though Rachel had asked him to use the cup. 'How's your love life? Still making eyes at your hunky personal trainer?'

Rachel let this one go, pulling her fleece jacket up round her neck and rubbing her hands together. 'I've got a party coming up. A "girls' night".' She wagged her fingers in quote marks, simultaneously pulling a face.

'Oh Christ, that sounds crap.'

'I know.'

'Anyway, Prince, do you actually *have* any female friends? I've never heard you mention any. Not one.'

'Not many,' Rachel admitted. 'I was never a girly girl.'

She thought back to her younger self. She had been overweight, and bullied, which accounted for many things. Her preoccupation with health and fitness, for one. Her wariness of commitment. There was one female in particular whose persecution had made her swerve her own gender: Lorraine Grassmore. A girl who had pretended to be her friend and to sympathise with her weight struggle, but had really been laughing at her behind her back the whole time. Thinking about her now could still make Rachel inhale forcibly, and she did.

'What?' asked Brickall.

She wasn't about to launch into a sob story about her miserable adolescence: not now, when she was tired and disorientated. 'Let's just say I was never part of the popular crowd at school and then, as you now know, I married very young, and my career took over. There's never been time for the girly stuff.'

'Because you're always too busy with men stuff.'

She swatted at him with a gloved hand. 'I've nothing against going out for a drink – you know that – but there's something about a bunch of women en masse…' She shuddered.

'So you're looking forward to it then?'

'It's going to be awful.'

The final light went out on the top floor, and the house lapsed into silence. A cat howled menacingly, followed by a volley of screeches as a fight broke out and a dustbin was knocked over. A dog barked persistently for a couple of minutes, then fell silent. A couple of pub-goers wove their way home down the middle of the street.

Brickall fished out a tube of Smarties and swallowed a handful, offering them to Rachel. 'I need to tell you something.'

'Go on.'

'You know Amber Crowley.'

'The hot lawyer?'

He nodded. There was a pause.

'Go on.' Rachel repeated, trying to recall a time when she had last seen Brickall looking this worried. It had been a while.

'She did something that makes me think… that she suspects I made use of her personal information when I shouldn't have done.'

Rachel stared at him. 'Go on.'

'Well, you know I found her number on file and texted her to try and get her to go out with me. And maybe I was a little…'

'Pushy?'

He sighed. 'It was just meant to be, you know… banter. But she sent me this.'

He held up his phone, showing her a text. There was no message; just a hyperlink. Rachel took the phone and clicked on it. It took her via a web browser to a site displaying legislative guidelines for crown prosecutors. Specifically, offences under Section 55 of the Data Protection Act, which police officers were prone to abuse through their privileged access to the public's personal information.

'Shit,' said Rachel.

'I know.'

'Maybe it's just…' she struggled to find a positive, 'as you said, just banter. Like a private joke.'

Brickall looked at her sideways. 'You don't really believe that.'

'Not really, no. Maybe it's just intended to be a warning to leave her alone.'

'I suppose.' He didn't seem overly reassured.

'Whatever happens, for Christ's sake stay away from her from now on. Promise me.'

'Promise.' Brickall finished the Smarties then bundled up his scarf and used it as a pillow, leaning against the door. 'Wake me up in a couple of hours, then it'll be your turn to have a kip.'

Rachel let him sleep for three hours, staring out at the silent, frosty street. Worrying. Eventually, when she could not keep her eyelids apart any longer, she woke Brickall and lay curled up on the back seat.

When she woke again it was still dark, but the clock on the dashboard said 6.45. Brickall went off in search of somewhere to empty his bladder, and came back with two cups of tea.

'Café round the corner's open if you want to go for a slash.'

Lights went on in the Urquhart household at 7.45, and once again voices were raised in parent–child discord. An hour later, the next-door neighbour emerged with a gaggle of children who appeared to be in fancy dress, knocking on the Urquharts' door. Lisa answered it in her pyjamas, and, after turning over her shoulder to screech at her offspring, ejected Chelsea and Connor into the street: one dressed as a princess, the other as a fireman. She handed them their lunchboxes and book bags, then lit a cigarette and slammed the door shut, leaving her children to walk to school with the neighbour's brood. One fireman, two princesses, a superhero and a penguin.

'Weird,' observed Brickall. 'Now I really know I'm sleep-deprived. I'm hallucinating fucking penguins.'

'There must be something going on at their school: World Book Day, or dress as your favourite character for charity or something.'

Of Michelle Harper there was no sign. She eventually emerged just before 10, just as Rachel and Brickall were about to give up. She was dressed in a shiny black Puffa coat and high-heeled boots, and wore giant sunglasses like ants' eyes. She strutted to her white BMW, parked further along the street, and climbed in.

'Mark, quick!'

He started the engine, and as soon as Michelle reached the junction with the main road, executed a fiercely efficient three-point turn and followed her. Michelle headed in the direction of Willow Way, driving quickly and confidently. When she glanced in her rear-view mirror, Rachel dropped her head so that her face was not visible. Brickall hung back out of sight until the BMW was on the driveway of number 57 and Michelle had gone inside, then parked about twenty metres away. He cut the engine and they waited.

Rachel's head was thumping, her knee was sore after fourteen hours in the car and she needed to pee again. So it was for personal rather than procedural reasons that she perked up when Michelle emerged from the house again after only thirty minutes. She was carrying a full black plastic refuse sack.

'Fucking hell,' said Brickall, reaching instinctively for his airwave set. 'That better not be body parts.'

He went to use the radio, but Rachel checked him with her right arm. 'Wait a sec.'

Michelle had gone back into the house, and a couple of minutes later came out again with a second bag. She dumped both of them next to the wheelie bin, then got into her car.

'We split,' Rachel ordered, climbing out of the vehicle. 'You go after her, I'll check out what she's dumped and phone you if we need backup.'

Right on cue, Michelle sped past them. Brickall took off after her, and Rachel walked slowly towards the black sacks, snapping on her latex gloves.

CHAPTER EIGHTEEN

Rachel laid out the contents of the bags on the back lawn, like a macabre jumble sale.

The first was full of Lola's clothes: not the durable denim and corduroy of Rachel's own childhood, but flouncy, sparkly dresses and shoes in pastel colours, white tights, a shrug made from white marabou. There was a grotesque studded white leather jacket and mini skirt, like a scaled-down version of what a streetwalker would wear. These were clothes for a human doll, not for climbing trees or riding a bike.

The second sack contained toys: mostly dolls and stuffed animals, though Katy Bear was still not accounted for. There were some girlie sets of pink Lego, child's make-up and hairstyling kits, a bead-encrusted mirror, nail polishes in candy colours, flecked with glitter. There were DVDs, and the CD player that Rachel remembered seeing in the photos of Lola's room. So Michelle was in the process of clearing it out.

Brickall phoned. 'She went to the nail salon where she works. Looked like there was a client waiting for her, and she put on her pinny thing and got on with it. All legit. How about you?'

Rachel paused for a few seconds.

'Am I calling for backup?'

'No, nothing like that. But it's a bit odd.'

'On my way back.'

The car screeched to a halt on the kerb a couple of minutes later, and Brickall appeared in the garden. 'What have we got here?'

They looked at Lola's belongings together.

'This lot has got to be her best stuff. Her favourites. So why get rid of it, unless…'

'Unless you know she's never coming back.'

'Could be too painful to look at if you fear the worst,' Brickall suggested.

Rachel was shaking her head. 'But you don't give up hope if you're not certain. You act as though your child's coming back. And if they're coming back, they're going to want their prized possessions waiting for them.'

Brickall put on gloves too, and they returned the morbid jumble sale to its bags and heaved them onto the back seat of the car. 'Let's drop these at the Surrey Police evidence store before we head back,' Rachel told him. 'I can't see Patten wanting them back at the office somehow.'

Brickall was subdued as they drove away. Eventually he ventured the obvious. 'So if she knows Lola's not coming back to the house, that means…'

'That she knows her daughter's dead.'

Two days later, Nigel Patten chaired the promised review of Lola Jade's case in one of the meeting rooms at the CEOP building in Vauxhall Bridge Road. Giles Denton and a female colleague were there, plus a representative from the surveillance team, and Rachel had invited Leila Rajavi to attend from Eastwell CID. Rajavi was now only a few weeks from giving birth, her body bulky and her ankles puffy.

'We're actively following up any new tips that come in with regard to Lola Jade,' said Giles Denton. 'And we'll continue to do so, and to liaise with DI Prince.'

He gave Rachel a warm smile and, unless her hormones were making her imagine things, the faintest wink. Brickall scowled and started tapping his pen rhythmically on the table.

'Those of you who know me are aware that I like to rely on visual aids…' Rachel gave the room a smile of apology as she walked up to the whiteboard, wrote Lola's name in large red letters at the centre and started filling in a spider's web of arrows and circled words. There was a circle with Gavin in it, and she drew an arrow leading to Andy, and another to the deceased baby Oliver. She drew a large question mark next to his name and wrote 'COT DEATH??' She talked the others through Gavin's arrest and the revelations from his divorce papers. Michelle took up another large circle – a purple pen seemed fitting – and Rachel outlined the findings from the Lewises' camera, the financial angle and the recent discovery that Lola's clothes and toys had been cleared out.

'That wasn't part of the covert surveillance,' said Patten. 'Which I was just about to come on to.' He flapped the file. Rachel coloured slightly. Carrying out your own rogue operation in the middle of the night was not sanctioned by the chain of command.

'It was part of our investigations,' said DS Rajavi, covering smoothly. 'We've got Lola's possessions in our exhibits room.'

Rachel shot her a grateful look.

Patten spoke about the thoroughness of the surveillance done by the NCA operations team, and the fact that it had thrown up no new information but merely confirmed what they currently knew about Michelle Harper's situation, and that she definitely didn't have Lola in her care.

'To sum up, I'm going to recommend the following actions: that Michelle Harper is re-interviewed and her son's death looked at again; that friends and neighbours not spoken to already are identified and interviewed. Also, in the light of Michelle throwing away her daughter's things, that another search for Lola's remains is conducted in the local area, with as much manpower and as many canine units as we can source. DS Rajavi, are you happy to liaise on this?'

Rajavi nodded.

'Then there's the media angle. We need to prepare an update, keep the press vultures quiet while reassuring the public we haven't given up the search. There's been inevitable speculation since the search in Portugal made the news. The usual gubbins about pursuing several new lines of enquiry should do.'

Patten rubbed his hands and passed round the hot drink flasks and chocolate biscuits like a vicar at a tea party. 'Excellent. Let's continue to work together, and do all we can to move this forward.'

Rachel had no idea what to wear for the girls' night.

She was assuming the others would be more practised at this, so she texted Louise, a former colleague from the Met and the organiser of the evening, to canvass her opinion.

Full-on glam! xx

The reply made her heart sink. She pulled out the black dress she had worn to dinner with Stuart, but decided it was a bit too restrained, too formal. She had a sleeveless checked sundress that she quite liked, but it was all wrong at the end of November. In the end, she dressed in black velvet jeans, a loose ruffled shirt in dark red silk and – reluctantly – black suede high-heeled ankle boots. After adding suitably vampy make-up, she viewed herself in a full-length mirror. Ridiculous. She looked like an expensive call girl.

She scrubbed off some of the cosmetic excesses, but by then she was running late and there was no time to change her clothes, so she called a taxi and headed straight to the Flirty Martini cocktail bar near St Paul's. Even the name was enough to fill her with dread.

There were seven other women in the group. Since Rachel was late, they were already assembled, all sporting short tight dresses and strappy shoes. She had worked with a couple of them in the past but didn't know any of them well apart from Louise. One of them, a redhead, definitely wasn't a former colleague but looked vaguely familiar. Disconcertingly, every time Rachel turned her head in that direction, the redhead was shooting her dirty looks.

The noise level was already high, and as more of the rainbow-hued cocktails were consumed, the shrieks and giggles rose to a glass-shattering pitch. Rachel reached into her bag and stealthily texted Brickall.

Girls' night = exactly as awful as I predicted 😞

These women were all roughly her contemporaries, which meant they were in their late thirties or early forties, with husbands or partners and children. And that was what they talked about. It made no sense to Rachel: these women planned a night out as an escape from humdrum domesticity, yet once they were out talked about nothing but their humdrum domesticity. She hovered on the edges of the conversation and immersed herself in a steady flow of vodka martinis.

When everyone was excessively tipsy, there was a lengthy debate over splitting the bill, and then more shrieking as the group tried to negotiate a path through the other customers to the front entrance. Alcohol had erased collective memory of how to walk in heels. A couple of the women had babysitting curfews, but the remainder were going to go on to a club.

'My husband's borrowed a friend's minivan and he's going to drive us,' said the redhead. 'We're probably all too pissed to organise taxis.' She and Louise sniggered.

'That's extremely nice of him,' said Rachel.

'Oh, he's a diamond,' affirmed a woman called Becky. 'Her Howard's the best, isn't he, Julie?'

Howard. The penny dropped in Rachel's vodka-muddled brain. That was where she had seen the redhead before: at the pub with Howard. She was Julie Davison. Rachel walked up to her, attempting to start a friendly conversation, but was again greeted with a disdainful look.

'Hi – Julie? I'm Rachel Prince. I know Howard,' she said, attempting to initiate a friendly conversation. 'He trains me at the gym.'

'Oh don't worry, darling, there's a whole army of you. All of them throwing themselves at my husband. It's pathetic, really.'

As she spoke, Howard himself loomed in the doorway, looking handsome in a navy reefer coat and waving car keys. The jolt of surprise when he saw Rachel was visible, to her at least. She hadn't planned on going to the club anyway, since she had to interview Michelle Harper the next morning, so no one paid much attention when she slipped past the group into the street.

All except for Howard, who turned and watched her as she walked away.

Back at her flat, she tugged off the ankle boots, made herself a herbal tea and started the process of removing her call-girl make-up. All that effort putting it on, only to scrub it off a couple of hours later: one of many reasons why girls' nights out were a ridiculous concept. She was slower and clumsier than usual, thanks to the three martinis. Or was it four? It could have been.

The intercom buzzed, making her jump. At 11.30, the only person it could be was Brickall, wanting to do an informal case review over a pizza or a curry.

'Hello?'

'It's Howard.'

She buzzed him up.

'I've got time to kill before I go and pick up your friends,' he explained, pulling off the reefer coat to reveal a navy sweater that strained over his substantial biceps and pectoral muscles. 'I said

I'd go back to the club and collect in…' he looked at his watch, 'an hour and a half.'

'Actually most of them are your wife's friends,' pointed out Rachel. 'Your wife who was about as friendly as… as a rattlesnake.'

'Ah.' He had the grace to look embarrassed. He was also sober, and therefore would be able to tell that Rachel was not.

'Cup of tea?' she ventured.

'Do you have anything stronger?'

She found a bottle of single malt and poured him a shot. He smelt of clean wool and expensive aftershave, and she found herself leaning in to inhale deeper as she handed him the whisky. He did not pull back; in fact he came and stood so close to her that their thighs were touching. After a hasty gulp of his drink, he set his glass down on the kitchen counter so that both hands were free, and placed them lightly on the small of Rachel's back.

She gave an involuntary shiver. 'So, according to your wife, I'm just one of many women who are throwing themselves at you.'

He raised an eyebrow. 'Throwing themselves, eh? How does that work?'

'Well now… let me show you…' Rachel leaned in, flattening herself against his broad chest. It felt wonderful: both exhilarating and somehow comforting. Howard reached for his glass again, draining the last of his whisky in one mouthful, then lifted her up as though she weighed nothing. They kissed furiously as he carried her into the bedroom, and continued kissing as he pulled off her trousers and shirt with a speed that bordered delightfully on roughness. And Rachel did not protest even though she knew she should, all sense and discretion washed away by one vodka martini too many.

'Oi, Cinderella, your carriage awaits!'

When Brickall phoned from the lobby of her apartment building the next morning, Rachel was grateful that Howard had already been committed to returning to the nightclub to collect Julie and her friends. It meant that there was no awkward scene when she woke, hung-over, the next day, and no walk of shame in full view of her detective sergeant. Nevertheless, she had a pounding head, which she richly deserved. She came downstairs and met Brickall wearing sunglasses and clutching a Thermos mug of strong coffee.

'Big night, was it? With the girls.'

'Don't ask.'

'I just did.'

Rachel silenced him with a glare, and was mute for most of the drive to Eastwell. The arrangement was that DS Rajavi would collect Michelle Harper and bring her to the local police station, where Rachel and Brickall would conduct an informal interview. Taking her to the NCA interview rooms in Great Queen Street, where criminal investigations were processed, was judged to be too heavy-handed on this occasion.

Rachel was in no mood to deal with a bolshy suspect, but Michelle seemed compliant and subdued, almost eager to please. She was dressed in a skirt suit and blouse and nude platform heels, as though attending a job interview. Her hair had been freshly boosted by extensions, and her gel manicure was immaculate.

'So, I wanted to start by asking you about these.' Rachel pointed to the bags from Willow Way, which had been brought into the room. 'For the purposes of the tape, I'm pointing to exhibits HAR/16/232 and HAR/16/233.'

Michelle gave a good-natured shrug. 'What is there to tell, really? I went back to the house to pick up my post and tidy round and I decided to have a bit of a clear-out.'

'This is more than a bit of a clear-out,' interjected Brickall. 'This is most of the stuff from your daughter's room.'

Michelle frowned, but her tone remained level, reasonable. 'I wouldn't say it was all of it. There's still stuff in her wardrobe. I just find it hard, you know, to have so many reminders.' She bit her lip, which was wobbling decorously, and pulled a tissue out of her bag.

'All right then, what if Lola Jade is found and comes home wanting her stuff? I imagine she *would* want her stuff.' Rachel took a swig of coffee, wincing at the jackhammer behind her temples.

'I'll get her all new, of course. I get her new stuff all the time. Got her new stuff,' she corrected herself, glancing down and inspecting her manicure. 'Kids grow out of clothes and shoes anyway. She's still growing.'

'So you didn't chuck her clothes and toys because you know she's not coming back?'

'Definitely not.' Michelle was firm, and quite unruffled. 'I'm still hoping you'll find her. You know, one day.'

One day. This struck Rachel as an odd choice of words, but she decided to change tack. 'Can we talk about the funds raised on the JustGiving page.'

'It's to help find Lola Jade.'

'Obviously,' said Brickall. 'But why would you need to withdraw £30,000 in one go? In cash.'

'Someone said to me I should hire a private investigator.'

'Really?' Rachel checked her notes. 'A few days after Lola disappeared, when the police investigation was still in full swing? Wouldn't that be something you would do when other lines of enquiry had failed?'

Michelle narrowed her eyes defensively, but Rachel could tell she was trying hard not to seem truculent. 'All I know is I was desperate. And when you're desperate, you're going to try anything.'

'So who was the PI?' demanded Brickall. 'And how much did you pay him.'

'He's called Mike Booker. I found him on the internet. I paid him fourteen grand, but it was a total waste of money. He was useless.'

'And the rest of the money?'

'I've still got it. Of course.'

'Not according to this. For the purpose of the tape, I'm showing Michelle exhibit HAR/16/219.' Brickall showed her the log from the second search of 17 Jubilee Terrace. 'Nothing written on here about a bloody big bag of twenties.'

Michelle scowled at him, but kept the same level, reasonable tone. 'I don't keep it at my sister's, obviously. It's at the salon where I work, locked in the safe.'

'And you'd be happy to let us verify that?'

Michelle smiled sweetly. 'Of course.'

'And what did you intend to do with the rest of the cash? Why take out 30,000 if the investigator was only charging you fourteen?'

'I was afraid he might get going with something… you know, find some proof or whatever, and then say he'd run out of money. I thought it was best to have the other fourteen grand ready, you know: in case.'

So plausible. So reasonable. Rachel smiled calmly. 'I thought you said the investigator charged fourteen thousand? That would leave another sixteen.'

For the first time, Michelle lost her composure, picking repeatedly at her right thumbnail with her forefinger. 'Booker could have charged more; I honestly can't remember the details.'

'Such a big sum of money, and for something so important: you'd think you'd remember.' Brickall folded his arms across his chest in a textbook 'don't believe you' tell.

'I can't remember stuff like that: my head's all over the place!' Michelle folded her head into her hands and started to cry; jagged breathy sobs. She straightened up and dabbed her face with the tissue. 'You've no idea how awful this is for me. It's literally a living nightmare. I just want my princess back, my little princess angel.'

The sobs were met with silence, and petered out. Michelle sniffed and raised her head, groping again for the tissue, which this time she used to dab at her nose. Her eyes, Rachel noticed, were completely dry.

CHAPTER NINETEEN

The following morning, Rachel's mobile rang for a third time, and for the third time the display said *No Caller ID*.

She had ignored the first two calls, but this time she answered it. There was an almost-silence, the kind that betrays the fact that someone is listening on the other end of the line but has no intention of speaking.

'Hello?'

No response. She cut the call and placed the phone face down on the table, switched to silent mode.

She was spending the first half of the morning working at home, which should have been a luxury. Instead she was made irritated and on edge by this intrusion. Brickall was in Tinworth Street making a start on tracking down Michelle Harper's PI, and they had arranged to meet up later and head back to Eastwell to check the safe at her place of work.

Once the previous day's hangover had receded, some exercise had been in order. Before sitting down with her laptop and a large mug of coffee, she had been for a run over Tower Bridge and back. Alone. She had cancelled her training session with Howard with a craven five-word text.

Sorry, can't make this morning.

Yes, probably she would have to face him again at some point, but not yet. Not today.

The message board on Find Lola Jade was her destination of choice this morning. Slowly, painstakingly, she read through all the comments. Most of them were anodyne displays of emotional support with emojis to match, or criticisms of the police. Michelle's cheerleader-in-chief seemed to be Stacey Fisher, who agreed with everything that she wrote on the page (which wasn't much) and leapt to her defence at every turn. Then, posted a few weeks earlier, during Rachel's extended stint in Portugal, was the following:

If you ask me, the mum knows far more about this than she's letting on.

The name of the account was simply 'TruthTella'.

A few days later, TruthTella cropped up again.

It's no coincidence police start by looking at the family, it's always the person who's closest to the victim.

The poster was eloquently shouted down by Stacey Fisher.

You don't know what your talking about you slag!!

Rachel printed off the comments feed and showed it to Brickall as he wove expertly through traffic, sighing. 'Why don't we just move to Eastwell: save ourselves the commute?'

He glanced at the printout while they were idling at a red traffic signal.

'Interesting. And shall I tell you what else is interesting? That Mike Booker guy.'

'Doesn't exist?'

'Oh, he exists all right. But the phone number on his website is out of date, and when I visited his registered office in Tulse Hill, it was all locked up. I shoved my card through the letter box, but the place looked dead as the proverbial donkey.'

Michelle greeted them at the Happy Nails salon as though they were merely enquiring about an unpaid parking ticket. She was wearing a pink beautician's tunic and had her hair tied back in an elaborate fishtail plait. Her manner was relaxed, friendly even.

'Come through to the back office,' she said, then asked, 'Can I get you anything? Coffee? Herbal tea? Water?' As though they were there for a pedicure.

'If we could just see the safe, please.' Rachel was still surfing the tail end of the martini hangover, and not in the mood to make nice. Brickall, on the other hand, was fascinated by the sample nail-colour wheels, holding the finger-shaped palettes over his own nails one by one.

Michelle unlocked the safe and pulled out a large manila envelope containing bundles of twenty-pound notes with an ATM slip wrapped round them. The date and the amount – thirty thousand pounds – matched her bank account record and the remaining cash added up to fourteen thousand pounds.

'Did you get a receipt from Mike Booker?' asked Brickall.

She shook her head. 'I never thought to ask for one. My head was all over the place at the time. Wasn't thinking straight.'

'And where did you meet him?'

'At his office.'

'Which was?' Rachel asked.

'In Tulse Hill,' Michelle said, without missing a beat. 'On Norwood Road.'

'Go by yourself?'

'Course not. I was a basket case. Kevin drove me. Lisa's other half.'

'Fucking hell, she's a slippery one,' Brickall muttered as they left the salon, his tone betraying a grudging admiration. 'You think you've got her cornered, and she comes up with the answers.'

'Speaking of answers,' said Rachel, tilting her head and scanning the street, 'this might provide some.' She pointed to a CCTV camera on the frontage of a newsagent opposite called Bangla Stores. Its lens was trained on the nail salon. 'Let's round up what they have, and then I think we have to get back to the good old-fashioned plod work Patten requested. Talking to witnesses. Including our pal Gavin, who's up for sentencing tomorrow.'

Her phone buzzed in her pocket. *No Caller ID*. She cut the call in disgust.

'Your ex again.'

'I doubt it,' said Rachel, very much fearing that it was.

Joanne Keen, whom Michelle claimed bore her a sizeable grudge, was at the top of Rachel's interview hit list. Followed by Lisa Urquhart's neighbour, Kirsty Wade, although she'd already been interviewed and not had much of interest to say.

Joanne Keen lived in a pin-neat executive detached and looked like a suburban Stepford Wife, in catalogue-fresh leisure wear and a neat bob without a single stray hair.

Her feisty manner belied her bland appearance. 'The woman is a psycho,' she said firmly, as she set down matching mugs of coffee on a dust- and smear-free glass coffee table. 'When I heard about what happened to her daughter I wasn't that surprised, to be honest.'

Rachel sipped the coffee gratefully while Brickall homed in on the biscuits.

'Don't get me wrong,' Joanne went on quickly, smoothing an imaginary crumb from her top. 'I'm not saying she'd hurt her. That girl was the centre of her universe: she adored her.'

'So why weren't you surprised?' Rachel pressed her.

Joanne sighed. 'I don't know… It's hard to put into words. It's just that she thrived on drama, you know? There was always something going on with her. Danny says she's the sort of person who would start a fight in an empty room.'

'Danny's your old man?' asked Brickall through a mouthful of shortbread.

'That's right. He put in some kitchen units for the Harpers, only they refused to pay him because Michelle claimed one of the units was crooked, only actually it was their floor that was uneven. Danny said it was because they had subsidence. Anyway, that's what I mean. About Michelle. She could always find something to kick off about.' Joanne gave a triumphant smile.

'She mentioned you when we asked if she had enemies,' Rachel said, unable to resist a smile.

Joanne made a snorting sound. 'Oh, come on! As if we'd have anything to do with taking her daughter!' She indicated the immaculate sitting room. 'I mean, why would we? Not only have I never had so much as a speeding fine in my life, but Danny's business is doing fantastic. We've just moved into our dream home. We're happy together, planning another baby. Okay, yes, I couldn't stand the woman, but I wasn't alone in that. Most of the mothers at school felt the same.'

'So there was a bit of a dust-up at the school gates.' Brickall rubbed the biscuit crumbs from his fingers. 'Michelle claims you threatened her. Like to tell us about that?'

'She was the one who got physical,' Joanne protested, the colour rushing hotly to her cheeks, 'She grabbed me hard. Really hurt me. She may not look it but she's pretty strong. I was just trying to defend myself. And when I said we were going to get her back, I was only talking about getting our money from them. Danny was planning on taking them to the small claims court.'

'And did he?'

Joanne shook her head. 'She paid up after that, like nothing had happened. Like I said, she's a nutter. When Danny was working round there, he said that Michelle and Gavin had the most horrendous fights. And he said when they fought it was Gavin who would get upset. She would just laugh at him, all cold; didn't give a crap about his feelings.'

'Did it get physical between them?'

Joanne considered this. 'I've only got what Danny told me to go on, but apparently he would chuck stuff and shout, but when she snapped she would fly at him and actually hurt him. And I heard on the grapevine when they split that Gavin was going for custody. But now, obviously…' She gave a rueful shrug, to indicate that things had changed.

'I can't see Little Miss Perfect there being our criminal mastermind somehow,' said Brickall ten minutes later as he drove them to Jubilee Terrace.

'Agreed. That would involve messing up her outfit… Interesting corroboration, though.'

'Patten's after us for more than corroboration. All we've got to show for our efforts is a fucking great bucket of circumstantial. Not good enough.'

Kirsty Wade's mother-in-law answered the door at 19 Jubilee Terrace. She was minding the youngest while the child napped, Kirsty having popped out to do a grocery shop. Rachel told Mrs Wade Senior that they would wait, and they sat in the car, both idly flicking at their phone screens. Like a teenager unable to stop herself from checking her social-media status, Rachel was drawn again to the Find Lola Jade message board.

'Ooh,' she said out loud, even though Brickall was not paying attention. 'Look at this! TruthTella's posted again!'

'Who the fuck's TruthTella?'

'Remember – the troll on the Lola Jade Facebook site. I showed you the comments page… "Why doesn't someone ask Michelle Harper about her boy?"'

'Let's have a look.' Brickall took her phone, frowning at the message. 'Whoever it is presumably knows about the cot-death baby. Gavin Harper's our next stop: we need to get him to talk about it.'

Kirsty Wade returned, and, while she unpacked bags of oven chips, sliced bread and cheese strings, chatted happily enough about what she knew of Michelle. She had seen her very rarely since she had gone to stay with her sister, just the occasional glimpse as she came in or out of the house. She would acknowledge

Kirsty but they didn't really speak. Kirsty was, however, on good terms with Lisa and the two of them took turns to take and collect their children from the nearby primary school: Overdale Infants and Juniors. All the children from the neighbouring streets tended to walk together in a group.

'Not especially helpful,' grumbled Brickall as they headed north again. 'Time to go and cheer on our mate Gav.'

Gavin Harper was being sentenced at Croydon Crown Court, and Rachel and Brickall slipped into the public gallery just as his case was called.

He did, after all, have a very good barrister, who made a meal of Gavin's grief and anguish over Lola Jade. The judge appeared to take heed of this mitigation and only handed down eighteen months in prison for the theft of the rhodium and six months for the passport fraud, to be served concurrently. A lenient sentence in light of the value of the goods, and the time he had already served on remand would be taken into account.

'I'd rather barbecue my own head than spend any time inside,' Brickall said to Rachel as they walked down to the holding cells in the basement of the court building. 'But I reckon Harper's a lucky beggar.'

'On this occasion, I agree,' she said, pleased to find she could now keep up with the ever-springy Brickall without limping. 'Strictly speaking he was looking at four— Oh Christ.'

She had switched off her mobile while she was in court, and now turned it on to find four missed calls from *No Caller ID*. It rang again in her hand.

'You need to sort that out,' observed Brickall. 'Have a word with whoever it is.'

Gavin Harper was sitting on a slatted bench in a tiny open-fronted cell, waiting for transport to arrive and take him back to High Down. Now that he had been sentenced, he would eventually be moved to a lower-category prison. He seemed calm and composed.

'I'm just glad that Andy's okay,' he told them when they asked how he was bearing up. Andy Whittier had been given a suspended sentence two weeks earlier, and his employers had very generously allowed him to return to work.

Rachel pressed her hand briefly on Gavin's shoulder, then sat down beside him on the bench. 'I want you to know that we're still offering operational support to Surrey Police while they're looking for Lola Jade,' she said. 'But I also need to ask you something. You mentioned your son, Oliver, in relation to Michelle's conduct as a mother. What did you mean by that?'

A look passed across his face; one she was unable to fully decipher, but which had elements of sadness, anger and despair.

'They said it was just one of those things.' He spoke quietly, looking at his prison trainers. 'They said there was nothing we could have done differently. It's just something that happens sometimes.'

'On the certificate, the cause of death was "unascertained". I understand that pathologists sometimes put that if they're not convinced it was Sudden Infant Death Syndrome.'

Rachel let the observation hang there. Gavin adjusted his position to avoid the possibility of eye contact. 'Look, I don't know for sure what happened. But the police… they acted like they were suspicious that Michelle had something to do with it. I thought that was a bunch of crap at the time. Just something they had to investigate. Michelle and I… we were both really upset, we just showed it in different ways. I'd lost my son; I needed to grieve for him. Michelle wanted to heal the wound by having another kid. It was only years later, when I'd actually got my head straight, that I started to wonder. When our marriage was breaking down and she was acting like a complete psycho… it got me thinking back to the way she'd acted when Olly was born.'

Rachel adjusted her position on the bench, but he still wouldn't look at her. She stood up and leaned on the wall in an attempt to give him thinking space. 'Which was?'

'We didn't get told the sex when we had the antenatal scan done: Michelle claimed she wanted to be surprised. But she was convinced it was a girl. She decorated the nursery all pink. And then he was born, and he was a boy, and she just didn't want to know. I mean, she looked after him. Gave him a bottle and changed him. But she didn't, you know…'

'Bond with him?'

'Yeah. They didn't bond. She pretty much ignored him. I thought that was just Michelle: she's not exactly the cuddly type. But then she was quite different around Lola when she was a baby, and that got me thinking… I remember in particular this one night when I got back from work and she was bathing Olly, and his head was under the water. She lifted him out again when I came into the bathroom, said she was just washing his hair—'

'You thought she might be trying to drown him?' Brickall interjected, blunt as ever.

'Who knows? Michelle could twist things, and she got *so* defensive if you ever suggested she was doing anything wrong. She was furious that night; said I was crazy to suggest she could hurt a baby. I remember that bit particularly: it was "a" baby, not "my" baby or "our" baby… But she was pestering me and pestering me, from the day of her six-week postnatal check, you know – to get her knocked up again. I said it was too soon to be thinking about another one, and of course that led to yet another row. So many rows.' He sighed and ran his fingers through what was left of his hair. 'Long after Olly's death, it came back to me what she'd said during that particular argument.' He lifted his face and looked straight at Rachel. 'She said: "I don't want a boy. I want a girl. I'm not going to stop until I get my little girl."'

CHAPTER TWENTY

Rachel had once again cancelled a training session with Howard.

Unfortunately, by the time she returned home the same evening, exhausted but with her brain buzzing, she had forgotten this. Grabbing her kitbag and a swimming costume, she headed to the gym, only to walk straight into Howard as she entered through the building's revolving door.

'Well, this is awkward.' She thought she might as well address the large, adulterous elephant in the room.

'Rachel, about what happened...'

'It's fine. No big deal.' She tried to dodge round him, but he filled too much space.

'Can we please just talk about it over a cup of coffee?' He indicated the café area to one side of the reception desk.

Rachel sighed. The last thing she wanted was a heart-to-heart with an inadvisable one-night stand. On the other hand, if they were going to keep on bumping into each other, it would be best to clear the air.

They sat in one of the ceiling-height windows overlooking a playing field, where a floodlit game of five-a-side football was under way. Rachel asked for a hot chocolate, and when Howard brought it over to their table it was buried under whipped cream and mini marshmallows. She set about removing them with a spoon, the task giving her an excuse not to look him in the eye.

'The thing is, Howard,' she said firmly, 'I'd had an awful lot to drink the other evening. I probably wouldn't have been so reckless if I hadn't.'

His expression was mildly disappointed.

'Come on, admit it,' she went on. 'Sleeping with me wasn't the best idea. I'm a client. And you're married.'

'For the time being,' he said grimly.

'Things that bad?'

'We haven't resolved the baby issue. She acts like she doesn't want me, but she's so paranoid every time I leave the house. Suspicious.'

'Well you can relax, on my part at least. I'm not going to make waves. Luckily you picked the most commitment-averse woman in London for your one-night stand.'

He did relax, enough to laugh at this. 'Fair enough.'

'And it was… fun.' She smiled as she recalled the heavy, solid feel of him. 'But speaking of making waves, you haven't been…' More awkwardness. For a few seconds she concentrated on arranging the marshmallows in a neat row along the edge of her saucer. Best to just come out with it. 'Have you been phoning me and withholding your number?'

Howard's horrified expression was the only answer she needed. She had been interviewing suspects long enough to know that you couldn't fake a reaction like that. 'Christ, no! Why would I do that? If I wanted to speak to you, I'd just call you and leave a message; all above board. Withholding your number's creepy. Not my style at all.'

'It's fine, I believe you.' She touched his wrist briefly and looked into his pale blue eyes. 'Someone's been making nuisance calls to my mobile and it started after that night we…'

'Not me, honest to God.' He placed a giant paw on his equally impressive pectoral. 'Hand on heart.'

Rachel stood up, kissing him swiftly on the cheek. 'I've got to go, but... good chat.'

'Our indiscretion is in the past.' Howard gave her a conspiratorial wink. 'Even if it's not quite forgotten.'

The following morning, Rachel carried out one of her now habitual checks on the Lola Jade Facebook page. TruthTella had been at it again.

Lola Jade hasn't gone very far. And I've got proof.

The other site visitors had stopped responding to her taunts, deciding that if she was ignored, she would go away.

The phone on Rachel's desk rang. It was Donna, the Tinworth Street receptionist.

'Is Detective Sergeant Brickall there? Only he's not answering his extension and there's a man in reception who wants to speak to him.'

'He's in the building somewhere,' Rachel told her. 'I'll send him down.'

She tore herself away from her screen and went in search of Brickall. He was sitting in the office kitchen morosely nursing a mug of instant coffee.

'Someone to see you in reception.'

'Who is it?'

'How do I know? I may leap tall buildings in a single bound, but I haven't mastered X-ray vision.'

'Can't you go down?'

'No. That's what I have *you* for. Jesus, Detective Sergeant, sometimes you're as much use as an ice tray in an igloo.'

Still grumbling, Brickall disappeared. When he returned, thirty minutes later, it was with a bit more of a spring in his step.

'Well, that was interesting.'

'Because?'

'The man who wanted to talk to me was our missing gumshoe – Mr Mike Booker. He does exist. He's the real deal.'

Rachel set down her pen. 'A classic turn-up for the books, just like in the best TV cop dramas.'

'For what books? Never known what that expression means… Anyway, the place was locked up because he was away for a couple of weeks in Swindon, on a case. All legit; he showed me the paperwork. When he got back, he found the card I shoved through the letter box and got in touch.'

'Interesting. And what did he have to say about the elusive Mrs Harper.'

'That bit's even more interesting.' Brickall dropped into his chair, slapping his notepad on the table for emphasis. 'Never met the woman. Never spoken to her and never been hired by her. And more importantly, never been paid fourteen grand by her. Or sixteen, or however much it was supposed to be.'

'So Michelle lied to us. Again.'

'No big surprise there, Sherlock.'

Rachel frowned. 'In that case, what's she done with the rest of that money?'

'When we interview her, I guess we'll find out.'

But Rachel was shaking her head. 'We're not going to do that. Not yet anyway. Because you know that if we do, she'll just come up with another lie: she got the name wrong, or Booker's not being truthful, or whatever. We need to come at this from a completely different angle, and hope we can get something watertight that way.'

Brickall was sceptical. 'By doing what?'

'Tell you on the way. It's going to involve another drive down to Eastwell.'

Brickall sighed heavily. 'I was afraid you were going to say that.'

'Where are we going this time?' Brickall asked as they set off on their ninth joint road trip along the clogged London-to-Brighton trunk road. It was a dour, squally early-December day, with damp leaves blowing on to the car windscreen and sticking there. 'Michelle's house or Lisa's?'

'Neither. Eastwell nick. When we were there last time, I asked them to go through the CCTV from the shop opposite Happy Nails, and Leila Rajavi just emailed to tell me they'd found something.'

While she was checking the contents of her inbox that morning, Rachel had also emailed Lee Knightley and asked him to try and track down TruthTella's identity. Statistically the odds were on him or her being a crank, a fantasist, but it still seemed worth investigating.

Rajavi led them into a vacant interview room and set up a computer monitor, arranging chairs in front of it so that Rachel and Brickall could watch the footage.

'The shop has an old-fashioned analogue system where you take out tapes and replace them with a fresh one when they get full. The owners were in the habit of keeping the tapes for several months before recording over them, rotating and re-recording in a loop. This is from late June.' She pressed play.

The image was of mediocre quality, but clear enough to show Michelle sitting across from a woman at one of the manicure tables. The time stamp showed that it was 8.30 in the evening, and there was no one else in the salon. The woman, who looked somewhere between thirty and forty, had her hair in a ponytail and was still wearing a parka, as though she didn't intend on staying. She and Michelle spoke for a few seconds, then Michelle went out of the room, heading in the direction of the office, where the safe was kept. She came back thirty seconds later with a bulging envelope, which she handed to the other woman. The woman took out a couple of bundles of notes and started counting them, then, once she had checked them, shoved the envelope into her coat pocket and left the salon.

'So what's that then?' asked Brickall. 'A bung? A bribe? Blackmail?'

'We don't know yet,' said Rajavi. 'It might not be any of those things. But we do know who this woman is.' She brought up another file, which showed footage from further down the street, recorded the same evening. The woman in the parka climbed into a small, rust-streaked hatchback along from the nail salon and drove off. 'We ran the plate and the car is registered to a Stacey Fisher, of 27 Merrion Drive, Eastwell.'

'Michelle's online mate,' said Rachel. 'At least she's the one who's always defending her honour on the Lola Jade message board.'

'Have you spoken to her?' Brickall asked.

'Not yet. I wanted you to see this first. But we can bring her in now if you like?'

'Excellent idea,' said Brickall. 'Send one of your trusty woodentops to get her, if you'd be so kind.'

The best way to describe Stacey Fisher was drab. She had drab mousy-brown hair, a drab complexion and wore a drab khaki top, teamed with the same fur-trimmed parka.

She was unmoved when DS Rajavi showed her the footage from the salon.

'Yeah, what of it?'

'Michelle Harper is giving you what looks like a considerable sum of money.'

Fisher shrugged. 'She owed me it. She bought a washing machine and tumble dryer off me. Seven hundred quid.'

Rachel thought of the small fitted kitchen in Willow Way, done up by Danny Keen some time ago, and the even smaller kitchen in Lisa's house in Jubilee Way, which on the most recent search had not featured newly plumbed appliances.

'So where are they now? These machines?'

Stacey shrugged. 'Dunno. Didn't ask.'

'You can't just hand them over like a packet of biscuits,' Brickall said. 'They put concrete in the base of washers, you know. You need a truck to put them in, some muscle to move them... So did she come to your house for them, and who with?'

Stacey chewed her fingernails, and her neck reddened slightly. 'Don't remember. My partner dealt with it.'

'And what happened to the seven hundred pounds?' asked Rajavi.

'Spent it. On Christmas presents.'

They let Stacey go, in perfect confidence that she was lying. The CCTV footage suggested bundles of notes that would amount to thousands, but the images weren't sharp enough to prove it.

'I can try getting them enhanced,' Rajavi offered. 'And we can speak to Fisher's boyfriend about the washing machine story.'

'Thanks,' said Rachel. She was just about to arrange a time for a debrief when her phone rang.

No Caller ID.

That evening, Rachel went for a long, solitary run, icy drizzle whipping against her cheeks and Lorde playing in her headphones. Her right knee protested but she ploughed on, slipping over the greasy cobbles of Shad Thames until her mind had emptied. After a long, hot shower and a bowl of tofu salad, she sat staring at her phone for a few seconds, then with a heavy exhalation picked it up. It had to be done. She couldn't avoid the issue of her non-marriage forever.

Stuart answered after a couple of rings, and sounded full of bonhomie.

'Rae! That's a coincidence. I was just about to phone you, actually.'

Rachel was thrown. 'You were?'

'I was,' Stuart said, maintaining his amiable tone. 'As it happens, I'm going to be in London tomorrow, for a symposium at the Royal College. I thought it might be a good idea for us to meet.'

Rachel's hackles went up. The last thing she wanted was another attempted interrogation on the sudden end of their union. 'Why's that?'

'I've got the outline divorce petition; I just thought it would be easier and quicker to agree on the statement of case together. Though since we've been separated so long and have no children, it should be pretty straightforward.'

'I suppose so.'

'Unless you're intending to file for spousal support?'

'Of course not,' said Rachel hotly. 'I have a perfectly good income of my own.'

'All right then. The next thing I think you should consider is the name of a solicitor.' Stuart: in control as ever. 'Not mandatory; you can represent yourself if you like. Cheaper.'

'Sure,' said Rachel. 'Whatever. Let's try and carve out some time tomorrow.'

'Was that why you phoned me? To ask what was happening with the divorce? Only I'm sorry it's not been quite as speedy as I hoped it would be: I've been lecturing in Singapore.'

'There was something,' said Rachel. 'But it can wait until we're face to face. I'll see you tomorrow.'

CHAPTER TWENTY-ONE

The following morning, Rachel and Mark Brickall had an argument.

This was not unusual; in fact, it was one of their standard case-solving techniques. They would take opposing positions and find the truth somewhere in between the two.

'I reckon we should get Michelle Harper in again,' Brickall said, as they sat at their desks ploughing through routine paperwork. Rachel was checking her inbox for word from Lee Knightley about TruthTella for the umpteenth time that day.

'What would that achieve?' she asked. 'We know she doesn't have Lola Jade. We can't charge her with anything at this point in time.'

'That's bullshit,' Brickall hissed. 'She lied to us about Booker in the course of the investigation: that's Section 89, perverting the course of justice by wilful obstruction of a police investigation. She's helped herself to the charity fund: that's a Section 4 fraud. Fuck it, looks like we could even have her under Section 5 of the Domestic Violence Act: causing or allowing the death of a child.'

Brickall had an encyclopedic recall of crime statutes, and loved to trot them out whenever possible.

'There's the not-so-small matter of evidence.' Rachel's tone was calm: the best way to draw the heat from Brickall's fire. 'Besides, our first priority still has to be finding out what happened to Lola Jade, and not ruling anything out. We've still got Gavin Harper

– now a proven criminal – leaving his semen on the bedroom floor. Okay, he says Michelle set him up, but we have zero proof that's true.'

Rachel kept her eyes on her screen as she spoke, going to the bookmark for the Find Lola Jade page.

'But if we haul her in and really put the screws on, maybe she'll cough. Tell us what she did with the rest of the money.'

'Knowing Michelle Harper, I doubt that. She's probably spent it on handbags and clothes. And if that's the case, we'll have her for fraud, I promise. Just not yet.'

Brickall threw his pen angrily across his desk. 'Fuck this!'

Rachel ignored him, as though he was a toddler throwing a tantrum for attention, and turned back to her online search. The previous afternoon, TruthTella had posted again.

Well, if none of you believe me when I say I know where Lola Jade is, I'm pretty sure the police will!

'Christ,' said Rachel. 'This could be interesting. Our online troll's threatening to come out into the open.'

Brickall merely grunted. Rachel turned and squinted at him. He was scowling, and for the first time she noticed that he looked paler than usual, and had shadows under his eyes.

'What's up with you?'

'I've got a bit of a… situation. Can we go to the Pin, grab a pint and talk about it?'

Rachel checked her watch. 'We'll have to be quick. I'm meeting my ex for lunch.'

'Don't you mean your husband?' Brickall managed a weak grin.

'Not for long, I hope.'

Rachel grabbed her bag and favourite winter coat – long and black with military-style frogging, which she liked to think gave her a Dr Zhivago air – and they headed for the lift.

'Hope you're going to tell him to stop phone-stalking you,' said Brickall, as they walked across the street to the Pin and Needle.

'Oh, don't worry, I intend to,' Rachel said firmly. She bought a beer and a bowl of chips for Brickall, a mineral water for herself and plonked them down on the table.

'Now, tell me what the hell's going on.'

Brickall sighed heavily, toying with a chip but not actually eating it. 'You remember the Data Protection Act business?'

'When the attractive lawyer warned you to stop misusing your access to her data: yes, I do.'

'And you told me to just stay away from her…' He mashed the chip into pieces on the edge of the bowl. 'Thing is, I saw her. Last night.'

Rachel set down her glass. 'Don't tell me you approached her again.'

'No, that's the thing – it was a total accident. You remember Chris Daish?' He named one of their former colleagues at Scotland Yard.

'Yep. I do.'

'Well, he invited me to a Christmas do being thrown by a firm of criminal solicitors. It was at a club near Chancery Lane. There were a load of people there: some CID, some CPS and lawyers…'

Rachel exhaled slowly. 'Don't tell me.'

'Amber Crowley was there with some people from her chambers. I swear I didn't know she was going to be there. I couldn't have been more fucking horrified when I spotted her. I told Chris I was leaving, but there was a real crush round the bar, and as I tried to work my way over to the door, I bumped into her. Literally. I banged her shoulder as I tried to get out.'

'Oh Christ.' Feeling the need for something stronger than water, Rachel took a sip of Brickall's beer. She didn't even like beer very much. 'Did she notice?'

'Oh, she noticed,' said Brickall grimly. 'She spoke to me. Said, "Thought you'd have got the message by now." I tried to apologise but she just went, "You haven't heard the end of this."'

Rachel sighed, checking her watch. 'Listen, I've got to go...
but here's what I think you should do. Pre-empt the situation. Go
to Patten and tell him what's happened, before she has the chance
to do anything. Tell him it was all a misunderstanding, admit you
made a mistake. It will be much better if you do.'

'You reckon?'

'I know.'

'Okay then, maybe I will.' He took a gulp of beer and started
smothering the chips in ketchup. 'Thanks, Prince.'

Stuart had asked to meet in a small Italian restaurant in Blackfriars
Road. It was a brisk twenty-minute walk from the Pin and Needle,
but to save her still-weakened knee, and because she was running
late, Rachel took a cab.

When she arrived, Stuart was already at the table and had
ordered. For both of them.

'I didn't think you'd mind,' he said, standing to kiss her on
both cheeks. 'It will save time.'

He produced the D8 divorce petition form, and they looked
at it together while they ate antipasti of olives, artichokes and
Parma ham.

'My solicitor says we should have the decree nisi within a
couple of weeks if there are no areas of dispute. The decree absolute
follows about six weeks later.' He looked up at Rachel with an
expression she couldn't read. 'Then we'll no longer be man and
wife, Rae.'

'We haven't been man and wife for a decade and a half,' she
pointed out.

'I know. It still feels a little like a loss, though. And I still wish
I knew what happened when you disappeared. Where you went,
why you cut yourself off from me.'

Rachel pretended to be reading the wine list. 'Can we please just leave all that in the past? There's nothing to be gained by rehashing it now.'

He gave her that steady, authoritative look; the one that could dismantle her when she was a naïve twenty-something. 'I disagree.'

'I'm sorry, Stuart, but that's all you're going to get out of me. But I have to ask *you* something…'

Her mobile vibrated on the table. They both looked at the screen.

No Caller ID.

Rachel cut the call and looked up at her husband. 'That's funny.'

'Why?'

'I've been getting anonymous calls. Nuisance calls. I was going to ask if it was you.' She chewed her lower lip. 'Clearly it's not.'

Her phone rang again, and this time Stuart reached over and picked it up. 'Hello?'

After a few seconds he handed it back to her. 'They hung up without saying anything. But maybe having a male voice answer will put them off. Whoever they are.'

'Sorry. I mean, that I thought it was you. It seems silly now.'

Stuart gave her hand a friendly squeeze. 'Well, I did phone you a few times when I first tried to make contact… and I showed up very suddenly after a long absence. That must have been unnerving, so it's not such a strange conclusion to draw, in the circumstances. But the truth is, I'm trying to get away from you, not closer to you. Yes, I would have liked a chance to talk properly about what happened, but I'm going to have to accept your decision. That you're not going to. And the best part is that I can walk away knowing you're okay – better than okay: thriving – and I can concentrate fully on my life with Claire.'

The waiter interrupted his soliloquy with two piping-hot plates of aubergine parmigiana, allowing Rachel to turn the conversation to Stuart's work.

'This symposium has been very interesting: a guy from Harvard – a medical examiner they call them there – talking about protocols in unexplained deaths.'

This brought Rachel straight back from his work to her own. 'Stuart, there's a case I'm working on… If I send you something, would you give me your professional opinion? Off the record.'

'Of course. Although I'm always happy to go on the record. I've lost count of the number of times I've given evidence in a criminal case.'

'Thanks, appreciated.' She lifted the glass of wine that Stuart had ordered for her – red this time, she noted. 'Here's to the most overdue divorce in history.'

'I'll drink to that.' He held up his own glass. 'To divorce.'

As Rachel was heading back to Tinworth Street, her mobile rang again.

'Jesus!' she said out loud, addressing her invisible stalker. 'Will you please just stop!'

She grabbed the phone from her bag, intending to switch it off, only to recognise the office phone number.

'What is it, dickhead?' she asked, assuming it would be Brickall.

'Um, Rachel? This is Lee Knightley.'

'Sorry, Lee, thought you were someone else. Obviously.'

He laughed. 'It's okay, I'm happy to answer to dickhead… I just went down to your desk, but you weren't there. I've got some news.'

'I'm on my way back into the office. Hang tight and I'll come to you.'

When she reached Lee's desk in the fifth-floor Tech Support department, his face wore an almost apologetic expression.

'I've traced the IP address that the TruthTella comments were posted from. That's the good news.'

'And the bad?'

'The computer is an open-access terminal in Eastwell public library.'

Rachel allowed this to sink in for a few seconds. 'Okay, well that's going to require a bit more digging, but the library should have a record of the people who are logged onto their computers at any given time. We just have to cross-match times and names.'

'Unless they're hiding behind a proxy server,' Lee pointed out.

'I don't think this is a sophisticated cybercriminal, so that seems unlikely.'

'And also assuming they're using their real name. If they want to avoid discovery, they're likely to use a fake one, surely?'

'Only one way to find out,' said Rachel, taking the printout he had produced. 'Thanks for this, Lee: you're a star.'

'Not a dickhead?'

'Whichever you prefer.'

She went down to the third floor with the intention of roping Brickall into a repeat road trip to Surrey, but he was nowhere to be seen.

'Have you seen Mark Brickall anywhere?' she asked Margaret, who was pottering about organising case files.

'He went out about half an hour ago, love. Face like thunder.'

'Did he say where he was going, or when he'd be back?'

Margaret shook her head.

Rachel's right leg was now finally capable of driving without pain, and once she had cleared a snowstorm of sweet and crisp wrappers from the passenger seat of the pool car – making way for the Lola Jade Harper file – she was quite content to have an hour of her own company. The Friday-afternoon rush hour had not yet kicked in, and the drive was relatively smooth. She tuned the radio to a classical channel – something Brickall would have sneered at – and enjoyed a bubble of relative peace.

Eastwell Central Library was a handsome civic building, one of the many built to celebrate Queen Victoria's golden jubilee. The head librarian, a grey-haired motherly woman called Nancy Poole, proudly pointed out its stained-glass windows, and the original book stacks just visible behind cheap plywood shelving units and peeling nylon carpet. Rachel spotted the row of desks in the corner where people were using the four public terminals. There was a ceiling-mounted CCTV camera trained in that direction.

'Do you ask to see formal ID before someone can use one of the computers?'

Nancy shook her head. 'Only if they want a reader's card. For time online, we just ask them to sign a register with their name and address, and they're given a time code. Maximum one hour, so people can't hog them.'

'That might make things a bit trickier.' Rachel showed her the printout of the IP log.

'We'll do all we can to help,' Nancy said, 'But it might take a while to go through our records. We're very short-staffed.' She grimaced ruefully. 'Public funding cutbacks: the usual story.'

'It is quite urgent.' Rachel was wondering whether she could offer Lee Knightley's support to speed things up. His line manager probably wouldn't be willing to spare him.

'Leave it with me, and I promise we'll get back to you as soon as possible.'

Rachel parked outside Eastwell police station and pulled out her phone. She tried calling Brickall, but he didn't answer. There were three missed calls from No Caller ID. Switching the thing off in disgust, she tossed it into the glovebox and went inside in the hope of finding Leila Rajavi.

'She's on a major incident,' the desk sergeant told her. 'They all are.'

Rachel produced her warrant card. 'I'll wait.' But she didn't have to. DS Rajavi appeared with a couple of constables in tow, all of them in stab-proof vests. Her own was straining over her pregnant belly.

'Sorry,' she said to Rachel when she saw her. 'I can't talk now: we've got a suspicious death on our hands. Young woman found dead in her home. I'm heading over to the scene now.'

'I could come with you,' Rachel offered. 'Not like I've not had plenty of DB experience.'

Rajavi shrugged. 'All right. I've got a forensic team there already, but a pair of extra eyes won't hurt.'

'It's a really sad situation,' she told Rachel, when they were in the squad car. 'The victim is Carly Wethers, twenty-nine. Single mother, raising her seven-year-old on her own. He found her dead in her bed this morning but was too terrified to do anything for a couple of hours. When he didn't show up at school and there was no reply on Carly's mobile, the headmaster phoned the grandmother, who went round and found the kid sitting on the floor next to his dead mum.'

Rachel shuddered. 'Poor little bugger.'

They pulled up in Albert Park, a few streets from where Lisa Urquhart lived. The whole road had been cordoned off, and two police officers were trying to discourage the small crowd that had gathered, some of them snapping pictures or filming with their phones. A third uniformed officer was stationed at the door of the shabby terraced house, and SOCOs in paper suits and overshoes tramped in and out to their van.

'Front bedroom,' said one of them, pointing up the stairs.

Carly's body was lying at the centre of a small brass double bed, tawny corkscrew curls forming a halo on the pillow, eyes closed. The duvet still covered her torso and legs, and at first glance she could have been asleep. But only at first glance. The skin around her eyes and mouth was pale, but the rest of her face was flushed a sickly shade of violet. A dark sliver of tongue was just visible between her lips and there was a shadow under her nostrils that turned out to be the faint ooze of blood.

One of the anonymous white suits was taking photos; another extended his hand and introduced himself.

'Adrian Christie, forensic pathologist.'

'I know you can't confirm cause until you've completed your PM, but it's looking like…'

'Suffocation from obstruction of the air passages. And with some force, too.'

'How did the perp get in?' Rachel asked. Thinking out loud, she went on: 'She's not going to answer the door in the middle of the night and then climb back into bed, is she? So it was either someone with a key, or a break-and-enter.'

'The front door had a single flimsy cylinder lock, and it's been "bumped" by inserting a specially adapted key and giving it a whack with a something like a spanner… well, with any hard object really. It's such a simple technique, we've known ten-year-olds do it,' Rajavi told her. 'We haven't found whatever was used. Yet. We're still searching nearby drains and bins.'

'A burglary gone wrong, perhaps?'

DS Rajavi was shaking her head. 'It's a technique burglars use, certainly, but there was nothing of value to nick, and the house contents are completely undisturbed. According to her mother, Carly didn't own a laptop, and her mobile phone was by the bed when Ben found her.'

Rachel was looking around the room. The floorboards were stripped bare, the door stripped and varnished, and the clothes hanging on the wardrobe door had an earthy, hippy-ish look. There were half-burned joss sticks on the simple pine dresser, along with a bottle of patchouli oil. A few ethnic necklaces, but no valuable jewellery, and no make-up. Downstairs, the furnishings had a colourful but homespun air. There was a simple woodburner in the living room, jars of muesli and leaflets for spiritual self-improvement workshops in the kitchen and a bicycle in the hall, fighting for space with two pairs of Scandinavian-style clogs. One adult-sized, one small.

'According to the neighbours, Carly was the tree-hugging type. Opposed to a digital lifestyle, into activism; that kind of thing,' Rajavi told Rachel as they came out onto the street and examined the damage to the front door.

'Is the little boy at Overdale Infants?'

'Ben Wethers? Yes. Same school as Michelle's sister's kids. Most of the kids in Albert Park go there.'

'And he's where now?'

'He's with his grandmother and an FLO. I'm headed over there next to see if we can get anything useful out of him.'

'I'll leave you to it,' Rachel told her. 'I was going to touch base with you about the Harper case, but it can wait. Finding the nutter who'd kill a twenty-nine-year-old mother is priority number one.'

CHAPTER TWENTY-TWO

Rachel drove herself straight home in the pool car. She would return it to Tinworth Street and switch it for her own car on Monday morning. For now, she needed a hot scented bath to wash the odour of death from her clothes and her hair. But still, lying in the fragrant steam, the sight of Carly Wethers' dead face kept coming back to her. She poured herself a glass of wine, put on some Ibiza chill-out music and sat down with the Harper file.

Were they looking in the wrong direction by scrutinising Michelle, and in doing so, were they mistakenly ruling out Gavin Harper? He might now be in prison, but could he have harmed Lola Jade accidentally in a bungled attempt at removing her from the wife he despised so much? She re-read the papers she had copied in the offices of Hepburn, Willis & Bell. Coming at them afresh, the commissioning of the psychiatrist's damning report seemed calculated, spiteful even. Who wouldn't come up short if our personalities were put under that sort of scrutiny? So much bitterness and resentment leapt off the pages. Each parent so determined that the other did not deserve to keep their daughter, with little Lola Jade herself getting completely lost in the process. Her photo gazed out from every news website in the world, and yet she was a victim without an identity or a voice. A pawn.

She looked at the copy of Oliver's non-committal death certificate again, and something occurred to her. She had already recruited the best help available, but hadn't yet got round to using it.

She phoned her soon-to-be-ex-husband.

Stuart didn't pick up straight away, but called her back after a few minutes.

'That thing I was going to send you, can I do it now?'

'Sure, if you're quick. We're going away to Aviemore for the weekend, but not for another hour or so.'

He gave Rachel his email address and she sent him the post-mortem findings and the police report on Oliver Harper.

'I take it you suspect infanticide?' he said when he phoned her fifteen minutes later. 'I can't think of any other reason you'd be asking me about this.'

'Correct.'

Stuart sighed. 'Okay, to start with, there are a couple of things that make me think it was asphyxia rather than an intercurrent infection that killed this child.'

Rachel took a mouthful of wine. 'Which are?'

'The presence of petechial haemorrhaging just below the eyes. Tiny rash-like red dots, from burst blood vessels. And internally, there was bloodstained frothy fluid in the back of the throat and oedema to the lungs. These are strong indicators of smothering, both when it happens by accident and when it's the result of a deliberate act.'

'So you can't be sure it wasn't accidental?'

There was the slightest pause at the other end of the line. 'Here's the thing: homicidal smothering is very difficult to detect in a small infant. Accidental smothering by bedclothes is usually the culprit in infants under four and a half to five months, at which point they become strong enough to roll themselves over. Before that, they can end up with their faces covered if they change position. And this child – Oliver – was less than four months. So the petechiae and fluid in the lungs are not in themselves proof of foul play. To know what happened in this case, I think you have to refer back to the police report.'

'Go on.'

'A child can be smothered if the weight of the bedclothes is above them, over their nose and mouth, or if they're face down with their face buried in a pillow, mattress or even a soft toy. But this was July. I checked the weather for that day in 2008, and sure enough there was a heatwave in the South East. The temperature that morning would already have been around twenty-five degrees. The police report describes Oliver as having been put to sleep on his back in a sleeveless onesie, with just a light woven cotton blanket covering his legs. Yes, potentially he could have wriggled sufficiently to get the blanket tangled round his face. But the mother's testimony is of being able to see his face when she came into the room, because at first she claims she thought he was still sleeping.'

'Which is inconsistent with accidental smothering…'

'… because his nose and mouth were free of obstruction. Precisely.' There was a voice in the background, and Stuart said, 'Listen I have to go. I hope that was helpful though.'

'Yes,' said Rachel. 'Very. Thank you.' She hung up and sank back in her chair. If Stuart was right, then Michelle smothered her own baby. It bore out Gavin's story about only wanting a girl. That still didn't mean she could, or would, do the same to her daughter. But was this what Gavin Harper wanted them to think when he'd instructed her to ask about their son: that his ex-wife was a killer? Was he just doing it in order to deflect attention away from himself? Rachel felt as though her mind was being flipped repeatedly through one hundred and eighty degrees and back again.

Her thoughts were interrupted by the dissonant squawk of the intercom.

'It's me.'

Brickall.

'Where the fuck have you been all day?' she said to him as he came in carrying a pizza box and a bottle of wine. Then she saw his expression.

'Fucking bitch had already done it,' he said, pulling off his overcoat and flinging himself uninvited onto the sofa.

'What are you talking about?'

'Amber. I went to see Patten first thing, as per your advice. To – you know – fess up. Get him on side. Only Amber had already spoken to him. Made a formal complaint about my conduct.'

'Oh shit.' At a loss to offer comfort, Rachel cut a slice of pizza and put it on a plate for him, finding a bottle of chilli sauce in the cupboard and handing that to him too, along with a glass of wine.

'She's basically really embellished the story, made me look like a full-on psycho rather than just, you know…'

'An opportunist? A Jack-the-lad?'

'Yeah, exactly.'

'Well look.' Rachel sat down next to him and gave his shoulder a tentative squeeze. 'So you happened to bump into her near where she lived. That could just be chance.'

'They'll cross-check my PNC log-in though, and see I looked up her address. And I took her mobile number from the Bogdhani case file.'

Brickall hung his head. She'd never seen him so wretched, and with good reason. Breaching data protection rules and accessing personal data for non-policing purposes was not only a sackable offence, in some cases it led to prosecution and could mean up to six years in prison.

'Look, Mark…'

He gave her a rueful grin. 'I know things are down the shitter when you call me Mark.'

'I'll speak to Patten. See if I can get him to go easy on you.'

'Fucking bitch,' said Brickall morosely. 'Not you: her. Amber Crowley.' He pulled a pack of cigarettes from his trouser pocket and lit one.

'You don't smoke.'

'I do now.'

Rachel went into the kitchen and fetched a saucer to act as an ashtray, placing it silently in front of him. She didn't know what else to do.

Brickall stayed until nearly 2 a.m., and when Rachel finally woke on Saturday morning she decided that instead of exercise, what she needed most was strong coffee and the weekend papers. Until, that was, she saw one of the headlines in her local newsagent.

LOLA JADE COPS IN MURDER PROBE.

There beneath the headline was a blurry photo of herself and Leila Rajavi on the steps of Carly Wethers' house, as a white-suited SOCO knelt beside them examining the front door.

'Shit!'

Rachel grabbed the offending tabloid, along with her usual paper, flung down the money and ran back to her flat. Twenty minutes later she managed to get through to the publication's on-duty lawyer and, by raising her voice and threatening sanctions against the editor, persuaded him to have that page pulled from later editions. A Pyrrhic victory: the damage had already been done.

Sure enough, first thing on Monday morning, she was summoned to Patten's office to listen to him huffing and blustering about Saturday's press leak.

'Put a call through to the PCC and let them know in no uncertain terms that I want to speak to them. Then tell your team at Surrey Police to put out a denial that there's any link between this woman's death and Lola Jade Harper. Take control of the story, as soon as possible.'

'Yes, sir.'

Rachel sighed and looked down at her feet, knowing only too well what was coming next. 'And send Mark Brickall in, will you. Straight away.'

'Suspended from duty, pending an enquiry,' he said glumly as he came back to his desk to clear out his things. 'It's with full pay, at least,'

'You'll still be able to buy me a Christmas present then.' Rachel gave him a playful thump on the arm, determined to try and keep things light, even though she was inwardly horrified at the prospect of losing her sidekick. 'How about the Christmas party? Are you going to come?'

The MCIS Christmas party was taking place that night: traditionally a rowdy affair, with a sit-down festive dinner followed by drinking, dancing and ill-advised fraternising at a local club.

Brickall shrugged. 'Can't say I'm feeling exactly festive.'

'Oh go on! It'll be fun.'

'Don't be fucking daft: work parties are never fun.'

But he showed up that evening, and Nigel Patten raised an eyebrow then turned a blind eye. The whole department – civilian support staff and analysts, uniformed officers and detectives – made themselves look foolish in paper hats while they ate dry turkey breast with lumpy gravy and khaki sprouts, then a core group went on to Shapes nightclub, in a basement near Smithfield Market.

Brickall cheered up, especially when he saw Patten take to the floor and execute a strange blend of skipping steps and flailing arms to Kool & the Gang's 'Celebration'.

'Patten's reached peak dad-dancing,' he observed.

'Well, he is a dad, so I suppose it fits.'

Rachel hovered on the sidelines, nursing a shot of tequila and watching, until an assistant crime analyst called Tim Marshall dragged her onto the dance floor. He was very drunk, and determined to wind his arms round her waist, despite her attempts to keep some space between them. She sent 'Help me!' looks to Brickall, but he ignored her, grinning to himself.

Out of the corner of her eye she spotted Patten leaving the dance floor and huddling in the corner to take a call on his mobile, the index finger of his left hand stuck in his ear. When he had hung up, he scanned the room until he located Rachel. He beckoned to her to follow him out into the foyer that housed the cloakroom, where the noise level was marginally lower.

'Sorry,' Rachel mouthed to Tim, grateful for the chance to escape.

'That was Nick Furnish in Intelligence,' Patten announced.

A wave of relief washed over Rachel: she had been afraid that the news was something to do with Mark Brickall.

'Apparently there's been a potential development in relation to the hunt for Lola Jade Harper.'

CHAPTER TWENTY-THREE

Over twenty years of policing, Rachel had learned to be sceptical about 'developments' and 'breakthroughs' in a case. So often they turned out to be a bid for attention or an attempt by an investigator to push a particular agenda.

At the 8 a.m. briefing, she had managed her expectations accordingly. She was also grateful that the call to Patten had come in while she was still only on her second drink of the night. Otherwise she would have been nursing a headache, and not just the feeling of missing her right arm. Now Brickall was no longer on the Lola Jade case, she was painfully aware of his absence.

'So,' said Nick Furnish, a portly man in his fifties, whose ginger hair had all but gone. His shiny pink pate gleamed under the harsh lighting in the Tinworth Street meeting room. 'Sussex Police received a report of a child being snatched yesterday afternoon, about fifteen miles from Eastwell, just over the border from Surrey, in Chilbourne. The MisPer is Chloe Atwell, aged eight. She was playing with a friend in the park, and they both had their bikes with them. The friend – Emily Taybridge, who's ten – told police that it was getting dark, and they were just about to head home when two men appeared and grabbed Chloe, bundling her into the back of a white Transit van that was parked at the entrance to the park. She wasn't able to give a detailed description, but one of the men was of slight build and wearing a hoody; the other was larger with a tattoo on his neck.'

Furnish wiped his head with his handkerchief, and nodded at Giles Denton to take over.

'Clearly there are some significant similarities with the disappearance of Lola Jade Harper. The location, the girl's age, the white van and the description of one of the men: short and of slight stature. A white Transit van was picked up by ANPR leaving the Chilbourne area shortly after Chloe was taken. The same number plate was recognised in the queue for the Portsmouth to Le Havre ferry a couple of hours later. Unfortunately, by the time Emily had been interviewed and her statement checked, that vehicle had already boarded the ferry and unloaded on the other side without us having a chance to notify the relevant border authorities. But…' Giles Denton gave a smile that betrayed more confidence than he could possibly be feeling, 'a yellow notice has been published by Interpol's central bureau, and there's every chance the vehicle will be located.'

If only the same could be said of little Chloe, thought Rachel.

Gilly Durante, an officer from the Slavery and Human Trafficking unit, said a few words, then Patten cleared his throat. 'We'll hold another debrief as soon as appropriate, and there'll be a press briefing later this morning. They are bound to speculate about a link, but you know the protocol: at this point we say we can't confirm one. In light of some recent press stories about Lola Jade, we need to keep a tight grip on this. As much as is possible where the media are concerned. DI Prince…' he glanced sideways at Rachel, 'you're still investigative support officer to Surrey Police, and I'll leave it to you and your colleagues there to share information with Sussex.' He addressed Giles Denton. 'Will you make sure that Sussex do the same and share any relevant intel with Surrey? We need cross-force cooperation to establish if the two cases are in fact linked.'

As they left the meeting room, Rachel hurried past the others until she had caught up with him. 'A word, sir…'

'Go on.'

'Can I come and talk to you about Mark?'

'I'm not sure that would be appropriate at this stage. Once the enquiry's under way, perhaps, but that won't be until the new year. You're going to have to keep across his workload as well as your own – a big ask, I know – so you may need to take a back seat on the Harper case. For now, anyway.'

Rachel responded with a bland smile. Back seat, my arse, she thought.

As Patten had predicted, it didn't take long for the national press to get hold of the news and run with it. They loved a missing child story, especially if the child in question was cute and photogenic. And they loved to think that a crime was one of a series.

DID LOLA KILLER TAKE CHLOE?

LOLA JADE GANG STRIKES AGAIN.

Underneath the inflammatory headlines was a smiley photo of Chloe Atwell, who had dark shiny hair and freckles, and was far more appealing than the glum Lola Jade. She would divert attention from Carly Wethers' murder at least, Rachel thought, with the cynicism of more than a decade investigating serious crime.

Leila Rajavi phoned her on Wednesday, soon after the Chloe story broke. 'Do you think it's true?' she asked Rachel. 'Do you think the same people took Lola Jade?'

'It's possible,' said Rachel cautiously. 'Why, don't you?'

She heard a hissing sound, as though Rajavi was sucking her teeth. 'No,' she said finally. 'I don't think so. Lola was targeted. Whoever took her knew she was in that house. With Chloe, it seems random: they drove past a playground and snatched a child because she happened to be there.'

'Those men could have been following Lola prior to that night, though.'

'Maybe. I'm not saying it's impossible.' Rajavi sounded unconvinced.

'Sussex are going to pass on any intelligence they get about the men in the van, so we may end up with more meat on that particular bone.'

'Good, thanks… Anyway, I know it's not your case, but since you were with me, I thought you might like to know we've had the pathology findings on Carly Wethers. Cyanosis, internal congestion and haemorrhaging consistent with deliberate suffocation. It would have taken several minutes, and required the application of some force.'

'Poor girl,' said Rachel. 'Poor family. Is there an obvious suspect – an ex-partner or boyfriend?'

'Ben's father isn't on the scene, lives in Ireland apparently. His alibi checks out. We're talking to everyone else that we can, but she doesn't seem to have had many friends or acquaintances. Not really in the inner circle of the mums' mafia.'

Rachel spent the next couple of hours fielding the inevitable press enquiries about Chloe Atwell and the possibility that the same person took Lola Jade. When she wasn't on the phone, she was gazing miserably at Brickall's empty desk, and ploughing through the sort of scut admin work that she usually delegated to him. She texted him.

What are you doing, loser?

He replied ten minutes later. *Watching Eurosport: now fuck off and leave me in peace.*

After staring at her screen for twenty minutes without taking in a single word, Rachel could stand the ringing phone of her office phone no longer. She diverted her extension to Margaret, grabbed her kitbag from under her desk and headed to the gym. A bit of Howard was in order, she decided.

*

'How about a live opponent?'

Rachel had been throwing punches at the bag for ten minutes, with Howard looking on. Her hair was plastered to her forehead with sweat and her mascara was running, but she didn't care. Hitting something felt good.

'What do you mean?' asked Howard, who was standing watching her.

'You and me. *Mano a mano.*'

He shook his head. 'It wouldn't be a fair fight. I'm a lot heavier than you, and – no offence – a lot stronger.'

'Oh go on…' she wheedled. 'Please. I want to know what it feels like.'

'Where's this aggression coming from? Still getting those calls?'

'Not for a while… no, it's work stuff. All uphill at the moment.'

Howard relented enough to put on some gloves, but only on condition that he was purely playing defence. He'd fend off her jabs, but not return them. He stripped off his tracksuit top and stood there in singlet and shorts, his heavily muscled and tanned torso like a copper sculpture under the light. At that moment Rachel wanted to drag him back to her flat and into her bed, but she couldn't; not after so recently banishing him to the friend zone. So instead she punched him. Hard.

Howard stood with his gloves six inches from his face, parrying the blows with his wrists or the flat of his hands. They kept this up for fifteen minutes, until Rachel slumped forward, gloves on her thighs, panting.

'Better?' Howard enquired.

'Much. The best alternative to therapy I know.'

She straightened up again and pulled out her mouth guard, dripping strands of drool.

'How about a drink once we've showered?' Howard asked, with his disarming smile.

'Remember what happened the last time I saw you after consuming alcohol?' She raised an eyebrow.

'Just as friends. I know my place.'

'Another time, I'd love to. But officially I'm still at work, and I've got stuff to do.'

As she left the gym and walked back towards Tinworth Street, her phone rang.

No Caller ID.

Enough was enough. She searched her web browser for her mobile network's customer service number and phoned them then and there, in the freezing street. They had a procedure for tracking nuisance calls, a sympathetic female operator told her, but the process took two to three weeks. In the meantime, they suggested picking up the call and telling whoever was on the other end that they had been reported and that the mobile company always gave information about offenders to the police.

'We find that usually does the trick,' the woman told her cheerfully.

No sooner had she hung up than she had the chance to put this advice into action, because her phone rang immediately. Only this time, although the number was an unfamiliar one, it had not been withheld.

'Yes?' Rachel was aware she sounded snappy.

'Is that Detective Inspector Prince?'

'It is.'

'This is Nancy Poole. From Eastwell library.'

'How can I help you?' She modulated her tone to sound more user-friendly.

'I think *I* can help *you*,' said Nancy. 'We've found out who was sending those messages.'

CHAPTER TWENTY-FOUR

Rachel had only been to Brickall's flat once, when she had dropped him off on the way back from a human trafficking job in Dover. He lived in Forest Hill, in a small Victorian first-floor conversion on a steep hill with views over the Weald of Kent.

She rang the button by the front door that said *M. J. Brickall*. No reply.

She rang again. And again. The speakerphone crackled. 'Jesus, who is it?'

'It's me, dickbrain. Prince.'

'I'm suspended, remember. Fuck off.' He hung up the intercom.

Someone from another of the flats came through the front door at that exact moment, hesitating as Rachel tried to get past him into a communal hallway littered with pizza leaflets and junk mail. She flashed her warrant card.

'Police.'

Brickall ignored the hammering on the door for about thirty seconds, then flung it open.

'What?' If he was surprised to see Rachel, he did a good job of covering it. He was unshaved and still in pyjama bottoms, his naked torso partially covered with an open towelling robe.

'You're coming with me. Go and shower and put some clothes on.'

He scowled, but complied with the order.

Unlike her own pristine flat, her sergeant's was chaotic and untidy. The coffee table was littered with empty lager cans and takeaway remains; the throw on the back of the sofa featured the Charlton Athletic strip. A large wooden dresser along the wall opposite the window contained a surprising number of books: mostly sci-fi and thrillers. There was one framed picture next to them, catching Rachel's eye because it reminded her of the photo of Gavin Harper and Andy Whittier. Two sunburnt, freckled little boys grabbed each other's T-shirts in a play fight, staring down the camera with cheeky grins. They were very alike, but Rachel could tell from his wiry frame and belligerent expression that the smaller one was Brickall.

'Who's this with you?' she asked when he emerged, shaved and dressed in jeans and a clean shirt.

'My older brother.'

'I didn't know you had a brother.'

'Well, I didn't know you had a husband,' he fired back as he followed her down the steps of the building to her car.

'So what does he do?'

'Mostly pushes up daisies. In the cemetery.'

Rachel stopped in her tracks. 'Jesus, Mark, I'm so sorry. What happened to him?'

Brickall climbed into the passenger seat. 'Don't want to talk about it.'

'Sure. Of course.' Rachel started the ignition without looking in his direction. She had heard the catch in his voice and didn't want to embarrass him by provoking tears.

'Where the fuck are we going?' he asked as they turned back towards the South Circular. His voice had returned to normal. 'Um, let me guess: Eastwell.'

Rachel smiled sweetly. 'That's right: your favourite Home Counties destination. I felt like some company, and since you've got nothing better to do than sit around farting in front of *Countdown...*'

'So what are we doing?'

'Paying a visit to the library.'

'Bloody hell, Prince, you know how to live life in the fast lane, I'll give you that.'

Nancy Poole was waiting for them at the front desk, shifting from foot to foot, her plump frame almost quivering with excitement. Rachel and a still-surly Brickall followed her into her office.

'So...' she spread a photocopied document on the desk, 'this is the sign-in page for the days in question. The messages coincide with the time slots when this user was active.' She pointed to the relevant line with the tip of her pen.

Under surname, the user had written: *Found*. Under first name: *Lola*.

'Lola Found,' read Rachel.

'It's the same here, here, here, here...' Nancy pointed to the other occasions when Lola Found had booked time.

'As a fake name, it makes a point,' observed Rachel drily.

'Doesn't really help us identify them, though,' muttered Brickall, hovering like a reluctant teenager on a family outing.

'Ah, but!' Nancy continued triumphantly, enjoying her role as bringer of important news. 'We also checked the footage from our closed-circuit camera, and on one occasion, the user who logs into Terminal One as Lola Found then comes up to the front desk and checks out a book. Using a reader's card that was registered with a real name and address.'

She slid a copy of the electronic book scan on top of the paper they had been looking at.

Title: Harry Potter and the Philosopher's Stone

Reader: Ben Wethers

Rachel caught her breath. 'Have you still got the footage? Can I see?'

Nancy bustled over to a computer and pulled up a black-and-white video file. Thanks to the bright strip-lighting in the library, the quality of the image was good. The woman at the desk was young and slender, dressed in baggy linen pants and a ripped T-shirt. She had her head dipped down, face partly obscured, but the abundant corkscrew curls were unmistakable. Rachel had seen them at close quarters only a few days earlier.

'Bloody hell!' she breathed. 'I know who she is.'

'You've met our TruthTella then?' asked Brickall.

'Not exactly,' said Rachel. 'By the time I clapped eyes on her, she was dead. Murdered. She's Carly Wethers.'

PART THREE

It matters little, at this point, where the exact truth lies in the maze of perjury, evasion, and of contempt for the normal.

Noam Chomsky

CHAPTER TWENTY-FIVE

Officially, Rachel was out of the office attending a victim-support training day.

In reality, she had emailed the course organisers first thing that morning to say that she was no longer able to attend, and had returned alone to Eastwell to talk to DS Rajavi. Giles Denton had emailed her to say that Sussex Police had a significant new lead, and she would hear about it as soon as it was confirmed.

'We're still running forensics on Carly's house,' Rajavi told her. Her olive skin had a grey tinge, and there were circles under her eyes from what had no doubt been a week of minimal sleep, compounded by the discomfort of late pregnancy. She had offered Rachel coffee, but after seeing her air of exhaustion, Rachel insisted on fetching drinks for the two of them.

'I've got the full post-mortem report here, if you want a look,' Rajavi said when Rachel returned.

Rachel skimmed through it. 'So there were marks on her wrists compatible with some sort on inflexible restraint… like a handcuff?'

'Possibly. Time of death is between two and four on the Friday morning, so the theory is that Carly was deeply asleep. Didn't hear the lock being bumped – it doesn't really make any noise other than a tapping sound – so was still asleep when the killer came upstairs. Then, to prevent her struggling, something was slipped round her wrists while she was still sleeping. She probably woke up at that point, by which time she was pinned down, unable to move her arms. Her mouth would have been covered before she could cry out. There wouldn't have been a whole lot she could do.'

Rachel closed her eyes briefly. What a terrifying way to die. It always made an investigation slightly less soul-destroying if a victim had the chance to fight back, and managed to inflict some scratches or bruises. Not only were relatives consoled that their loved one had not given in, but there was often valuable DNA gathered under the fingernails from skin or hair.

As if reading her mind, Rajavi said, 'Whoever did this wasn't stupid. They used fabric gloves – we found some dark fibres around her mouth. So there were no prints on the door and no DNA left on Carly's body. They probably closed off her mouth with one hand and pressed a pillow down hard with the other. It's usually pretty difficult to achieve suffocation unless the victim is a child, or very frail, but the fact that Carly couldn't move her arms would have made it possible. Once she was dead, the pillow was returned to its position under her head, but we know for sure that it was used because of the saliva and traces of blood on it. The handcuffs or restraints were removed and taken away. The whole episode probably only took ten minutes.'

Rachel sipped the cup of machine coffee, though she felt that brandy would be more appropriate. 'You probably know what I'm going to ask next.'

'If it's about CCTV, then we're still going through it,' said Rajavi wearily. 'I'll let you know what we find. We're doing all we can. Taking Ben Wethers' formal witness statement has to wait until we've held a CWIP meeting with Surrey Children's Services.' Rajavi referred to the Child Witness Interview Planning regulations. 'You know how it is: all the boxes have to be ticked, an officer with the correct training has to be assigned, and we can only go ahead when he's ready.'

'In that case, I have something that could be relevant when the time comes.'

Rachel told Leila about their discovery that the individual claiming online to know what had happened to Lola Jade was none other than Carly Wethers. 'In her last post as Truth Tella, she claimed she was going to take what she knew to the police. Less than forty-eight hours later, she's permanently silenced. There has to be a link between Carly and the Harpers.'

Rajavi took a moment to let this sink in. 'All I can say is that Carly never came up in any of our original enquiries. There's no reason she and Michelle would have known each other, or moved in the same circles. Ben Wethers is at Overdale, but Lola Jade went to St Mary's C of E Primary, over on the other side of Eastwell.'

'Lisa's kids are at Overdale. And Michelle Harper is living under her roof, mixing with Lisa's friends and acquaintances,' Rachel pointed out.

'But if these comments – Truth Tella's – are anonymous, how would anyone with an interest in Lola have known they were written by Carly?'

'Maybe Carly spoke to someone about what she knew.'

Rajavi smoothed a strand of dark hair away from her face, placing a hand over her swollen abdomen. 'We can't exactly ask her now, can we? All we can do is question as many people as possible about it; see if they heard anything.'

'There's Stacey Fisher,' Rachel reminded her. 'She of the mysterious disappearing washing machine. She used that message board too. There were others. And the neighbour – Kirsty – she might know more than she was letting on…' Rachel suddenly thought of something. 'Hold on, let me see your copy of Lola's file.'

She flicked through until she found Kirsty Wade's original statement, reading it out loud. '"I'm married to Darren", blah blah… "I have three children…"'

She looked up at Rajavi. 'Her youngest is a baby or toddler. We saw that when we called round to speak to her. She has three kids, but only two are school age. So when we saw Lisa and Kirsty's children going to school together, who was the fifth child?'

She was thinking aloud now, and Rajavi stared at her, mystified. 'There were the two Urquhart kids and the two Wades. A fireman, a Superman, a couple of princesses and a penguin... so who on earth is the penguin?'

In her flat that evening, Rachel paced restlessly, thinking about Carly Wethers. Did her killer also kill Lola Jade? In an attempt to untangle the spider's web of connections in her mind, she used the longest blank living room wall as a canvas, pinning up pictures of Lola, Michelle, Gavin, Andy, Lisa, Carly, Kirsty Wade, Stacey Fisher and Chloe Atwell. Black silhouettes served to represent the mysterious men with the white Transit van. She tried drawing lines between the key players, but it ended up looking like a ball of knitting wool and provided no answers.

She rarely watched television in the evening, but switched it on now in an attempt to relax. After pouring herself a glass of wine, she settled down to watch a documentary about the ways in which Mexican cartels smuggled drugs across the US border. They were hidden inside a surfboard, in breast implants, even fired across the border in a cannon. There was one method that caught her eye: the creation of a secret compartment along the inner sides of a pickup truck, packing plastic-wrapped bundles all the way around the edge of the flatbed and then covering them with a false front of panelling. It was ingenious: unless you knew about the fake sides, you would have sworn it was a regular unmodified vehicle.

Rachel sat bolt upright, splashing an arc of wine over her new rug. That was it! There had been something nagging away at the back of her brain, and looking at the concealed partition in the Mexican drug lord's truck had made her realise what it was. She snatched her phone and trawled back through the call history, hoping she still had a record of his number. She found it, and pressed call.

'Mr Lewis… sorry to phone so late, but I need to speak to you about something. Urgently.'

Philip and Sally Lewis, the son and daughter-in-law of Michelle Harper's next-door neighbours, lived in a 1920s semi-detached in the prosperous but dull wasteland between Wimbledon and Mitcham.

Philip Lewis was clearly proud of his home, insisting on giving Rachel a full tour and bragging about how much its value had surged, and how good the local schools were. Inside, everything was orderly to the point of obsession: every surface devoid of clutter, shoes in the hallway neatly aligned, mugs in the kitchen with their handles pointing the same way. Rachel tried to imagine what it would be like to live with a Philip Lewis. The thought made her shudder.

'Well, this is certainly a surprise, Detective Inspector,' he said, as he led her into the converted breakfast kitchen, almost vibrating with curiosity. 'How may I be of further assistance? Refreshment? Can I offer you tea or coffee?'

Rachel accepted tea, since it was still early, and sat down at the table. It was neatly set with four place mats, but the chaos of family breakfast and the school run was already spirited out of sight.

'You have two children, is that right?' She already knew this, having just seen their abnormally tidy bedroom. Philip Lewis had lectured her on how houses like this built in 1926 had three large double bedrooms, while the standard 1930s semi had two doubles and a box room. The Lewises' third bedroom was used as a home office, with two desks and a lot of computer hardware.

'Yes, Felix and Finlay.' He looked concerned, which was understandable given that Rachel was investigating the abduction of a child.

'It was something your mother said that got me thinking… She said they liked staying with her because at her house they get to have a room each.'

Lewis frowned. 'A small room admittedly – they're both singles, and one has the computer in it – but yes, the boys sleep separately there. I suppose it's a novelty for them.'

'So your parents' house was built as a three-bed? When they bought it.'

He nodded.

'But the house next door – the Harpers' house – is only a two-bed.'

Philip looked perplexed. 'No, no, that's not the case.' He shook his head firmly. 'My parents bought from new, off-plan, in 1991. They had the choice of either 55 or 57, the point being the two houses were identical: mirror images of each other with their garages adjoining in the middle.'

'You're quite sure?'

'I'm not only sure, I can prove it to you.' He gave her a smile of triumph. 'If you'd care to come upstairs, I can show you the plans.'

They went up to the office and Philip pulled out a box file from a cabinet. A typed label on its spine read: *Purchase of 55 Willow Way*.

'My parents had never bought property before, so I helped them with all the paperwork.' He pulled out an architect's blue-print and laid it on the desk, then produced a floor-plan outline that was probably drawn up by the estate agent or property developer. Numbers 55 and 57 Willow Way, Eastwell.

And there they were. Two identical houses, with living/dining room and kitchen on the ground floor, a large bedroom taking up the full width of the front of the house, a bedroom along the vertical edge of the landing – Lola's room in number 57 – and a bathroom and single bedroom next to each other at the back of the house.

Rachel pulled out her phone and sorted frantically through the camera roll until she found the pictures she had taken in number 57. The headache-inducing poppy wallpaper on the landing, with two doors at the garden side, a bathroom and a storage cupboard. Except that it hadn't started out as a cupboard; not when the house was built. It had been another room.

CHAPTER TWENTY-SIX

A couple of hours later, Rachel was back on Victoria Embankment.

This time, she was not visiting the offices of Hepburn, Willis & Bell, but 6 Bailey Court, a barristers' chambers. There on the brass plate at the entrance listing the incumbent lawyers was an engraving that read *Miss Amber Crowley.*

The clerk at the front desk was unmoved by Rachel's warrant card: police officers routinely attended criminal-case conferences in chambers. Miss Crowley was in court, but would be back when the morning session ended, at 1 p.m. It was now 12.45, so Rachel decided to wait.

She recognised Amber as soon as she walked into the building. Brickall's description had been minimal, but this girl was a real head-turner, with olive skin, glossy dark brown hair that fell in waves almost to her waist, a figure that wouldn't disgrace a catwalk, and arresting chartreuse-green eyes. Small wonder Brickall had been so obsessed with her that he had risked his job.

'Ms Prince.' She extended a hand in a perfunctory handshake when the receptionist told her Rachel was waiting to see her. She smiled, but there was a hint of irritation that her lunch break was being interrupted.

'Detective Inspector Prince.' Rachel returned the smile. 'Could I have a quick word?'

Amber led her into her room, shared with a colleague. It had antique keyhole desks piled high with pink-ribboned briefs and the paraphernalia of court dress: wig tins and starched white neckbands. Bookshelves of legal texts lined the walls.

'Sit down,' said Amber, pointing to her colleague's empty chair. She sat opposite Rachel and started puffing on an electronic cigarette. 'How may I help you? Is this concerning evidence in a criminal case?'

Rachel shook her head. 'Mark Brickall is my DS.'

'Ah.' Amber pursed her lips round her e-cigarette and blew vapour at the ceiling.

'I understand you made a complaint about him?'

'Damn right I did,' Amber replied coolly. 'What he did constituted harassment. Coming to my address – which I assume he found on the vehicle registration database – and then lifting my personal number from the case file and using it to message me. Following me around. It's totally unprofessional and unacceptable.'

'I agree,' said Rachel. 'And I told him so myself, believe me. But that last time you saw him: that was a genuine coincidence. He was going to leave you alone, and he had no idea you'd be at the same event. It wasn't deliberate. I can vouch for that.'

'I see.' More scented vapour floated to the ceiling.

'I may as well get to the point: I'm here to ask you to retract your complaint. His style may be a bit brash, but Mark's a bloody good police officer, and a great colleague. Someone I trust implicitly and can rely on completely. It would be a great shame, and a loss to the force, if he was fired from his job because of an idiotic mistake. He thought you and he had chemistry, and he acted on it. It was a bad judgement call, but there was nothing sinister behind it, just overconfidence.'

Amber gave Rachel a long look. 'Are you and he an item?'

'Good God, no!'

'Just the way you speak about him… So what is your relationship?'

'Friends,' Rachel said firmly. 'Good friends. We've worked together on and off for years. He's a good guy; really he is.'

Amber raised her hands to indicate defeat. 'All right, you win.' She gave a reluctant smile. 'That mitigation was worthy of a top QC. I'll contact your boss – Patten, is it? – and tell him I don't wish to complain. Hopefully my point will have been made.'

'Oh it has,' said Rachel, standing up. 'You can be sure about that.'

'What I want,' Rachel told Brickall over the phone, as she walked back to Tinworth Street, 'is for you and me to go round to Willow Way and have a look ourselves.'

'We can't, you muppet,' Brickall scoffed. 'Since Michelle's not been charged with any crime, you need a warrant to search her house. And I can't go with you because – in case it's somehow slipped your mind – I've been suspended.'

'About that…'

Rachel told Brickall that she'd successfully persuaded Amber Crowley to have a change of heart. He swore copiously, blustering that she had no right to interfere in his problems. Once he'd calmed down, he did concede that he was grateful.

'Patten didn't want to know, when I tried him,' Rachel said. 'I thought going direct to Amber was the only option I had. And by the way: you're right. She is stunning.'

Brickall ignored this. 'Speaking of Patten, are you going to tell him you want a warrant to search 57 Willow Way again? I guess you could use the Chloe disappearance as a reason to re-examine the scene.'

'No,' Rachel said firmly. She had arrived at the NCA building and was now walking up to the third floor rather than taking the lift, to see how her right knee stood up to the climb. To her delight, it was fine. 'You know how Patten works: he'll start faffing about getting Ops involved again. I thought I'd go straight through Surrey Police. It's on their patch after all, and they've probably got a tame magistrate on hand to sign off a warrant. I'll phone them the second I'm back at my desk…'

She walked into the office as she spoke, glaring at the empty chair where Brickall should have been sitting at that moment.

'… which is now. Better go.'

'Hold on,' said Brickall quickly. 'While we're on the subject of phone calls, are you still being stalked?'

Rachel thought about this for a second. 'Actually, now you mention it, the calls seem to have stopped. I spoke to the phone company – maybe that did the trick.'

She logged onto her computer, checked her emails, and was about to contact Leila Rajavi when a text arrived from Brickall.

Think you should check news headlines.

At exactly the same time, she saw a flagged email from Giles Denton, an earlier missed call from him on her mobile and a Post-it note on her screen from Margaret, asking her to phone Giles. Laying her phone down again, she went to the BBC news site.

BODY OF MISSING GIRL FOUND

The body of missing eight-year-old Chloe Atwell has been found at the edge of a field near the village of Terrest in Belgium. She had been sexually assaulted and strangled. Chloe was snatched from a children's play area in a park in Chilbourne, Sussex, four days ago. Officers from Sussex Police are on their way to Belgium now, and are known to be investigating links between Chloe Atwell and the disappearance of six-year-old Lola Jade Harper from nearby Eastwell seven months ago.

There was a link to a video of the Chief Constable of Sussex Police breaking the news.

Rachel buried her face in her hands for a few seconds, then phoned DS Rajavi's number. Predictably, her line was engaged.

'Bad day at the office?'

Howard intercepted Rachel as she headed into the gym building. The place was now decked with tinsel and paper chains, and there were carols playing. There were only a couple more working weeks until Christmas – and the obligatory tense family lunch with her sister and brother-in-law.

'You could say that.' Rachel smiled wearily. She had fielded at least half a dozen media enquiries asking if the search for Lola Jade was about to move to Belgium, denying it while simultaneously knowing that this was a real possibility, and that it would be she who would be tasked with leading the operation. 'I think I'm going to skip the boxing and have a swim instead. It'll make me more zen.'

Howard put out a hand and stopped her in her tracks as she headed for the ladies' changing room.

'Hold on a minute, can we have a quick chat?'

'Can't it wait?'

'No, not really. Won't take long.'

'Okay.' Sighing, Rachel trudged after him to the café, thinking longingly of the warm, blue water of the pool.

'I'll get straight to the point,' he said when they had sat down. 'I know who's been making those unwanted calls to your mobile.'

She stared at him. 'You do? How?'

He looked down at his hands. 'Because it was Julie.'

'Your *wife*? Are you sure?'

Howard nodded. 'I opened a letter to her from her phone company, and it said that they had been tracing some calls that had been made from her number. So I checked on her mobile and found a whole load of withheld calls to your number. She must have lifted it from my phone without me noticing.'

'But why?' Rachel tried to engage eye contact. 'That stuff about women here chucking themselves at you… is that what she thought I was doing?'

He grinned. 'I seem to remember that's actually what you did.'

'Only after she put the idea in my head.' Rachel was also smiling. 'What happened was *her* fault.'

'She'd heard me mention teaching you to box, and that night you apologised to me in the pub, she saw us talking and was able to put a face to the name. Then she found out we were doing PT sessions together… and that night at the cocktail bar, first you left, and then I went out of phone contact for a while.'

'She'd make a good detective.' Rachel smiled ruefully. 'And I'm happy to report that the calls have stopped.'

'I think that letter gave her a fright. Shocked her out of her stupid behaviour.'

'And our sleeping together… you could say it was a self-fulfilling prophecy.'

'She still doesn't know we actually did it. She just suspects. And frankly, that's the least of our problems at the moment.'

'Will you confess?'

He shook his head. 'If we do stay together, it will just create friction. Although that's looking more and more unlikely.'

'Oh God.' Rachel sighed loudly.

'Don't feel bad: none of this is your fault. The irony is that Julie hasn't always respected our marriage vows herself. She's had… close friendships with people she's worked with.'

He let this revelation hang, but Rachel was too stressed for a discussion of someone else's marital shortcomings, and could think only of the soothing swimming pool water surging over her body. She stood up.

'Sorry to hear that. But it's best we just forget it. For now, anyway.'

She couldn't resist turning as she walked away. Howard was giving her retreating back a long, wistful look.

The following morning, early, she was back in Eastwell, standing outside 57 Willow Way with DS Rajavi and a group of uniformed policemen in stab vests.

At 10 p.m. the night before, she had finally got hold of Rajavi, who had filed an urgent request for a search warrant. The house was still empty, and the tactical squad felt like overkill, but Rachel was tense nonetheless. More than anything she wished that Brickall could be with her. Tactical operations were where he came into his own, never panicking or losing his cool.

The door was forced open and the rooms swept for either humans or weaponry. Then Rachel led Rajavi upstairs to the landing.

'Here,' she said, opening the door next to the bathroom, surrounded by the blaze of distracting purple poppies. She banged on the partition at the back of the cupboard. It made a hollow sound.

'Shall I get an Enforcer?'

'No, wait…' Rachel pressed her fingers against the back of the cupboard, which was about a foot deep. 'Let me just test my theory first.'

She cleared the shelves of their tangle of shoes, toilet rolls, cleaning materials and spare light bulbs, then grasped the edge of one of the shelves and pulled. The whole of the back panel, shelves and all, lifted away in one piece, like the separation between layers in a box of chocolates. It was heavy, and Rachel staggered a little. Rajavi beckoned for the armed officers to come up the stairs, and they all crowded onto the narrow landing to see what had been concealed behind the partition.

It was a small room, empty apart from a few plastic crates stacked against the walls.

Rajavi gave her a look, and Rachel knew only too well the mixed emotions it conveyed. A strange blend of disappointment that Lola Jade was not there, and relief that her remains were not there either.

With the false front removed, the room was about six feet wide and nine feet deep. It smelt stuffy and stale, but other than a few dead flies on the windowsill, there was no sign of recent habitation. Rachel put on two pairs of latex gloves and opened the top crate on the pile. It contained baby clothes, most in sickly shades of pink. The box below that held clothes for a toddler, and the ones below that some outgrown school uniform: grey pinafores, white blouses, blue cardigans. She knelt down and took a closer look at the beige carpet, but at first glance it seemed clean. In fact, there were track marks in the pile where a hoover had been used.

'Get a forensics unit down here,' Rajavi told one of the uniformed officers. 'And someone go and bring in Mrs Harper, either from Jubilee Terrace or the Happy Nails salon.' She turned to Rachel again. 'Do you think this has something to do with Lola Jade, DI Prince?'

'Right now, I honestly have no idea. But I'm hoping her mother will be able to tell us.'

CHAPTER TWENTY-SEVEN

Michelle Harper wore an off-the-shoulder dove-grey top, revealing that she had recently topped up her fake tan. Her oval talons were painted in a dusty-pink colour, featuring nail art made from dozens of miniature diamanté gems, some of which had become detached. Her toenails matched, visible through open-toed boots. Rather than being shocked or upset at being swooped on by a tactical squad, she seemed annoyed. The offer of a solicitor had been disdainfully refused.

Rajavi pressed the taping device to on, and it made a loud bleep to show that it was recording. She made her introductory statement covering time and date and people present, then pushed her glossy mane away from her face and leaned forward as far as her pregnant belly would allow. 'So, Michelle, you're aware that the third bedroom at 57 Willow Way has been concealed behind a false partition.'

Michelle wrinkled her nose. 'Of course. I put it there.'

'But when your house was searched on the tenth of May this year, following your daughter's disappearance, you didn't think to mention it to the officers involved in the search?'

Michelle shrugged, unperturbed. 'Why would I have done? It would just have wasted their time.'

'What was the purpose of closing off the room like that?' Rachel asked. 'Most people want to add bedroom space, not lose it.'

'I've only got one kid, I don't need a third bedroom. It makes much more sense to use it for storage. There's only a tiny loft and it's impossible to get in and out of. I'm going to turn that room into a walk-in wardrobe eventually. Well, I was going to. Before…'

She looked down at her lap.

'A walk-in wardrobe with a false front?' persisted Rachel.

'I wanted it to be like one I saw on *Cribs* on MTV,' said Michelle earnestly. 'This rapper had it in his house in Hollywood, which cost like twenty million dollars. There was a wall of shelves and you pressed a button and it swung open to this huge wardrobe. That's what I was basing it on.'

Leila Rajavi seemed at a loss. The room was indeed being used for storage, just as Michelle said. And Michelle was the sort of person who would see a rapper's home as aspirational, even though replicating the arrangement in her modest house was bizarre.

'We'll need to have a look at your laptop.'

Michelle's mouth twitched as if she was suppressing a smile. No longer annoyed, she was enjoying herself. 'Knock yourselves out.'

'Excuse me?' Rajavi glared.

'I don't have one. I. Do. Not. Own. A. Laptop.'

'What about a tablet?'

Michelle shook her head. 'I bought one for Lola, for her to watch cartoons and stuff.'

'Where is it now?'

'Still in her bedroom, as far as I know. I just use my phone if I want to look up stuff online.'

'We'll need your phone then,' Rajavi told her.

Michelle's eyes widened. 'You're kidding.'

Rajavi smiled. 'Obviously not.'

'But I'll get it back?'

'It depends what we find.'

*

Back in Tinworth Street, Rachel could barely tolerate sitting at her desk, thanks to the combination of Brickall's absence and the morning's frustrating dead end.

Michelle Harper had been released without charge, pending further investigation, and DS Rajavi had promised to update Rachel about the forensics on the 'walk-in wardrobe' and the examination of Michelle's phone. After answering a handful of emails and deleting about fifty more without reading them, Rachel abandoned her paperwork and went to find Nigel Patten.

'Sir, I—'

He held up his hand to forestall her speech.

'If you're here to tell me that Giles Denton's calling an emergency meeting at CEOP regarding Chloe Atwell, I already know.'

'I wasn't, actually.' Rachel thought back over the past fifteen minutes, realising that in her distracted state she had probably just deleted an email about the meeting by mistake. 'I wanted to talk to you about DS Brickall.'

'Go on,' said Patten warily.

'I've spoken with the barrister who reported him, and she's agreed to retract her complaint. There was a degree of misunderstanding involved, and she doesn't want to proceed with it now she has all the facts.'

Patten sighed. 'DI Prince, you know full well that once it's been passed on to the PCC, it's out of our hands. They're duty-bound to investigate anyway.'

'So you can't stop it?'

He shook his head, but his tone softened. 'I'm afraid not. Listen, Rachel: I do know how much you value DS Brickall, and therefore how difficult this is for you. If I can pass on a formal statement of retraction by...'

'She's called Amber Crowley.'

'… Ms Crowley, it's certainly going to be in Brickall's favour when the case against him is weighed up. So you weren't wasting your time by speaking to her.'

Rachel smiled weakly. 'Thank you, sir.'

'I'll tell you what: the meeting at CEOP's not until five and you look worn out from covering both your job and Mark's… Why don't you take a couple of hours off? Go and do some Christmas shopping.'

The streets of the West End were a riot of jewel-coloured globes, miniature Christmas trees, ice-white snowflakes and gold shooting stars with shimmering tails. Rachel wandered up Bond Street and down Regent Street, staring at the inviting shop windows, which sparkled with yet more lights and heaps of improbably fancy wrapped gifts. Gifts which were almost certainly empty boxes beneath their metallic gold paper and gauze ribbons.

This summed up Christmas for Rachel: a glittery mirage with very little at its heart. She was not religious or even remotely spiritual, and although she enjoyed living in a comfortable flat, its functional interior was testament to her disdain for material possessions. That was all Christmas was about, she thought, as she watched shoppers hurrying past with handfuls of bulging carrier bags: stuff. Just more and more stuff. Stuff no one really needed.

She tried to remember the last time she had been Christmas shopping. Not in years. Usually she ordered a handful of presents from the comfort of her laptop and stayed away from the shops completely. This afternoon she found herself in an upmarket department store and, seduced by the feeling of entering Aladdin's cave, buying gifts. A pashmina for her mother, a book about military history for her brother-in-law, and a bottle of expensive gin for her sister, who, when pressed, would admit to enjoying a G&T as though it were smoking a crack pipe. Her niece and nephew would receive cash. She had no idea of their tastes, but they were old enough to appreciate having spending power of their own.

Finally, in a fit of uncharacteristic sentimentality, she bought a burgundy cashmere scarf for Brickall, to wear with the Crombie overcoat that she teased made him look like a second-hand car salesman.

She was paying for her purchases when her mobile rang. It was Leila Rajavi.

'Hold on,' said Rachel through the deafening hubbub of canned Christmas music and chattering shoppers. 'Let me call you back in a second when I can actually hear you.'

She went to the top-floor restaurant, ordered a pot of tea and sat down at a window table to return the call.

'The bloody mobile's clean!' Rajavi didn't even try to hide her frustration. 'The only interesting thing we found was frequent calls to a contact saved as 'Sunny', a number that turned out to be a burner when we traced it.'

'Can you triangulate its location?'

'We're working on that. Forensics wasn't quite a total blank. There were minute traces of Lola's DNA on the carpet in the blocked-off room: saliva and spots of blood.'

'Blood? Not what you would expect, surely?'

'Maybe. But given that the child lived in the house and could have gone into the room frequently to play, it's not definitive. There wasn't enough of it to suggest foul play. And Lola's iPad was in her room, just like Michelle said: nothing on there but cartoons and kids' stuff. So now DCI Manners wants me to organise someone to go out to Belgium.'

'I have a feeling that could end up being me,' observed Rachel drily. 'Whoopee.'

'Well it can't be me, obviously, given that I'm about to pop… Other than that, I'm not sure what our next move is.'

'Ben Wethers?'

'Still too traumatised, according to family liaison and the social worker. But the relevant people are on standby, and we're hopeful we might be able to try tomorrow. I'm about to go over all the CCTV from the night Carly died.'

'Baby steps,' Rachel told her firmly. 'The pieces of the puzzle will come together. We just need that first solid connection, then everything else will fall into place. I'm just heading to a meeting with Child Protection, but I'll get back to you with an update afterwards.'

'Mince pies.'

Giles Denton put a plate of them at the centre of the meeting room table, as though offering up a sacrifice. 'To thank you all for coming at such short notice,'

His dark eyes twinkled in Rachel's direction, and hers alone. Brickall would have a field day with this if he were here, she thought. Evidence for his Denton romance conspiracy theory.

'Okay, let's get to it: I'm going to keep this brief. Belgian police have arrested two men in relation to the murder of Chloe Atwell. They're Romanian nationals…' He pulled up two scowling mug shots on the wall-mounted screen: one huge, hulking and blank-eyed, the other smaller, with a sneering expression. 'Gavril Vasile and Danut Petrescu. Intelligence have confirmed that they're both known members of a human trafficking organisation. It's not yet clear what they had planned for Chloe after they snatched her, but it appears that something went wrong in transit and she ended up dead before reaching her final destination…'

He paused and looked at the other five people round the table. Rachel recognised all of them but one, whom Denton had introduced as the CID liaison from Sussex Police.

'Obviously one of the first things we needed to establish was a possible link to the case of Lola Jade Harper. Both men deny having any involvement in her disappearance, and the alibis they've provided appear to support their claim that they were both in Romania on the ninth of May. Until we've had the chance to double-check this, I suggest we don't mention Lola Jade in any press statement we put out. Depending on what we find, we may have to get someone from that enquiry out to Belgium to question them.'

'The press will speculate anyway,' said Nick Furnish, biting into his second mince pie.

'Of course: that's the nature of the beast,' agreed Patten. 'And up to a point, that's their job.'

'So if the alibis *are* confirmed and we can officially rule these men out of Lola Jade's abduction, we will need to reassure the public that efforts to find her are still ongoing,' said Gilly Durante. 'Can we confirm that's the case?'

Nigel Patten gave a little nod in Rachel's direction.

'Yes,' said Rachel, 'absolutely. I'm still working closely with Surrey Police on a couple of leads.'

At that moment her phone buzzed with a text from Leila Rajavi.

I think we've got something.

CHAPTER TWENTY-EIGHT

It was Rachel's first ever experience of the school run.

She set her alarm for 5.30 on Monday morning, left her flat an hour later and drove straight to Eastwell. Leaving before the rush hour was under way gave her a comfortable margin for error, but also meant that she reached Albert Park by 8.00. From her recollection of the night she and Brickall had spent on informal surveillance, the local children didn't set off until at least 8.30. The nearest café was opening to capitalise on the pre-commute rush, so Rachel bought a double espresso and sat in the car to wait.

At 8.39, the door of Kirsty Wade's house opened, and she emerged wearing a fluffy dressing gown and checked pyjama bottoms. Her youngest child – still in a sleepsuit – was hoisted under one arm, and she herded the older two towards the Urquharts' front door, then retreated, shivering visibly, into her own house. Beneath a sky of pale watercolour blue, a visible frost coated every surface, and the two Wade children were dressed in thick coats, scarves and woollen hats.

Lisa Urquhart emerged thirty seconds later, lighting up her first cigarette of the day and tugging on a padded gilet. Her daughter followed her out of the house, followed by two boys. They were around the same age and had the same indeterminate brown hair, long on the top and shaved at the sides. Both wore the navy and maroon uniform for Overdale School.

Rachel stared, trying to work this out. Did Lisa have twin boys? No, that wasn't possible: when the house was searched, Michelle had been sleeping in Chelsea Urquhart's room, and there were two single beds crammed into the bedroom the children were temporarily sharing, one with a pink cover and the other featuring the West Ham football strip. Chelsea and Connor. And the child wasn't Kirsty Wade's: her three were accounted for.

As the group reached the end of Jubilee Terrace, Rachel put the car into gear and followed at a discreet distance, keeping them in sight but not drifting close enough to be noticed. Lisa and the five children were eventually swallowed up by a larger gaggle of children and parents as they neared the school gates. Lisa waved them goodbye and turned back towards Jubilee Terrace, lighting another cigarette. Connor Urquhart and the Wade boy darted off together, leaving the other boy trailing behind the girls. Rachel recognised the hesitant walk. This was the child in the penguin costume.

The CCTV images had been recorded on a foggy night, in poor visibility, and as a result were a montage of indeterminate grey.

'Look – there.' Leila Rajavi pointed to the screen, and Rachel squinted to see. 'We don't have a camera covering the front door of Carly Wethers' property, but this was picked up just at the end of her street.'

There, just about discernible, was a slight figure in black jeans and shoes and a dark top, with its hood pulled up over a black beanie hat. The sweater's roll neck covered the person's mouth and nose, so all that was visible was the eyes.

'See…' Leila pointed again and zoomed in. 'Look what he's holding.' In the gloved hand, there was a shiny metal object that looked like some sort of wrench. The time stamp on the image said 3.17 a.m. on the morning of 2 December.

'This has got to be our killer,' said Rajavi. 'The time, the gloves, the lock-breaking equipment. It can't be a coincidence. Not possible.'

'I agree,' said Rachel. She turned to Rajavi, who was calm as ever but with a gleam in her eye. 'What happens next? Does the camera pick him up again?'

'Here.' Rajavi opened another video file. 'On Fairfield Road, at 3.47 a.m.' There was the same dark-clad figure, walking briskly in the other direction, still holding the wrench. 'I'm afraid that's all we've got.'

Rachel sighed. 'This backs up our theory, which is a good thing. The problem is, you know as well as I do that it isn't going to stand up in court. The images of the face simply aren't distinct enough for a positive ID. Even if we think we've found this person, they're simply going to say, "Not me, your honour."'

Rajavi sighed. 'I know. We traced the burner phone belonging to "Sunny" to an address in Whiteley, but the owner of the property – a guy called Sunil Khara – denied all knowledge of the phone, and of Michelle Harper. We're trying to find out a bit more about him, and we've applied for a warrant to search his house. And most importantly…' she exhaled heavily, 'we're talking to Ben Wethers later today.'

Rachel told her about the five children on the school run, but Rajavi was dismissive. 'Probably some school friend who's been on a sleepover. I've got nephews and nieces that age and they're forever staying at each other's houses. Or it could be a kid who lives further up the street, who gets dropped off by a working parent.'

'DS Brickall and I would have picked that up on our overnight surveillance.'

'Possibly. But then we don't know for certain that this is the child you spotted wearing the penguin costume.' Rajavi gave a conciliatory smile. 'I'll get a uniform to go and speak to Kirsty Wade again if you like.'

*

Before she left Eastwell, Rachel drove back to Albert Park, left the car and walked around the neat geometric grid of streets. The two-up-two-down cottages had been built for workers in the area's nineteenth-century paper mills, and the rows were arranged back to back, with rear yards connected by 'ginnels' to those of the houses in the next street along. Rachel walked to the end of Jubilee Terrace and turned left into the perpendicular street that linked it to the next row of terraces. Immediately on her left was the cobbled alleyway that ran along the back of Jubilee Terrace's back yards, their gates facing the gates to the yards of the next street in the grid: Osborne Terrace. With Eastwell's train and road links to the capital, the Albert Park area was being gentrified by commuters, and many of the humble cottages featured plantation shutters, hanging baskets and pretty dove-grey and almond-green front doors.

She continued past the turning into Osborne Terrace to the gates of Albert Park itself: a modest green recreational space created for the mill workers, with a bandstand and a duck pond. It was then that she saw the sign for the street she was on. Fairfield Road. The location of Carly's killer as they left the scene of the crime. And also, she remembered, mentioned in a possible sighting of Lola Jade Harper. The pieces of the puzzle shifted position yet again, tantalisingly close to falling into place.

The text was innocuous enough.

How about a training session?

That was it: no kisses, no innuendo.

And in life, timing was everything. The message found her strung out and stressed, missing Brickall, her human sounding-board, and in need of diversion.

Great. Come round at 6.30?

Howard appeared at her flat on the dot, dressed in sweatpants, gilet, baseball cap and fingerless gloves.

'Chilly out there; make sure you bundle up.'

'I'm wearing lightweight thermals,' Rachel grinned, zipping up her jacket.

'So that's your secret. And there I was thinking you were made of Teflon.'

'It has been said.'

They bantered back and forth like this as they ran – over London Bridge and along the Embankment – and for a while Rachel forgot about the Harpers, and Penguin Boy, and dead Carly Wethers.

'How are things with Julie since the…?'

'Since she stalked you? Still not great. Still not sure where we're headed.'

'Sorry to hear that.'

They slowed down to a walk as they neared Rachel's flat. Howard pressed his huge paw on her forearm. 'I don't have to be back for a while… I could, you know, pop up for a chat.'

Rachel shook her head firmly. 'Not with things the way they are for you at home. I know it looks likely you're not going to work it out with Julie, but while you're still married, you need to be trying to resolve things. And it's almost Christmas: not the best time to rock the boat.'

'Statistically it's the time of most marital break-ups.'

'Well in that case…' Rachel pressed her hand against his broad chest. 'If you're single come the New Year, you know where to find me.'

'Are you serious about that?' he asked, trying to read her expression in the winter gloom.

'As serious as I ever get.'

She allowed him to reach in for a brief hug, before pulling away and hurrying into the building alone. *Wine*, she told herself, *wine is what I need.* Wine never lets you down. She ran a hot bath, put some Massive Attack on her iPod and lay back in the water with a glass of rosé. A couple of hours later, with the bottle empty and the water cold, she crawled straight under her duvet.

Just after midnight, she woke suddenly, her senses tingling as though she had just been told something very important. She'd been dreaming, a flashback to childhood when her father was alive, and Rachel, Lindsay and their parents used to drive to Devon for their summer holiday. In the dream, their father was trying to stack the cases on the roof rack – something he had prided himself at being good at in real life – but no matter how much he persevered, they kept sliding off.

That was it.

She groped for her mobile and pressed Brickall's number.

'What the fuck…'

He had been asleep; she could tell from his voice.

'The suitcases.'

'What are you talking about?'

'The two big purple suitcases Michelle took from her house just after Lola Jade disappeared. It was on the neighbours' CCTV… She loaded them into her car and took them to her sister's.'

'Prince, seriously, what are you on about… Call me in the morning when you're making more sense.'

'They weren't there! When we searched Lisa's house, there was no sign of two huge suitcases.'

'And there was no teddy bear and framed photograph either. We've been through this: she must have just stored some stuff elsewhere. That house of the Urquharts' is tiny.'

'No, don't you see? She's got a room for storage in Willow Way; she's got all the space she needs. And she was chucking stuff out. So she wouldn't remove something just to store it at a different location. Whatever was in the suitcases, wherever she's put them: that's how we're going to find the answer to this whole thing.'

'I'm hanging up now,' her detective sergeant said tersely. 'And I seriously think you need to take some time off. If I weren't suspended, I'd be going to Patten and telling him to make you take leave.'

'Will you come with me to Eastwell tomorrow?'

'Fuck off, Prince,' said Brickall, with a little more warmth this time. 'Like I said: I'm suspended. I'll be in even deeper shit if I try and work the case…'

'I could—'

'… and even if I weren't, I'd still tell you to fuck off.'

He hung up.

CHAPTER TWENTY-NINE

Goose or turkey? Mum wants turkey. L x

Also, not doing sprouts this year. Kale? L x

And so it begins, Rachel thought. The Christmas period was officially under way when her sister started firing off daily texts about menus and other details, despite the fact that there were still two whole weeks to go. She deleted the texts without replying and went back to reading through the original Lola Jade Harper file, specifically the reported sighting of Lola on Fairfield Road, written up on a standard MG11 witness statement form and dated 30 September.

> *It was 18.55, and I'd just popped into the Sava-Mart to buy milk. I was on my way back from work. I saw a woman pulling a child by the wrist. The child seemed unhappy and was crying. I don't know why, but it just made me think of the missing child, Lola Jade Harper. I think the woman had dark brown hair, but it was getting dark, and it was hard to be sure. Because of the poor light, I couldn't be sure if the child was a boy or a girl. I watched them as they continued down Fairfield Road and turned into Osborne Terrace.*

Her phone buzzed with another text. Sighing, she picked it up to check the latest on the rights and wrongs of Christmas crackers, or brandy butter vs rum butter. It was from Leila Rajavi.

Something you need to see. Check your email.

There was a file attached to the email: *Transcript of Special Measures recorded statement, Ben Wethers 12/12/16.* She opened it and began to read.

DC 5019 TANSLEY: *Okay, Ben, my name's Jess, and I'm from the police. Now before we begin talking, I have to tell you that we're recording our chat on that camera there, and to check that it's okay with you that we record you? Is that okay?... For the transcript, Ben is nodding. And Ben, with us here is Sandra, Sandra Newland. You know Sandra, don't you? She's here to support you and to help you. Is that okay?*

BEN WETHERS: *Yes.*

DC 5019 TANSLEY: *Good, great. All right, Ben, we need to talk to you about the day that your mummy died. I know it's hard to talk about, so we'll take it very slowly, and if you need to stop at any time, you can just say so to me, or to Sandra. Okay?*

BEN WETHERS: *Okay.*

DC 5019 TANSLEY: *Right. So can you tell me what you remember about that morning? Take your time.*

BEN WETHERS: *I woke up, and I wondered if it was time for school. But Mummy didn't come into my room.*

DC 5019 TANSLEY: *And would she normally come in and wake you up?*

BEN WETHERS: *Yes. Every day. If it was school. Sometimes on Saturday and Sunday I went and woke her up. I jumped on her bed.*

DC 5019 TANSLEY: *Okay, Ben, you're doing really well. Things you can remember are really helpful, little things or big things. So this day was a school day?*

BEN WETHERS: *Yes. I called to her. I called, 'Mummy!' But she didn't come.*

DC 5019 TANSLEY: *And what happened next?*

BEN WETHERS: *Got out of bed, went into her room. (Inaudible)*

DC 5019 TANSLEY: *It's okay, Ben, I know this is very difficult, and it makes you upset. We'll take this as slowly as you like. What did you see when you went into your mummy's room?*

BEN WETHERS: *I thought Mummy was asleep. But she didn't move. I shook her like this.*

DC 5019 TANSLEY: *For the transcript, Ben is pushing on Sandra's shoulder. And what happened when you did that?*

BEN WETHERS: *She didn't wake up. She looked poorly. Her face was all funny.*

DC 5019 TANSLEY: *I know this is difficult, Ben, but can you tell me how it was funny?*

BEN WETHERS: *A funny colour.*

DC 5019 TANSLEY: *I see. And you thought she might be poorly?*

BEN WETHERS: *Yes. I was scared.*

DC 5019 TANSLEY: *I'm sure you were very brave, though. Can you tell me what happened next?*

BEN WETHERS: *I sat down on the landing and I waited. Waiting for her to get better.*

DC 5019 TANSLEY: *You waited all by yourself?*

BEN WETHERS: *For someone to come.*

DC 5019 TANSLEY: *That was very brave, Ben. And what happened next?*

BEN WETHERS: *Granny came, and she cried. She cried and cried. And then the policemen all came. And then I went to Granny's house, and she said Mummy wasn't coming back because she'd gone up to heaven. 'Cause she'd gone dead.*

DC 5019 TANSLEY: *I expect that made you very sad, Ben.*

BEN WETHERS: *I was scared.*

DC 5019 TANSLEY: *And why were you scared, Ben? Was there something that happened before Mummy died that made you scared? For the transcript, Ben is nodding.*

BEN WETHERS: *I thought Mummy had gone to heaven because it was my fault.*

DC 5019 TANSLEY: *What was your fault, Ben?*

BEN WETHERS: *Because I told the secret to her.*

DC 5019 TANSLEY: *What was the secret, Ben? Can you tell me?*

BEN WETHERS: *It was what I saw at school, and then I told Mummy and then she went dead.*

DC 5019 TANSLEY: *Can you tell me what you saw at school?*

BEN WETHERS: *Can I have a drink?*

DC 5019 TANSLEY: *Of course you can.*

BEN WETHERS: *And a biscuit?*

DC 5019 TANSLEY: *No problem, Ben. Sandra will get them for you. Can you remember what you saw at school?*

BEN WETHERS: *It was in the changing room at PE.*

DC 5019 TANSLEY: *And just so I'm sure, Ben, this was at your school? At Overdale?*

BEN WETHERS: *Yes, in Form Three, in Mrs Maudsley's class. After PE time. We had PE outside and it was raining. And Mrs Maudsley said we had to hurry up and change out of our wet things so we didn't get chills.*

DC 5019 TANSLEY: *I see. So you were in the changing room. Is it a boys' changing room?*

BEN WETHERS: *Yes, it's different to the girls' one. The girls are all together too.*

DC 5019 TANSLEY: *So what happened when you were changing?*

BEN WETHERS: *Harry Brown took his shorts off and he didn't have any willy.*

DC 5019 TANSLEY: *Sorry, can we just go back a bit, Ben. Is Harry a boy in your class?*

BEN WETHERS: *Yes. In Mrs Maudsley's class. He wasn't there at the beginning of Mr Faire's class; he came at the end,*

DC 5019 TANSLEY: *So Harry got undressed and he didn't have a penis? A boy's private part? Like this? For the transcript, I am showing Ben the male anatomical doll and he is shaking his head.*

BEN WETHERS: *He had a girl's front bottom. When I looked at it, he started to cry.*

DC 5019 TANSLEY: *Like this? For the transcript, I am showing Ben the female anatomical doll and he is nodding his head.*

DC 5019 TANSLEY: *Did you say anything else to Harry?*

BEN WETHERS: *In the playground I did. I said why haven't you got a willy like a boy. And Harry said it's a secret and you can't tell anyone or something bad will happen. But I told it to Mummy.*

DC 5019 TANSLEY: *You told her about Harry?*

BEN WETHERS: *I said Harry Brown's pretending to be a boy but he's really a girl. Why is he dressing up as a boy?*

DC 5019 TANSLEY: *What did your mummy say?*

BEN WETHERS: *She said, 'Oh my God.'*

DC 5019 TANSLEY: *You're doing really well at remembering, Ben. Really good job.*

BEN WETHERS: *I told her it was a secret and bad things would happen if we told. She said it was okay, because we were going to keep the secret. But it wasn't okay. Is that why Mummy's in heaven?*

Rachel was hunched forward in her chair, staring at her screen. They only had a traumatised child's word, but if this was true, then a seven-year-old girl was being passed off as a seven-year-old boy. A boy called Harry. Lola Jade's middle name was Harriet.

Why doesn't someone ask Michelle Harper about her boy? Carly hadn't been referring to baby Oliver; she was talking about Harry Brown.

She shut down her terminal, grabbed her coat and bag and headed for the lifts, texting as she went.

I'm heading to Overdale School now. Meet me there.

CHAPTER THIRTY

'Damn, the kids are all going home!'

Rachel and Leila Rajavi stood in the playground of Overdale Infants and Juniors and watched as children came out of the old Victorian schoolhouse; a trickle at first that swelled to a flood.

'I'm sorry,' said Rajavi. 'But I had the devil of a job rounding up a couple of available bodies who also happen to be trained in child protection.' She indicated the uniformed officers: one male, one female. 'Took me an hour to find these two.'

Rachel took in the curious stares of the parents as they led their offspring past. 'It means going in mob-handed,' she sighed, 'but in the circumstances I suppose we have no choice.' She had been sitting in her car for forty minutes, with a host of possible scenarios going round and round in her brain. She had even phoned Brickall in an attempt to anchor her whirling thoughts.

He had been sceptical. 'Come on: you know kids and toilet talk. They're obsessed with private parts at that age, and the differences between them. This kid without a winky is probably a bit under-endowed. I remember that being the cause of endless hilarity in the changing rooms when I was at school.' He added hastily. 'Never happened to me, of course.'

'I know I only read the transcript – and possibly it would have seemed different if I'd watched the video—'

'Maybe you should have done. Belt and braces, the old pet mantra. Or one of them.'

'This child, Ben, seemed so certain what he'd seen: I didn't want to waste any more time.'

'Take a breath, Prince. Let it play out: it could be something and nothing.'

The school was in the throes of festive end-of-term celebrations. Glitter-encrusted Christmas pictures decorated the walls, along with those for Hanukah and Diwali, and rustling swags of home-made paper chains dangled from every spare inch. Rajavi asked the uniformed officers to wait outside the head teacher's office and went in with Rachel.

Chris Sewell was one of the new wave of progressive primary heads, a fact that was signalled by his wearing jeans and sweater rather than a suit. 'I was expecting another visit, to be honest,' he said, indicating that they should sit on the chairs opposite him. 'This business with Ben Wethers' mum being found dead. Dreadful thing.' He adopted a suitably sombre expression, which looked out of place on what was a naturally cheerful freckled face.

'We're here to talk to you about a pupil called Harry Brown.'

He looked blank for a second. 'Brown… oh yes, Harry. One of Mrs Maudsley's lot. I was struggling to picture him for a minute: he hasn't been with us long. Let me just get his details.' He stepped into an adjoining office and came back with a file. 'Registered towards the end of the summer term, which is unorthodox, but the mother was quite insistent. Quiet child. Not a troublemaker, but doesn't have much to say for himself.'

'Did you meet the mother?' asked Leila Rajavi.

'Briefly. The school secretary takes care of most of the registration business.'

Rachel pulled up a photo of Michelle Harper on her phone. 'Is this her?'

He squinted at it. 'Oh gosh, no! I mean, I know we're not supposed to pass comment on the parents'…' he groped for a PC phrase, 'personal style, but I would have remembered someone as glamorous as that lady.' He peered a bit closer. 'Also, isn't she the mother of that missing girl?'

Rachel found Lisa Urquhart's Facebook profile shot. 'How about her?'

'Definitely no. I'd have remembered something as distinctive as pink hair! No, this lady was quite the opposite. Very... indistinctive.'

'Hair colour?' demanded Rachel.

'I don't like to—'

'Mr Sewell, this is vitally important. Please just tell us everything you can remember.'

He puffed out his freckled cheeks, making himself look about fourteen years old. 'Like I said, there was nothing distinctive about her. In fact, she was distinguished by a lack of distinguishing features. And clothing.'

'Dull, in other words?'

He flushed slightly. 'Well. Yes.'

Rachel went into her Facebook app and pulled up another photo, this time of the drab Stacey Fisher.

'Yes, that's her. That's Mrs Brown.'

Rachel and DS Rajavi looked at each other. 'Do you have a photo of Harry?'

'You know the rules have tightened up about us taking and using photos of pupils without parental consent...' Sewell stood up and rummaged in a filing cabinet. 'But we do have some class photos taken at the end of the last academic year, in July.'

He placed the photo, taken by a professional, on the desk. The teacher was sitting at the centre of the front row, with twenty-five or thirty children arranged around him. 'That's Harry there. In the back row.'

Two large boys either side were jostling for space, so not much of Harry was visible. His face wore a familiar glum expression.

And the style of the brown hair, shaved at the sides and long and floppy on the top, looked familiar.

'That's him. It's the penguin,' breathed Rachel.

'I'm sorry?'

Rachel and Rajavi were both on their feet. 'Will he have been picked up?'

It was twenty to four.

'Normally his class would have gone home by now, but Form Three have all been to the pantomime at the local theatre. Parents had the option to pick them up there or for them to be bussed back here. The coach should be arriving round about now. I can—'

Before he had finished speaking, Rajavi had opened the door and started running down the corridor, clutching her bump, followed by the two uniforms, Rachel and Mr Sewell. They reached the car park just as a minibus with the Overdale logo was pulling in. A dozen or so over-tired children were herded off by a harassed middle-aged teacher clutching a clipboard.

Harry Brown was not among them.

'It's been about, ooh, a week? He was fine on the Friday, but come Monday morning there was a note saying Harry was poorly and wouldn't be coming to school for the remainder of term. A chest infection apparently.' Mrs Maudsley seemed personally offended that Harry had not been at the pantomime with the rest of the class.

Rachel calculated. Harry mysteriously became ill the weekend after Carly Wethers died. The same weekend she and Leila – the 'LOLA JADE COPS' – had been on the front page, investigating Carly's death. 'Is this a common occurrence?'

'No, I'd say Harry's attendance has been good up until now. He's a timid child; you don't get very much out of him. Likes to stay in the background.'

DS Rajavi dispatched the WPC to Jubilee Terrace, with instructions to wait for backup, then to bring in Michelle if she was there. She and Rachel and the male officer set off for Stacey Fisher's house. Before they had arrived, Rajavi's airwave set bleeped.

'Sarge – Michelle Harper's not at the property, or at her workplace. The sister's there with her children, claims she doesn't know where Michelle is.'

Rajavi pressed the button to respond. 'Sort someone to look after the children, then bring Lisa Urquhart to the station. And get someone to check at Willow Way.'

Stacey Fisher did not seem surprised to see them, but then she did not seem pleased either. She had deep bags under her eyes and, despite it being tea time, was swigging from a bottle of Jack Daniel's. 'Like I told you, I just sold Michelle the washer-dryer. I don't know nothing else,' she whined. 'I've never heard of no Harry Brown.'

'Maybe a little trip to the police station will refresh your memory,' Rachel told her briskly.

'I ain't going nowhere.'

Rachel pulled the PC's handcuffs from his belt and dangled them in Stacey's face. 'With or without? Your choice.'

'You can take me where you like, but I'm not going to tell you anything.'

Quick as a whip, Rachel pulled Stacey's arms behind her back and cuffed her, knocking the bottle of bourbon to the floor, where it splashed over their feet. Enough was enough: no more softly-softly.

'Stacey Fisher, I am arresting you on suspicion of making a false statement, contrary to Section 89 of the Criminal Justice Act. You do not have to say anything, but it may harm your defence if you do not mention when questioned something you later rely on in court. Anything you do say may be given in evidence.'

At Eastwell police station, the charge was formally read to Stacey. That officially began the twenty-four hours they had to prise the truth out of her, or they would be required to let her go.

'I'll stick her in a cell and leave her there without contact for a couple of hours,' Rajavi told Rachel. 'That usually makes them more inclined to talk.'

They were interrupted by a scuffle at the front door as Lisa Urquhart was dragged in, screaming, swearing and generally resisting.

'You can't bring me in here, I haven't fucking done anything! What about my human rights? I'm going to fucking sue you lot!'

'Much as I'd like to leave *her* to cool off, we can't afford to waste any time.' Rachel pointed the officer manhandling Lisa in the direction of an interview room. The tint in her pink hair had been boosted from pale candyfloss to bright fuchsia, and it flew out like a Catherine wheel as she twisted her head and tried to bite his wrist.

'What is it they teach us about establishing a rapport with suspects?' Rajavi muttered. 'Lovely job for whoever's duty solicitor too.'

She watched as three uniformed PCs wrestled Lisa into a chair and cuffed her. This did not stop her from jumping to her feet and kicking the chair over. Her ankle was then cuffed to the chair leg, with difficulty.

'So, Lisa.' Rachel sat down calmly once the solicitor had arrived and taken his seat. 'This is a lot of fuss when all we want is to ask you where your sister is.'

'And I've said: I don't fucking know.'

'She's living in your house and working locally. You must have some idea.'

Lisa tried to shrug, which didn't really work when three of her four limbs were restrained, so she adopted a sneering tone instead. 'She's gone away for a bit. She is allowed to leave town, you know.'

'Where has she gone?'

'I've no idea.'

'Come on,' said Rajavi calmly. 'She must have said something about where she was headed.'

'She was thinking of going to the seaside.'

'The British seaside? In mid December?' Rachel was incredulous.

'Why not? It's not against the law, you know.'

'Has she gone on her own?'

'Of course she has. Who else is she going to go with?'

Rachel adopted her crossed-arm pose. 'Do you know who Harry Brown is?'

There was a microsecond of hesitation before Lisa answered. With her years of interview experience, Rachel sensed it. 'No idea. Don't know no one called Harry Brown.'

'All right then,' Rajavi said levelly. 'Who's the other child who goes to school with your two kids and the Wade children?'

'Which other kid?' Lisa's eyes shifted slightly, to the door and back again.

'There are always five of them walking to school together. You've got Chelsea and Connor, and Kirsty Wade's got two—'

'She's got three kids actually.'

'Two at school. So who's the extra boy?'

Lisa shrugged. 'Dunno.'

'He goes to school with your children, how can you not know?'

'Loads of the Albert Park kids walk to Overdale together, always have done. It'll be a neighbour's kid who calls next door.'

Rachel straightened up and stared straight at Lisa. 'You really expect me to believe that you don't know who your own children go to school with every day?'

'It'll be one of the Ellis boys. They live round the corner on Fairfield Road. Dean and Bradley, I think they're called.'

The duty solicitor looked up from his notepad. 'Unless you're going to charge my client, I suggest we leave it there. She's answered all your questions.'

Rajavi gave a heavy sigh. 'Make sure you stay in the area: we may need to speak to you again.' She nodded at one of the PCs to unleash Lisa, who whirled out of the room, swearing at the top of her voice.

CHAPTER THIRTY-ONE

'You know when you said I should just move to Eastwell?'

Rachel phoned Brickall that night from the budget chain hotel she had just checked into.

'Don't tell me…'

'Yup. Here I am. One of the locals now.'

She had decided to stay in town overnight. By the time Lisa Urquhart had been released pending further enquiries, it was nearly 8 p.m. Talking to Stacey Fisher was like firing questions at a brick wall, and when a breathalyser test revealed she had drunk enough Jack Daniel's for her testimony to be unreliable, Rajavi had called a halt to proceedings at 10 p.m., leaving her to sober up in her cell.

Rachel found a large twenty-four-hour supermarket and bought a sandwich, toothbrush and toothpaste, plus a plain white T-shirt to add to her existing work wardrobe of black trousers and plain white tops. Only when she sat down on the edge of the bed did she realise how bone-weary she was. The room was basic, and not altogether clean, and the bathroom had a tatty shower curtain and toiletries nailed to the wall, but she was too tired to care.

'If you're staying down there overnight, then something must be happening,' Brickall observed. 'Did the kid without a weeny turn out to be Lola?'

'We don't know yet,' sighed Rachel. 'Every time we get what feels like a break, we end up down another blind alley. We have no idea where Harry is. And now Michelle Harper's disappeared too.'

The officers who had been to check on Willow Way had found neither Michelle nor her car.

'Anyway, what about you?'

'Had a bunch of stupid paperwork through from the PCC.' Rachel could tell that Brickall was trying to sound blasé. 'Going to talk to my union rep about it tomorrow.'

'The timing couldn't be worse,' Rachel sighed, lying back on the pillows. 'I could really use you here with me now. Not in this room, obviously,' she added hastily.

'Fuck, no,' agreed Brickall. 'Never mind, it'll all look better in the morning.'

Stacey Fisher definitely looked worse in the morning, not better.

The whisky had worn off, and the lack of sleep had amplified her drabness. Her colourless hair hung in limp strands and her skin had the damp sheen of glazier's putty. Armed with a cup of tea, she started out by repeating last night's mantra that she knew nothing about Harry Brown. But exhaustion caught up with her, and just before the twenty-four-hour time limit rolled round, when Rajavi threatened her with an identity parade, she admitted that she had gone to Overdale Infants and Juniors, given false details and enrolled a seven-year-old child called Harry Brown; a child she had never even met.

'Why?' demanded Rachel.

'She paid me, didn't she?'

'Who did?'

'Michelle. Michelle Harper.'

'Seven hundred pounds?'

Stacey's putty skin took on a slightly warmer tinge. 'Three grand, actually.'

'And why did she want you to do this, Stacey? What was this child to her?'

Stacey shrugged. 'Don't know. She never said.'

'Come on, Stacey, we both know you've been on the Find Lola Jade site.' Rachel adopted the tone of a teacher dealing with a wayward sixth-former. 'So you know all about Michelle Harper's life. She suddenly shows up needing a school place for a random seven-year-old and you don't think to ask questions?'

Stacey took a sip of her lukewarm tea, shivering and pulling the thin prison-issue blanket round herself. 'She said she would give me the money to help her out, but I wasn't to ask her any questions. So I didn't.' She shot a defiant look at her interrogators. 'Okay, yeah, it did seem a little weird. But I've got a payday loan and store cards to pay off: I needed the cash. So I agreed to do it, and to mind my own business.'

Stacey was released on police bail and Rachel and Rajavi took a pool car and drove to the home of the Ellis family on Fairfield Road. The children were at school, but their mother, one Samantha Ellis, showed them photographs of her two sons. Both boys had the same high top haircut as Harry Brown 'They all want it like that now,' Samantha confirmed. The younger one's was chestnut brown, like Harry's. When asked if her boys ever walked to school with the Wade children, Samantha was vague.

'Well yeah, they could do. A lot of the kids gang up and go together. I just kiss 'em goodbye and boot 'em out the front door. Not sure what happens between there and school.'

'Damn,' said Rachel as they walked away, stopping at the café for cappuccinos and doughnuts. 'Unfortunately that kind of corroborates what Lisa Urquhart said.'

'Shall I get her in for questioning again? The uniform who brought her in said Michelle's dog was still there, at Lisa's house. They couldn't find a passport for Michelle in Jubilee Terrace, but she wouldn't necessarily have taken it there from Willow Way.'

'No.' Rachel shook her head. 'But see if you can organise some surveillance on her place. If you can't, let me know and I'll get our operations unit onto it. Maybe there should be another search at Willow Way, to locate the passport if nothing else. Okay?'

Rajavi's expression was unreadable, but Rachel could take a fair guess at how she was feeling. 'Look, Stacey's admission is a huge step. It's evidence tying Michelle Harper to Harry Brown, something that's a bit more than circumstantial.'

'That may be true. Only now we've got a missing child *and* a missing mother.'

Rachel returned to Tinworth Street and called an emergency briefing with Patten, Gilly Durante, Nick Furnish and Giles Denton. She outlined the new evidence from Ben Wethers' statement and Stacey Fisher's admission.

'Even without the Romanians' alibis standing up, it's looking less and less likely that the two girls are linked. Our priority now is to find Michelle Harper. Surrey Police has set up an ANPR alert for her car and we've requested a blue notice from Interpol, in case she's tried to leave the UK.'

'Well done, DI Prince.' Patten gave a rare smile. 'You've really helped the local force with pushing the investigation forward.'

Giles Denton suggested they all adjourn to the Pin and Needle for a Christmas drink and she accepted with alacrity, not because of his swarthy Irish looks but because she was ready to forget about Lola Jade Harper for a few hours. She texted Brickall and demanded that he joined them, adding cryptically:

Santa's paying a visit.

Brickall stared at his cashmere scarf with an opaque expression.

'I haven't got you anything.' He was gruff, to cover surprise or pleasure or both.

'That's okay. You can go and buy me a drink.'

He grinned, wrapped the scarf twice round his neck, and came back with two large glasses of mulled wine. The pub was decked with bushy swags of tinsel and wreaths of fake holly. There was also, Rachel noted, a bunch of mistletoe very prominently placed on the customer side of the bar.

'See that…' Brickall pointed at the mistletoe.

'I see it.'

'And see that…' He pointed to Giles Denton. 'Your Pierce Brosnan lookalike. Just saying.'

'So immature, Brickall.'

But as the evening wore on and the number of empty mulled wine glasses on their table grew, Rachel found herself hovering near the mistletoe in the hope that Denton would notice it. Eventually he did.

'It's a pagan tradition,' he told her.

'What is?' Rachel asked innocently.

'Kissing under the mistletoe. Wouldn't be at all suitable for a good Catholic boy like myself.' He winked at her.

'Just as well I'm a pagan then.' Rachel stared him down, her body language daring him to do it. And he did. He leaned in and kissed her full on the mouth, lingering longer than was strictly necessary, parting his lips slightly.

'Merry Christmas, Rachel Prince.' He gave her an intense look with eyes as dark as the North Sea, then walked away.

'Fucking hell, Prince, what is it with you and the men round here?' Brickall, who had been watching the entire encounter, frowned in mock-disapproval. 'You're law-enforcement kryptonite.'

CHAPTER THIRTY-TWO

'I knew we should have remanded the silly cow.'

It was Monday morning, and Rachel had not even made it out of her flat before her phone rang with a call from Leila Rajavi. Before she had even pressed accept, she already knew what Rajavi was about to say. Yet again the story had had been emblazoned in black-and-white two-inch-high capital letters across the front of a Sunday tabloid. This time it was a competitor for the paper that Rachel had locked horns with over the Carly Wethers leak.

LOLA JADE MUM IN SEX-CHANGE BOY MYSTERY

Michelle Harper, mum of missing seven-year-old Lola Jade Harper, has been sighted in the Eastwell area with a mystery boy the same age, a source told us.

'Stacey must have blabbed,' Rachel concurred with a sigh. 'Well, the papers don't name their source but I think we can assume it was her. It isn't even accurate: Michelle hasn't been "sighted" with Harry at all. She's far too canny for that.'

'And Stacey doesn't know anything about what Ben Wethers told us in his statement either,' said Rajavi. 'In fact, if you read the article, it's a bit of a non-event, mainly because Stacey's too dim to really join the dots. She just saw a chance to make a few quid on the sly.'

'And yet again a paper's opened itself up nicely to a charge of contempt of court for prejudicing legal proceedings,' Rachel pointed out. 'Although since Michelle's not been charged with anything yet, that's a moot point. She'd already done a runner before Stacey sold the story.'

The line went quiet, while Rajavi weighed up what Rachel had said. 'So are you saying we should hold off on making any public response?'

'Absolutely,' said Rachel. 'It will only make us look like we don't know what we're doing and open the floodgates to the crackpots. Right now, we have other fish to fry.'

She wanted to swim, but today she would need to forgo her exercise fix and go straight to the office. Before she had even reached her desk, she picked up a text from Rajavi.

Those other fish: one of them has just turned up.

Michelle Harper's white BMW was in a private car park in Feltham, Middlesex, parked in a far corner against the wire perimeter fence. At first glance, it was empty, and clean of any possessions or the usual detritus that accumulates in a car.

When Rachel and Rajavi arrived, a forensics team was standing by while a canine handler set his springer spaniel bitch to work. The spaniel first extensively inhaled from a piece of Lola Jade's clothing, then jumped into the open rear hatchback and started sniffing, so absorbed in her task that her body was vibrating with energy. Then she sat, frozen and staring, with her nose pointing to the carpet on the floor of the boot. One of the suited forensics officers stepped forward and started gathering microscopic samples.

'She's indicating,' whispered Rajavi.

'A cadaver dog?' Rachel wanted to know.

Rajavi walked over to speak to the handler. 'Not human remains specifically, just "human material",' she told Rachel when she came back. 'We'll know more when we get the forensics back.'

Rachel pivoted on the spot, staring around the car park. A jumbo jet screamed over their heads, on the south-eastern flight path. She pointed up at it. 'If we're looking for reasons to dump the car here, then there's the obvious one. We must be – what? – three, four miles from Heathrow. There's a bus that goes straight there, on the road we turned in from. Or it's a very short taxi ride.'

'Her passport wasn't in 57 Willow Way,' Rajavi added. 'We turned the place upside down. And her mobile's completely dead, so we haven't been able to track her that way either.'

'Can you get some manpower to check local hotels and B&Bs? And I'll get onto my contact at Border Force and ask them to scan through their exit checks data. They've got access to airlines' advance passenger data too, though I've no idea how long it would take to find what we need.' She smiled at Rajavi, who was crammed into a stab vest over her pale grey maternity top. 'And speaking of what we need: I could murder an espresso.'

'How would you feel about coming to the pub with me?' asked Rajavi.

Rachel checked her watch. 'Bit early, even for the festive season.'

'Don't worry, we can stick to coffee – or decaf in my case,' Rajavi said regretfully. 'While we do a little bit of intelligence gathering.'

The Hand and Flowers was in full Christmas drinks mode, with Slade and Wizzard blasting from the jukebox and a chalkboard menu that included several variations on a turkey theme. A Find Lola Jade collection tin perched on the bar, its label faded almost to illegibility. The pub was also very busy, given that it wasn't yet midday.

'This is Terry Harper's local,' Rachel said, as they corralled a free table in the corner. 'You know: Gavin Harper's dad. Lola's grandfather.'

'It's also the preferred boozer of my pet nark...' Rajavi went to the bar and came back with two mugs of passably decent coffee. 'And actually, that trashy story Stacey Fisher leaked to the paper has done us a favour on this occasion. After he read that, he reckoned he might have some information that's of interest to us. For a price, naturally.'

'Naturally,' Rachel sighed. 'Welcome to policing in the age of information technology.'

'And because it's Christmas, and he has extra cider and fags to pay for, of course his rate has doubled.'

Rajavi's nark arrived twenty minutes later. 'Spud' was a wizened, hunched man with the physique of a jockey, crossed front teeth and a nose that ran constantly, causing him to sniff, or wipe his nose on the sleeve of his jacket. Rachel could stand this for less than two minutes before offering him a tissue from her bag. He stared as though unsure what to do with it.

Rajavi ordered him a double brandy and Spud launched into a long, self-serving preamble, punctuated with much sniffing.

'Wait, hold on!' Rachel had just glimpsed a familiar figure on the other side of the bar. Terry Harper. Of course. He recognised her and looked startled and ill at ease, glancing over in her direction frequently. 'I think we're going to have to take our chat elsewhere. We can't risk him hearing any of this.'

Next door to the pub there was a restaurant called the Taj of India. Although it had not yet formally opened for lunch service, the manager let them in when Rachel showed her warrant card, and brought them complimentary beer and poppadoms.

'I'm not very good with spicy food,' Spud whined. 'I think I'll just stick with the English menu.'

'Probably best,' said Rachel briskly, picturing the impact of chilli on Spud's sinuses. She ordered a bowl of dhal and some steamed rice to placate the restaurant staff – even though she wasn't hungry – and Spud chose chicken and chips and a bowl of fruit salad and ice cream, shovelling the food into his mouth as though it was the first meal he'd seen in days. Perhaps it was.

Only after he had consumed most of it did he start to talk, still punctuating his speech with sniffs.

'You know that missing kid from Eastwell in all the news… Lucy, Lulu…'

'Lola Jade Harper,' Rajavi prompted.

'Yeah, that's the one.' Spud scraped the remainder of the vanilla ice cream from the bowl then waved it at the waiter to indicate that he wanted another one. 'So, a mate of mine, Bestie, that drinks at the Flowers sometimes, he's in this card school. Plays a bit of poker late at night in a room over that dry cleaner's on the Whiteley Road. Anyway, one of the geezers he plays with is this Asian guy, right?'

'Right. Go on,' said Rachel, wishing that she hadn't had to abandon her coffee next door at the pub.

'So they were playing one night, and he told Bestie – after they'd had a fair few whiskies – that he'd rented out a property to the mum of the girl. The missing girl.'

'Michelle Harper?' said Rajavi, giving up on her poppadum with a wince. She pressed her hands into her diaphragm and blew out hard. 'Heartburn.'

'Yeah. Michelle. Hard-faced bint, apparently.' Spud gave a long, liquid sniff before embarking on his second bowl of ice cream. 'Nothing wrong with that, you're thinking, Detective Leila. Only she wants to pay cash and keep it all very hush-hush. Doesn't want anyone knowing she was in the property. No written agreements and the like. She was willing to pay over the odds for that. Bestie says the place was only worth about six hundred a month and she paid nine hundred, a whole year's worth up front, and a deposit, just for him to keep it on the QT.'

'That's around twelve grand in cash,' said Rachel. 'And we know where she got that from.'

'Where is this house?' asked Rajavi. 'We need an address.'

'Don't know the exact address, just that it's over Albert Park way.'

Rajavi took a bunch of twenty-pound notes from her handbag, counted out ten and laid them on the table between the dhal and the ice cream, her hand hovering over them. 'You know how this works, Spud. I'm going to need at least a name from you.'

'The guy who owns it, the landlord, is called Sunny. Sunil Khara.'

CHAPTER THIRTY-THREE

As Rajavi drove them back to the police station, Rachel checked the balance of the Find Lola Jade JustGiving account. *Total raised: £64,761.*

She phoned Lee Knightley. 'Lee, quick as you can: get me an update on the amount in Michelle Harper's JustGiving account.'

Rajavi walked slowly into the station, one hand pressing into the small of her back, the other radioing a patrol car to go and find Sunil Khara.

'These interview rooms are earning their keep this week,' she quipped, lowering herself awkwardly into her desk chair. 'Are you okay to wait around a bit longer, or do you need to get back?'

Rachel shook her head. 'And miss out on being there when you find Lola Jade? No chance.'

As they waited, she checked her email inbox.

Crowdfunding account currently has a zero balance. Remaining £34,761 transferred to M. Harper's account on Friday, then same amount withdrawn in cash. See below.

Lee had attached a screen grab of the statement.

'Don't know nothing about no rental house.'

Sunny Khara was a short, good-looking young man, his black quiff glossy with hair product and his mannerisms distinctly cocky. Having declined legal advice, he leaned back in his chair, arms folded, crotch pushed forward as close to Rachel as possible. The heavily pregnant Rajavi was ignored.

'We've had information regarding an arrangement you've made with a woman called Michelle Harper. Basically her paying to live in a house you own in Albert Park.' Rachel crossed her legs and swivelled her body sideways to delineate a physical barrier between herself and the thrusting groin. This was why she never wore a skirt to work.

'Don't own no house in Albert Park.'

Rajavi sighed and tapped her pen on the table. 'Mr Khara, we can very easily cross-check with the Land Registry. That will tell us what you own and where.'

He grinned smugly, tweaking his quiff. 'Seriously, though. You think any of my investments are in my own name? Ladies, please, I'm a businessman! Never heard of the concept of a holding company?'

Rachel ached to slap him. Since this wasn't possible, she pulled herself up straight, emphasising that she was a couple of inches taller than he was.

'Given that you know so much, you'll also know that the maximum sentence for perverting the course of justice is life in prison. *Life*, Mr Khara. A "businessman" like yourself…' she made air quotes, 'is going to struggle to run his empire from behind bars.'

His chin jutted forward in the same plane as his crotch.

Rajavi hauled herself to her feet. 'Perhaps you'd like some time to think about it? I'm sure we can accommodate you in one of our best en suite cells. But first you'll need to accompany me to the front desk so our lovely custody sergeant can charge you.'

Khara held up his hands. As Rachel suspected, he didn't want any moral issues to get in the way of his ducking and diving. 'Okay, okay, ladies: you win. The house is number 16 Osborne Terrace.'

*

In the end, it all boiled down to numbers, and symmetry.

In Albert Park, the even house numbers ran down the south side of the streets; the odd numbers were north-facing. So, with Jubilee Terrace and Osborne Terrace running back to back, number 17 Jubilee had number 16 Osborne directly behind it, separated by the ginnel, their back gates only a few feet apart. You could leave Lisa Urquhart's house via the kitchen door, cross the back yard and enter the yard of 16 Osborne Terrace within a second, without being seen from either street. It meant that the two properties were effectively adjoined.

Rachel stood in the ginnel, admiring the staggering neatness of the plan, while she and Leila Rajavi waited for the tactical support vehicle to arrive. How easy it had been for Michelle to give the impression she was living at her sister's house when in fact she was in a separate home only feet away. To pass 'Harry' through the back gate so he could go to school with Lisa and Kirstie's children. Not to Lola Jade's school, but a different one, where no one knew her. And Michelle herself could come and go through the front of Lisa's house, with no one suspecting she was actually living in a different building altogether.

The inside of number 16 was dark and dismal, the sort of tatty leased property where the landlord was happy to take the rent while letting the place go to rot. The walls were covered with Artex wallpaper stained ochre with tobacco smoke. There were signs of recent habitation in the kitchen: tea bags, a wine bottle and crisp packets in the bin, clean dishes on the drainer. Upstairs, in the two bedrooms, the double bed and the single bed were made but had clearly been slept in. At the foot of the single bed was a familiar sight. Katy Bear. And in the larger bedroom, propped behind one of the curtains in a hasty attempt to hide it, was the huge airbrushed portrait. Lola Jade Harper leaning on a plastic Doric column in all her glory.

Leila Rajavi came to stand beside Rachel, and for a few seconds they were silent.

'My God. We found her.' The usually calm DS Rajavi sounded close to tears. 'Only she's gone again.'

Rachel touched her arm briefly before pulling on latex gloves and starting to search through the main bedroom. In the wardrobe there was a large purple suitcase: one of the matching pair Michelle had taken from Willow Way. She searched through the entire house and the storage shed in the paved yard, but the other suitcase was nowhere to be found.

She turned her attention back to Michelle's bedroom, rooting through the drawers in the cheap plywood chest. Suddenly she stopped, her heart racing. A pair of dark blue gloves made from a thin thermal fabric. She examined them, then turned them inside out when she felt something lumpy in the fingers.

There in her palm were three tiny rhinestones.

Rachel recognised them instantly. They were from Michelle Harper's sparkly manicure. On the top shelf of the wardrobe was Michelle's missing passport and a box for a new, unregistered mobile phone. The handset inside was gone, but Michelle had failed to realise that the barcode label had a record of the phone's number in tiny print.

In the single bedroom, a forensic officer was pulling items out of the wardrobe: boys' school uniform and sweatshirts and some pastel-coloured girls' clothes in the same size.

'Look.' Rajavi, who had been helping to search the bathroom, came in with a packet of brown hair dye and a pair of hairdressing scissors. 'There are still a couple of strands of blonde hair trapped in a crack in the bathroom lino. What's the betting it's Lola's, from when Michelle cut it off and turned her into Harry.'

'Ma'am.' One of the Tyvek-suited men handed something to Rajavi. 'I think you need to see this: we found it in the waste bin.'

It was a screwed-up piece of paper: a half-completed school registration form. The school was St Francis of Assisi Catholic Primary School, Inglewood, and the name of the pupil Jasmine Gabrielle Hutchins. Born 13 September 2009. The space under 'Names of Parents' was still blank.

'Of course,' said Rachel with a wry smile. 'The name of a Disney princess and the name of the chief of the angels. What else for Michelle's princess angel?' She turned to the forensics officer. 'Was there anything else with this surname on? Any mother's details?'

He shook his head. 'Just this, with the kid's name. But there was a laptop hidden under the sofa cushions. Maybe that will give us more.'

On her way back into London, Rachel took a short detour off the South Circular and drove to Mark Brickall's flat. There was no response when she rang his doorbell, even though she could see the faint gleam of a light behind the curtains of his living room. She phoned him instead.

'What?' His tone was terse.

'I was just passing your flat, and I wondered if you wanted to go for a drink and a chat. Or even a meal and a chat.'

'What for?'

She sighed. 'I really need a sounding board. Looks like I was right about the teddy, and the purple suitcase. And the picture.'

'Prince, are you smoking crack?'

'No. My brain is fried, that's all, and I need to download before the circuits burn out.'

'Well, sorry, boss, but I'm at five-a-side footy. And right now I don't even know if I still have a career as a copper at all. So if you need a cosy little chat about case evidence, I suggest you phone your gal pal at Surrey Police.'

He hung up.

Despondent, Rachel drove the mile and a half to the western edge of Crystal Palace Park. She bought a cup of tea from a truck serving hot drinks, and walked into the maze, her feet making a satisfying crunching sound on the frozen gravel. It was bitterly cold; the dove-grey sky streaked pale pink, and heavy with snow. A few dog walkers made the most of the last remaining minutes of daylight, but otherwise the place was deserted. So rare ever to be alone in London, thought Rachel, to have time to think. That was why she liked to run very early in the morning, rather than after work.

And how appropriate to find herself in a maze. That was what this case had been: a series of false turns and blind alleys leading nowhere. And at the centre of the maze was Michelle Harper. After many years as a criminal investigator, Rachel understood that offenders didn't sit around congratulating themselves on the genius of their evil plan. Most deviant behaviour was either stress-based or environment-based, and as a result, felons had no problem justifying their decisions to themselves. Increment by increment, their actions could become more and more extreme, and yet they could still rationalise what they had done. Some – like Michelle – were so personality-disordered that they saw themselves as the ones who were being wronged. Their starting place was the normal sort of life challenge that can face any of us, and the end point was behaviour that most human beings would regard as abhorrent. In between there was a logical pathway that in their minds justified every step they took. Rachel was quite sure that in Michelle Harper's mind she was victim, not villain.

For Michelle, the first step had been giving birth to a child of the wrong sex. She wanted a girl, not a boy. And because she hadn't got what she wanted, because that rendered her hard done by, quietly suffocating her infant son was what she needed to do. It gave her the chance to start afresh. And when she had her little girl – her princess angel – this appalling act was vindicated. She probably told herself that it could have been an ear or chest infection that finished him off as easily as a gently placed hand over the mouth and nose.

But then Gavin threatened her with not only divorce, but losing custody of her hard-won prize: her daughter. How alarmed she must have been when she realised that he had a good chance of winning that battle, and it was that alarm that prompted her next step. She calculated how public knowledge of Gavin's desire to take Lola Jade from her could work to her advantage. Because if Lola disappeared, everyone would assume that Gavin was responsible. All she needed was to set the scene – the 'abduction' attempt, the suggestion of sexual abuse – and ultimately no one would believe that Gavin deserved Lola Jade more than she did.

Lola Jade was only required to disappear for a short time: hence the secret room at 57 Willow Way. Michelle just needed to keep her shut away, adequately silenced by whatever pharmaceutical means, until the immediate fuss died down. She had injected her daughter with some kind of sedative – clumsily, which explained the telltale specks of blood on Lola's bed and the carpet of the hidden room.

Rachel's guess was that it was during this initial period that the penny dropped for Michelle. If Lola was miraculously 'found', the custody battle clock would simply be reset. Gavin would be exonerated of taking his daughter, and instead of her husband being scrutinised, the spotlight would be directed onto her: Michelle. Awkward questions would be asked, and would put her role as mother at risk.

So Lola Jade had to stay hidden. Another location had to be found, and another identity. Even a mother as warped as Michelle was going to struggle to keep her daughter locked in a room forever. By renting Osborne Terrace and inventing Harry Brown, Michelle could release Lola Jade back into the world and simultaneously take a step back, distance herself. There was nothing to connect her to Harry, until Ben told Carly Wethers the secret and she threatened to intervene.

Having come so far, and created such a successful illusion, Rachel doubted Michelle would struggle to justify using murder to silence Carly. She had suffocated her own son and got away with it; and in patterns of criminal behaviour a success like that greatly boosted the perpetrator's confidence and daring next time round.

But Rachel now saw clearly the one remaining problem for Michelle. She wrapped her hands tightly round her takeout cup to keep them warm as she walked, turning back in to where the maze started just as the first flake of snow floated silently from the sky. Harry Brown was ultimately no use to Michelle, because Harry was a boy and Michelle wanted a daughter, a mirror image of herself to mould and control. And she had to be stopped before she could carry out the final step in the process: the incarnation of Jasmine Gabrielle.

CHAPTER THIRTY-FOUR

'Do you remember our friend at Bangla Stores?'

Rachel looked blankly at Leila Rajavi. She had returned to Eastwell at first light having barely slept, and was exhausted. Rajavi, too, looked tired and uncomfortable, repeatedly shifting in her chair and pressing her fists into the small of her back.

'Sorry, cramp,' she explained. 'The place opposite Happy Nails. We used their security camera to pick up Michelle giving Stacey Fisher the cash.'

Rachel nodded.

'The owner heard about Carly Wethers' death, and remembered seeing her on his own camera footage. So he brought it in last night.' She opened a file on her computer and Rachel stood up to see it better. Carly's curls were partially obscured by her Peruvian-style knitted hat, but it was definitely her. She went into the salon and stood near the door, gesticulating at Michelle. Michelle stood up and said something back, shaking her head. The date on the footage was 1 December, about thirty-six hours before Carly died.

'We'll get a better idea what was said by interviewing the other salon employees,' Rajavi said. 'But this gives us a clear possibility that Michelle knew Carly Wethers was TruthTella.' She winced again, and rubbed at her back, squirming in her chair. 'And we have Carly's DNA found on Michelle's gloves, the ones in 16 Osborne Terrace. Plus, DNA from Lola Jade was found on the inside of that big purple suitcase.'

'She probably used it to transport Lola from the house in Willow Way to their new rental. It must be just about big enough to fit a young child. God knows what she thought was going on, poor kid.'

Rajavi shuddered. 'The good news is: the CPS are now happy that we have enough to charge Michelle with Carly Wethers' murder.' She gave a rueful smile.

'The bad news is: we can't find her,' Rachel supplied. 'She disappeared at exactly the moment that first leaked headline came out; the one we had to deny. I'll bet my mortgage that's what sent her to ground. Until then, I reckon she thought she'd pulled it off.'

'They're working on the log from the burner phone that was found at 16 Osborne Terrace, and the laptop data should be back…' Rajavi waved a hand at DC Coles, who was holding up some papers triumphantly, 'right about now.'

'The browser history,' he said, fetching a second copy for Rachel so that the two women could read in unison.

'I love search-engine histories,' said Rajavi with satisfaction. 'They're like how-to-commit-a-crime manuals.'

It was all there, interleaved with a myriad innocent domestic enquiries such as *How to replace a fridge light* and *When is my recycling collected?* Back in May, Michelle had asked the internet what dose of propofol would sedate a child weighing fifty-five pounds, and how long it would take to wear off. She wanted to know where to buy it online and how to inject it. Much more recently, she wanted to know what sort of implement would disable a Yale lock, how long suffocation by smothering took in a small adult, how to obtain a fake passport.

'Jesus,' said Rachel. 'I'm looking forward to hearing her explain this lot.'

Rajavi turned to the last part of the printout. 'Have you seen this? She's been googling cheap long-haul flights.'

'Let me guess – to Australia.'

'How did you know?'

'Because I looked up St Francis Assisi primary school in Ingle-wood, at two in the morning when I was still awake. It's in Sydney.'

Rajavi went to give her a high-five, then turned away and grimaced.

'Are you okay? Not a contraction, I hope.'

'Just heartburn. And horrendous lower backache. All a normal part of late pregnancy, apparently.'

Rachel turned back to the printout. 'There's no sign of her booking any e-tickets, though… Of course not!' She slapped her forehead. 'She can't use a credit card in her own name: that would leave a digital trail. She's got to use cash: the cash she withdrew from the crowdfunding account. And that means using an agent.'

Rajavi read down the last page. 'She's googled "Travel agents near me" and then clicked on one in West Croydon called Magic Tours.'

'Very apt.' Rachel stood up and pulled on her coat. 'Time for our own magical mystery tour.'

Magic Tours was at the down-at-heel end of the London Road. It had a scruffy shopfront and was just big enough to fit one desk and three chairs. This morning it was manned by a heavy woman with dyed auburn hair and a name badge that read *Magda Sokolova*. She was still in the process of opening up the shop, and reluctantly admitted Rachel and DS Rajavi, sighing at the inconvenience even after they had showed their warrant cards.

'We need to know if you've completed a booking in the name of Hutchins.'

Rachel showed her a photo of Michelle Harper. 'For this woman.'

Magda shrugged, her expression dour. 'Yes, I have,' she said matter-of-factly.

Rajavi, pressing her hands against her back, sighed. 'We need the details, obviously.'

In no hurry to cooperate, Magda settled herself at her desk with exaggerated care and booted up her ancient-looking terminal.

'Is slow,' she commented unnecessarily.

Eventually her connection fired up, and after much tutting and frowning over the printer, which jammed repeatedly, she handed them the reservation details.

There were not two, but three tickets to Sydney via Dubai: one for Lauren Hutchins, one for Jasmine Hutchins and one for Lisa Urquhart.

'Of course,' Rachel observed. 'She can't risk travelling with Lola Jade herself: far too risky. And Lola can't travel as Harry, because her official identity in Australia needs to be that of a girl. Harry Brown's over and done with now.'

'Did she pay cash for these seats?' Rajavi asked.

Magda nodded. 'Cash, yes.' She said this as though it was not unusual to bring nearly seven thousand pounds' worth of notes into the shop.

Rachel was reading the dates on the ticket, which had been printed in a tiny font. 'Michelle's flight's tonight. And Lisa and Lola Jade tomorrow... Okay, we need to get a car over to Jubilee Terrace right now!'

Rajavi picked up the airwave set and called for a patrol car to go straight to Jubilee Terrace and arrest Lisa Urquhart for assisting an offender. While she was speaking, Rachel was re-reading the details.

She shot to her feet. 'Shit!' She clapped her hand to her forehead, waving the printout. 'It's the connection from Dubai that leaves tonight. The flight *to* Dubai leaves in...' she squinted at her watch, 'eighty minutes.'

They raced outside to the car, but Rajavi doubled up, wincing again and handing the keys to Rachel. 'You drive. This heartburn is killing me.'

The airwave set crackled into life. 'Attempt to locate negative at 17 Jubilee,' said the muffled disembodied voice.'

'Go for a warrant and set up an ANPR,' Rajavi gasped, pressing her palm down hard on her upper thigh.

Rachel filtered onto the M25, switching on the light bar on the car's roof and activating the siren. She glanced over at Rajavi, who was sitting in a strange position. 'You okay, Leila?'

She responded with a strangled grunt.

'Listen, even with the blues and twos on, it's going to take at least forty-five minutes to get to Heathrow… I think we should call ahead and get Michelle held at the gate, in case we're not there in time.'

Rajavi inhaled sharply and held her breath for a few seconds, letting it out in a rush as the pain passed. 'I don't think I can get one of our patrols to arrive there any quicker than we will.'

'Try the Met's Heathrow station. They'll have someone on the ground at Terminal 3.'

Rachel glanced in the rear-view mirror and floored the accelerator up to ninety-five miles an hour, trying to remember when she had last used her pursuit-driving skills. She usually let Brickall do the macho car-chase stuff: it made him happy.

Rajavi threw her mobile down in disgust, still clutching at her abdomen. 'I've got no signal.'

'You'll have to radio control and get them to phone it in.'

As they approached Heathrow, the M25 grew thick with people travelling for the Christmas holidays, and Rachel was having to use the lights to clear a path through the traffic, weaving from lane to lane and struggling to keep up her speed.

'Oh… oh God!'

Rajavi had pulled her airwave set from the shoulder of her vest, but clutched it aloft as she stared down at her lap. A huge wet pool spread across the crotch of her trousers and over the seat upholstery, trickling down into the seat well.

Rachel glanced sharply across at her. 'Please don't tell me…'

Rajavi nodded. 'My waters have gone.'

'When are you due?'

'Not for three weeks. I've been feeling crampy on and off for the past twenty-four hours but I assumed it was just Braxton Hicks.' She looked at Rachel. 'Those are practice contractions.'

'I know what they are,' said Rachel tersely. She had to keep her eyes on the road, but was aware of Rajavi tensing up and catching her breath. 'This is no practice… Is that a contraction now?'

'I think so.'

Rachel stretched across her and took the airwave set, pressing the button and holding it against her left ear as she steered with her right. 'Control, this is 1819 Prince. I need a location ID for nearest maternity hospital…' she consulted the GPS, 'in the Byfleet area. And a unit to Heathrow Terminal 3 to intercept Michelle Harper, checking in for flight EK209.'

'It's okay,' panted Rajavi. 'We don't need to stop now; we'll be at Heathrow in half an hour or so, and they have medical facilities. Anyway, nothing's going to happen for hours yet.'

'Are you *sure*?'

Rajavi spoke through gritted teeth. 'Sure. I'll be fine. Just keep going.'

'Sorry, cancel that.' Rachel switched off the radio set and returned her hand to the steering wheel, but she still glanced at Rajavi every few seconds. Her fists were pressed against her upper thighs, and sweat was breaking out on her forehead.

'Leila? You *sure* you're okay to keep going?'

The DS managed to nod her head, but she was holding her breath so forcibly she couldn't speak.

'Leila? Talk to me!'

As they approached Junction 14, Rajavi finally let out a long, low moan and began to pant.

'I think it's coming,' she said, her dark brown eyes wild with panic. 'The head's really low; I can feel it between my legs.'

'Oh fuck.'

Rachel screeched onto the hard shoulder, hit the hazard lights and snatched up the airwave set again, barking at them to dispatch an ambulance. Then she half pulled, half lifted Rajavi out of the front seat and laid her along the rear passenger seat, removing her boots, underwear and trousers and arranging her own coat across Rajavi's lower abdomen in a makeshift attempt at modesty. She had undertaken five days of intense medical training in order to become an authorised firearms officer, but – unsurprisingly – it did not cover delivering babies. That scenario had been touched on during her training at Hendon, but she remembered precious little about it.

'It's fine,' she said to Rajavi, even though it very much wasn't. 'I've got this.'

She retrieved the medical kit from the boot of the vehicle and pulled out a sterile pad, which she placed under Rajavi's hips, and a foil heat blanket to wrap the baby.

'Don't try and fight it; just go with it. If your body's telling you to push, then you have to push.

Rajavi bellowed in fear and pain, and a few seconds later Rachel was astonished to see a glistening purple-black dome appearing between her legs, topped with dark wet hair. She took surgical gloves from the medical box and pulled them on, reaching in quickly to guide the head's crowning. Rajavi lowed like a wounded farm animal.

'Don't push too hard,' Rachel said, hoping this was right. 'Nice and gently does it.'

There was a pop and a gush, and the baby slid out into her hands, little fists clenched, curled body seeming strangely small compared to the head. As she cleaned it off with another of the pads, rubbing briskly at the chest, the baby gave a gargling cry, quickly drowned out by the howl of an ambulance siren. A green-suited paramedic rushed over and took the foil-wrapped baby from Rachel's hands; it looked for all the world like a plump oven-ready chicken.

It was only when she relinquished her hold that Rachel realised quite how hard her hands had been shaking. She took some deep breaths to dissipate the build-up of adrenaline.

'Is it all right?' whispered Rajavi, trying to sit up.

'*He* is perfect.' Rachel squeezed her hand. 'Congratulations: you have a son.'

CHAPTER THIRTY-FIVE

'I'm sorry, the flight had already gone by the time the request came through.'

'And "Lauren Hutchins" was definitely on it?'

Rachel was met at the entrance to Terminal 3 by the on-site liaison for the Metropolitan Police, and an Emirates flight dispatcher.

'She was.' The dispatcher nodded. 'And two items of luggage.'

Rachel had been expecting this to happen, given that she had waved off the ambulance bearing Leila Rajavi and her new son at more or less the same time the gate was due to close.

'The positive is we currently know exactly where she is,' added the police officer, who introduced himself as PC Ryan Mead. He pointed out of the viewing window at the sky above the runway to make his point. 'And when that flight lands, she's not going anywhere. Will you have her picked up in Dubai?'

Rachel shook her head. 'Dubai isn't a member of Interpol, so we have no jurisdiction. It's going to have to be Australia. So this development is completely embargoed for now, okay? Whatever you do, don't let the press get hold of this. It's because of a recent press leak that she's decided to do a bunk now.'

They both nodded solemnly.

'The last thing we want is Harper getting wind of us having a blue card out for her, and not reboarding in Dubai. If it's Australia, that gives me a bit more time to organise the warrant. I'll speak to my contact at the National Central Bureau in Sydney in a minute. But first…' Rachel turned to the airline representative, 'can I see your security cam footage from the check-in desk?'

She was taken to the airline's control centre and shown the images that were captured as standard procedure when passengers checked their baggage. Michelle was wearing over-the-knee boots and skin-tight jeans, and had her face partially concealed by the ant sunglasses. She kept the interaction to a minimum, taking frequent furtive glances around at security staff and her fellow passengers. Rachel stopped the recording on the frame when the cases were handed over to be weighed. They were two large Louis Vuitton knock-offs. No big purple polycarbonate case. The one in Osborne Terrace, now in the Surrey Police forensic lab, was proven to have contained the person of Lola Jade at some point. So where was the second purple case?

PC Mead was looking at the arrest paperwork that had been sent through. 'Michelle Harper… Hold on, isn't she the one whose little girl went missing. Lola Jade?'

'Yup.' Rachel nodded as she searched through her phone for the number of her contact in Sydney. 'The very same.'

'So if the mother's on her way to Australia, where's the kid?'

'Due to follow on with her aunt,' said Rachel. 'Who must know where Lola is right now.'

With nothing more she could usefully do at the airport, Rachel drove back to Eastwell. She felt she ought to return their squad car, and break the news that their colleague had successfully – if unexpectedly – become a mother.

As she approached Eastwell from the north-west, the car radio set crackled into life. 'Suspect Lisa Urquhart mobile, heading north-west on the A420, over.' Her trained ear picked up the faint sound of a police siren, probably a few hundred yards away.

A car sped past her on the opposite carriageway, exceeding the speed limit. She caught a flash of cyclamen hair through the front window, and recognised the beaten-up blue VW Passat belonging to Kevin Urquhart. Kevin was at the wheel, with pink-haired Lisa beside him. A police squad car followed, lights flashing.

'Christ on a sodding bike!'

Rachel executed a brisk U-turn and followed at a safe distance, switching on her own lights and siren. The blue Passat picked up speed as the police squad car closed the gap, causing it to veer erratically across the lane to the right. The steering was corrected – over-corrected – and the back wheels hit a patch of melting slush at speed, sending the car spinning, sliding and eventually flipping over into the ditch, plumes of steam punctuating the December air. The squad car swerved and braked, narrowly avoiding hitting the same slippery patch.

'Jesus!' Rachel pumped her brakes and skidded to a halt as safely as she could, hitting her hazard lights and jumping out of the car. She pulled fluorescent bollards from the boot and dropped them across the road behind her, forcing all the traffic in her wake to slow down and form a queue. The officers in the pursuit vehicle were already out of the car, one shouting into a handset and the other scrambling down the bank towards the crashed Passat.

Rachel ran in the same direction, her boots sliding on the frosty tarmac. Kevin Urquhart was moving slightly, blood trickling down the side of his neck. Lisa Urquhart was motionless, thrown forward so far that her head made a pink patch on the windscreen.

'Is she alive?' Rachel asked, reaching her warrant card from her back pocket and holding it up.

The officer shook his head slowly. 'Hard to tell. Touch and go, I reckon.'

'No one in the back of the car?'

The officer scrambled further down the bank and cupped his hands against the glass. When he stood up again, he shook his head. 'No. Small mercy, eh?'

'Check the boot!' Rachel urged.

There was a short struggle, followed by swearing, and eventually the boot lid was prised open. The officer staggered backwards under the weight of a suitcase. Rachel reached over and took it from him, pulling it up the side of the bank and laying it down on the gravelly edge of the lay-by. She unzipped it to reveal a tangled mess of patterned neon beachwear, flip-flops, large grey bras and sun cream.

'Looks like they were off on holiday. Why, what were you expecting?'

'I thought there might be… Never mind. Was that it?'

'Empty apart from the case.'

Rachel gave him a weak smile. 'Thanks for checking.'

More sirens wailed in the distance, and for the second time that day, Rachel watched as an ambulance pulled up, followed this time by a fire engine. The fire crew set about cutting the Passat apart and removing the passengers. Kevin was lifted out first wearing a neck brace, badly injured but conscious. It took longer to remove Lisa. She lay on the back board, her hair fanned out like the petals of a chrysanthemum, lurid against the greyish white of her face.

While the paramedics worked at stabilising her, the police finished photographing the wreck of the blue Passat and the fire crew set about winching the car from the ditch and loading it onto the recovery truck that had just arrived.

Rachel hovered near Lisa as the crew established cardiac output then lost it, employing the defibrillator to get it back again.

Eventually one of the paramedics shouted, 'Okay, she's back. I've got a pulse.'

With an oxygen mask over her face and a fluid drip attached, Lisa was loaded into the back of the ambulance and it sped away.

Rachel watched it go, a heavy sinking sensation in the pit of her stomach.

'I could put a nip of something stronger in there. You look like you need it.'

DS Rajavi's colleague, DC Matt Coles, brought Rachel a mug of scalding tea with two sugars in it, and waggled a silver hip flask in her direction. 'Scotland's finest.'

Rachel shook her head. 'Not while I'm on duty, thanks. But you're right, I could do with it. It's been one hell of a day.' She swigged her tea. 'So far. It's not over yet.'

She had broken the news of Rajavi's baby – met with whoops of jubilation – and the Urquharts' crash – met with anger and consternation – when she eventually got back to Eastwell police station. She had no idea what time it was, only that it was almost dark.

DC Coles sat down opposite her. 'I hate to drop even more on you, but there are a couple of new developments.'

'It's fine.' Rachel sipped her tea, fantasising that it had whisky in it. 'Go on.'

'Our enquiries from the area where we found Michelle's car have thrown up a lead. The manager of a small hotel about half a mile away phoned and reported booking out a room to someone matching Michelle Harper's description. I went to speak to him this morning, and I've got his MG11 if you want to take a look.'

He handed Rachel a copy of a witness statement form.

I work at the Crossgates Manor Hotel, Feltham, as assistant manager. On 19 December 2016, I was at the reception desk when a woman came in with a little boy. She had three cases with her: she was pulling two and the little boy had the other. I'd say the child was about seven or eight years old, quite stocky, with short brown hair. The child didn't speak, and I thought he seemed unhappy. The woman reserved a room in the name of Lauren Hutchins. She showed me a UK passport in that name. She said she wasn't sure when she was leaving and asked if it was okay to pay for the first two nights up front. I agreed and she paid for the room in cash. At 6.30 a.m. this morning, 20 December, as I was unlocking the reception desk, she came downstairs with a large purple suitcase. I asked if she wanted a taxi, but she said that she had already ordered one and would wait for it outside on the street. She said she was coming back shortly and would settle the bill then. The child wasn't with her, but I didn't give it too much thought as she was coming back.

At 8 a.m. she returned, and around an hour later came downstairs to settle the bill, with two more cases. I asked where her son was and she said he was playing outside. There is a small garden at the rear of the property. She paid the outstanding amount on the bill, in cash, and didn't want a receipt, but asked me to call her a taxi for the airport. The taxi arrived ten minutes later and she went outside with the luggage. When the chambermaid went to clean the room at 11.30 a.m, it was empty.

This statement is true to the best of my knowledge and belief and I make it knowing that, if it is tendered in evidence, I shall be liable to prosecution if I have wilfully stated anything in it which I know to be false or do not believe to be true.

Signed by: Piotre Zelinski
Witnessed by: DC 4371 Coles

I work at the Crossgates Manor Hotel as a part-time waitress. On the evening of 19 December, I was on duty in the restaurant. A woman came downstairs with a child and sat at a table for two. I don't remember the exact time but the restaurant was about to close so it must have been around 10.30 p.m. I thought it was a bit late for a small child to be eating. The child was wearing pyjamas with unicorns on. They looked like girls' pyjamas but the child's hair was cut like a boy's. He didn't speak, and from his eyes I thought he looked as though he was sedated. She ordered a pizza for the child but he barely ate any and his head kept drooping onto the plate, like in those YouTube videos of toddlers falling asleep in their dinner. I made a comment about it being past the child's bedtime and the woman told me it was none of my business. She paid with cash but didn't leave a tip.

The second statement was signed by a Jessica Kingdon.

Rachel handed them back to Coles. 'Well, we know where Michelle Harper is now, at least. But we need to know what she did with the purple suitcase.'

He stared. 'Are you saying…'

'That Lola Jade, the "boy" with the short brown hair, was in it? Yes, that's exactly what I'm saying.'

'Okay, well maybe this will help.' Coles handed her another document, which Rachel recognised as a telecoms intelligence unit log. 'The phone that was found in Osborne Terrace has just been analysed by our TIU. The texts are all to one number, which we've identified as belonging to Lisa Urquhart. That's the one called Phone B; Phone A is Harper's burner.'

Rachel skim-read through them. The first two texts were from three days earlier, on 17 December.

PHONE A: *Can't drop LJ with u: too risky. Pigs watchin ur place.*

PHONE B: *Where will u take her then? There's 24 hours before she and me fly.*

PHONE A: *Will find somewhere to leave her safe. Is only for a little while. Will make sure you have full deets don't worry! X*

The next day, Sunday 18th, there was a call from Phone A to Phone B lasting twelve minutes. At 8.20 a.m. that morning, there was a final sequence of texts.

PHONE A: *Okay, she is there safely, in place we discussed. But please, NOT FOR LONG, okay? Gave big dose of stuff to last till you can fetch her but make sure you're not late because of suffocation risk. And don't tell Kev.*

PHONE B: *Don't worry, he thinks I'll just be picking up some of your XS luggage to take with me. Still thinks it's a girls' trip! X*

PHONE A: *Okay, well be careful Leess. Please. Tickets and L's passport are in zipped pocket of case.*

PHONE B: *Not long now! Can't wait babes. X*

PHONE A: *Whatever happens make sure you don't screw up collecting L. Can't tell you how URGENT this is. Nothing must go wrong.*

PHONE B: *Don't stress, have memorised address of place like you said and will leave plenty of time to get there. X*

PHONE A: *Nearly there now. Fucking Gavin; he's going to have no idea.*

Rachel tossed the printout onto the desk and grabbed her bag and keys, trying to remember where she had left her car that morning.

'Code red, Constable!' she snapped, when Coles didn't imme-diately jump to his feet. 'There's only one person who knows where the case is: Lisa Urquhart.'

'Two people if you count Michelle Harper,' Coles pointed out. 'Why don't we try asking her first?' He was pulling on a jacket and hat as he spoke. 'She's going to have to talk to us when she finds out her daughter's at risk.'

Rachel consulted her watch. 'Michelle will be arriving in Dubai around now. But like I said before, we don't have any jurisdiction there to intercept her.'

'No, I meant we can call the plane. When she takes off for Sydney.'

She stared at him. 'Christ, of course! Why didn't I think of that sooner?'

Coles had already started running out to the car park, climbing straight into a patrol car.

'So how does it work?' Rachel asked as she jumped into the passenger seat and they headed, lights flashing, to Heathrow Terminal 3.

'Any ground station – like an airline dispatcher or a control tower – can establish two-way communications using VHF frequencies. Well, sometimes they can; it depends on the range.'

'How do you know all that, Einstein?'

'My dad used to be a pilot.'

They left the car in an emergency bay and ran to the Emirates control centre, only to have an apologetic ground-crew supervisor explain that because Michelle had just boarded her connection from Dubai, her flight was automatically out of range of the UK ground antenna.

'But you can try MedAire,' she suggested. 'They have special satellite phones to communicate with all aircraft about medical emergencies. Their operators are based in Farnborough, but they have a rep here, I believe.'

'I'll go,' offered Coles, taking in Rachel's washed-out face. 'Why don't you go and track down some coffee?'

He returned fifteen minutes later, shaking his head. 'They haven't been able to make contact with the flight – something about weather conditions – but they're going to keep on trying. Should we wait here?'

Rachel shook her head firmly, handing him a paper cup of coffee. 'We can't afford to sit around and wait: this is too time-critical. We'll have to try the only other person who knows where that suitcase is.'

CHAPTER THIRTY-SIX

The Accident and Emergency department of Ashtead Hospital was filling up with drunk and disorderly Christmas partygoers, along with a smattering of fractures and sprains from falls on icy pavements. Rachel and DC Coles had to fight their way through to the reception desk.

'We can't give out information about patients,' a weary-looking black woman told her. She didn't seem to have noticed that Rachel was flanked by a man wearing a police-issue stab vest, or perhaps she assumed he was fresh from a party and wearing fancy dress.

Bristling with impatience, Rachel whipped out her warrant card. The woman glanced at her screen.

'Mrs and Mrs Urquhart have both been taken to the Trauma Unit. It's back there, at the end of the corridor.'

They found a harassed nurse in scrubs who told them they would have to wait until someone could speak to them.

'This is a critical situation: I'm sorry, but it can't wait.'

Rachel pushed past the nurse into the triage area and started looking in the curtained cubicles, trailing a shell-shocked Coles in her wake.

'Excuse me, you can't do that!' The nurse trotted after them, pulling the curtains closed again. 'I'll get you a doctor.'

She came back a few seconds later with a doctor, also in scrubs, who she introduced as the trauma registrar.

'We need to speak to Mr and Mrs Urquhart urgently.' Rachel forced herself to slow her breathing; she was gabbling now. 'We've reason to believe they know where Lola Jade Harper is.'

'Lisa Urquhart is in surgery right now.'

'Where?'

'Downstairs in theatre. But I can take you back to speak to Kevin Urquhart. He's quite badly hurt, but he's awake.' He led them into the resuscitation area, which had four bed bays with their curtains pushed back. Kevin Urquhart was just about recognisable through the drips and bandages. His face was cut and bruised and his left leg was in plaster.

'Kevin, I'm DI Rachel Prince; I'm investigating the disappearance of your niece. I need to speak to you about today's accident.'

He couldn't move his head, but his eyes flicked in Rachel's direction. 'It was Lisa, she told me to speed up when she saw the panda car. I didn't know why; she just said we didn't have time to be stopped by the cops. And then I skidded on the ice and… bang.' He lifted his bandaged arm and let it drop on the bed as illustration.

'Mr Urquhart – Kevin – what I'm really concerned about at this moment is where you were going. You were on your way to collect Lola Jade so she could travel with your wife?'

He stared at her, dazed. 'No. She didn't say nothing about Lola. We were on the way to pick up some of the stuff Michelle couldn't take because she was over her weight allowance. Lisa said she checked it into left luggage and we had to pick it up.'

'Yes, but where? What was the address?'

Rachel was trying to work out how much Kevin knew. He must have been aware that Michelle wasn't living under his roof, that this was a fiction. But did he think she'd just disappeared back to Willow Way, or did he know about Osborne Terrace? If so, did he know about Harry, or did the sisters keep his appearances to the hours when Kevin was at work? There simply wasn't time to go into it all now.

'She didn't give me the actual address; she just said head up the A420. I assumed we were heading for Heathrow because that's where I work and that's where Lisa's flying from, you know, when she goes on her holiday. Tomorrow.' He looked anguished. 'Except she's not going on no holiday now. The doctor said it's only fifty-fifty that she'll even make it through surgery.'

Kevin closed his eyes, and a nurse darted forward to adjust his opiate drip.

'I think he's had enough for now.'

Rachel turned to the registrar. 'What about Lisa?'

He shook his head. 'Even if she's out of theatre, she's not going to be in any condition to speak to you.'

Rachel felt her whole body quiver with undiluted frustration. Each bed in the room had a blood pressure cuff: if someone hooked her up to one, her reading would be at the top of the scale. 'She's the only one who knows where Lola Jade is: this is a young child who has been missing for more than seven months now, and who is currently in serious danger.'

'I'm aware of that.' The registrar seemed sympathetic. 'Look, I'll take you down to theatre and you can speak to her surgeon. That's the best I can offer right now.'

They were led down to the basement theatre suite with its strange scent of chloroform and singed flesh, and waited in an anaesthetic room for what felt like hours. Rachel refused to sit, pacing and glancing constantly at her watch. Eventually the surgeon appeared through the dividing door, still in his cap and gown.

'DI Prince – I won't shake your hand if you don't mind: I'm still sterile.'

He stood, holding his gloved hands at right angles as though he was about to start cutting and stitching imminently. 'Lisa Urquhart. I've just finished working on her. She's got a pneumothorax, multiple rib fractures and a fractured femur, and her spleen was badly damaged: I had to perform a splenectomy. There was a lot of internal bleeding, which I've just about managed to get under control.'

'Is she going to survive?' asked DC Coles.

The surgeon bunched his lips. 'I'd say she has a chance. If she makes it through the next twenty-four hours.'

'When can we speak to her? Obviously we wouldn't normally… but this is extremely urgent.'

'That's not going to be possible today, or tomorrow. She's in a medically induced coma, and will be for at least forty-eight hours. I'm sorry.'

Rachel had already turned away and was racing back upstairs to Resuscitation. She flew over to Kevin Urquhart, with Coles in her slipstream, bending so that her face was near his.

'Where's Lola?' she shouted at the top of her voice. 'You've got to know *something*!'

A nurse darted in to intervene, as Rachel bore down on him. 'WHERE IS SHE?'

Rachel and DC Cole sat in darkness in the squad car outside the hospital entrance. She was physically shaking and completely empty, like a deflated paper bag.

Cole had bought a bar of chocolate from the shop as they left, and insisted on giving half to her.

'Come on, it's late. When did you last eat? You need to keep your energy levels up.' He gave her an encouraging smile, for which she was grateful. She took the chocolate and did indeed feel better for it, gathering herself sufficiently to engage lateral thinking.

'Nothing from the MedAire people yet?'

Coles shook his head.

'Okay, so if we can't reach Michelle's plane, and neither of the Urquharts can tell us Lola Jade's location, our only hope is to work out where she is for ourselves. I'd say the likeliest place is the left luggage facility at Heathrow. We need to radio backup and get some manpower over there as soon as we can; start searching.'

'Which one, though? There's one in every terminal except Terminal 1, so that's four in total.'

'Good point.' Rachel just about managed a smile. 'Although she was flying from Terminal 3, so that's got to be the most likely location. We'll start there, but get as many bodies onto it as you can. I'll phone Ryan Mead, the Met Police officer I met earlier, and get him to start the process immediately, using his bodies. We can't afford to waste another minute.'

Coles radioed in the request, then slid the car out onto the M25 and headed back to Heathrow, lights flashing, siren screaming.

Five Metropolitan Police officers took an hour to conduct a thorough search of all large suitcases in the left luggage lockers at Terminal 3, while their colleagues – joined by available officers from Surrey Police – did the same thing at Terminals 2, 4 and 5. The purple suitcase was not found. Nor was Lola Jade.

By the time the search was complete it was after midnight and Rachel was gritty-eyed with exhaustion. She left DC Coles chasing up the staff in the MedAire office again, sank on to a bench with a Coke she'd bought from a vending machine and pulled out her phone.

'Don't hang up!' she said as soon as Brickall answered. 'Please don't hang up.'

He heard the sheer desperation in her voice and stayed on the line while she unfolded the events of the day as succinctly as she could, aware that emotional exhaustion was detracting from the narrative thrust.

'You delivered a kid, Prince? No fucking way!'

'I did. But unfortunately I didn't find the kid we've been looking for.'

He made a tutting sound. 'That's because you made a very basic mistake.'

'What?'

'Michelle would never have been able to leave Lola Jade in a suitcase at an airport left luggage place.'

'Why not?'

'Because they all have a weight limit of thirty-two kilos. And a big solid-sided case with a clothed kid weighing getting on for sixty pounds is going to be over that. Kevin Urquhart's a baggage handler, so she'd probably already have known that. She needed to leave it in a storage place nearby where the thing isn't going to be weighed or handled. Where did you say her car was found?'

'About five miles from here, just outside Feltham.'

'Hold on…'

Rachel felt as though she could hear Brickall thinking. *Hurry up*, she said over and over in her mind. *Please just hurry up.*

'Let's have a look, shall we… Okay, the obvious solution is a twenty-four-hour place in Feltham offering personal storage for – among other things – people who are travelling. Sending it to you now.'

Rachel's phone pinged with a text containing a map pin.

'I suggest you head straight over there.'

'We're still checking to see if MedAire can manage to speak to Michelle in-flight.'

'Belt and braces, Prince, remember? In this situation you need to do both. Leave someone else trying to make radio contact with the plane and get your fucking backside over to Feltham. 'Hold on…' She could hear background noise, including the jangle of car keys. 'Sorry – just putting my shoes on. I'll meet you there.'

'But Mark…'

He had hung up. Rachel had been about to say that she had arrived at Heathrow in a squad car, the keys to which were currently in the trouser pocket of a DC whose mobile number she didn't know. And she didn't have an airwave set to contact him with either. For a fleeting moment she considered phoning Ryan Mead and asking him to organise a car for her, but that would take too long. She was on the exit level for ground transportation so walked straight outside into the frosty, sulphurous gloom and jumped into the first of a line of black cabs with their orange 'For Hire' lights on.

She gave the cabbie the map location and told him there was a big tip in it if he put his foot down.

'Easy, treacle,' he said in a thick East End accent. 'Don't want to get in trouble with the Old Bill.'

She held up her warrant card. 'I am the Old Bill. And I give you permission to break the speed limit.'

He whistled. 'Sweet. Always wanted to do that… So, to clarify, fast as I like?'

'Faster.'

CHAPTER THIRTY-SEVEN

Despite its claim of twenty-four-hour service, the storage warehouse was closed for the night.

A sign outside said: *For on-call duty manager phone 07831 560516.* There was a security light above the front entrance, but otherwise the building and car park were in complete darkness.

'Don't really like leaving you here, darlin',' said the cabbie, who had introduced himself as Jim. 'Doesn't seem right.'

'I've got a colleague on the way over. I'll be fine,' Rachel reassured him.

'How about I hang around as your wingman till he gets here? I've always fancied being one of the Sweeney.'

Rachel left Jim sitting in his cab with the interior light on and pulled out her phone. It was a toss-up – did she summon the manager or call for a support vehicle? She remembered Brickall's diktat on deploying belt and braces and decided to do both. First she summoned a tactical unit, who would be able to break into the place and search it. Then she called the manager, who answered after a couple of rings.

'No problem: I'll be there in three minutes.'

'Make it two.'

And he was: a cheerful young Turkish man wearing a padded coat over a T-shirt and tracksuit bottoms.

'I'll need to check the records on the computer; give me a sec.'

Rachel shifted from foot to foot while he switched on the lights and waited for the system to boot up.

'Everything okay, guv?' shouted Jim from the cab. She gave him a thumbs-up.

'Harper… Harper. No, we ain't got no unit reserved to Harper.'

'Or Hutchins?'

He searched again, whistling as he flicked slowly through the spreadsheet. 'I'm going to have to ask you to hurry.' Rachel couldn't help snapping. She glanced out at the front car park but there was still only Jim there. 'I've reason to believe there could be a child in one of your storage units.'

The man's eyes widened. 'You're kidding!'

'No, I'm not.'

'Well there's definitely no Hutchins, sorry.'

'Are you sure?'

'One hundred per cent, look.' He swivelled the screen to show her.

Rachel could feel sweat running down her back, despite the chill in the office. Brickall had landed on this place, but how many other businesses with the capability to store a suitcase could there be within a five-mile radius of the airport? Dozens? Hundreds? This was a child-sized needle in a metropolitan haystack. Lola Jade had been drugged and imprisoned for over eighteen hours now: time and oxygen could already have run out.

'How about Brown?' she asked.

'Got a couple of Browns, but they've all been here long-term. House contents and that.'

Her heart racing, Rachel performed a mental scan of everything she knew about Michelle. Then it came to her: something that had been on the divorce paperwork. Her maiden name: Kenny.

'Try Kenny.'

'Yeah, we've got a Kenny. Opened the account yesterday. Wanted one of our smallest units.'

'Get the key.'

They ran down the aisle between numbered steel-fronted units until they reached Unit 148. A few feet away, Rachel heard vehicles skidding to a halt on the gravel, footsteps running.

And there it was. The second purple suitcase.

She tipped it onto its side, trembling as she fumbled for the zip. Two officers in tactical gear appeared in the doorway, and she heard another, familiar voice shouting into a phone for an ambulance.

Curled up in a foetal position, wearing unicorn pyjamas, her skin a sickly purplish grey, was the missing child.

'Oh Lola,' whispered Rachel. She brushed tears from her eyes and stroked the short, damp hair, blonde roots starting to show through the brown dye.

Brickall darted forward and pushed Rachel aside, pressing two fingers against the child's neck. On her ear lobes there were faint dot-like scars where her ear piercings were starting to heal over.

'Have you got a pulse?' asked one of the officers.

'I'm not sure.' Brickall lifted the girl from the base of the suitcase, laid her on the floor and started chest compressions.

Somewhere outside, there was the insistent whine of an ambulance siren; more footsteps.

Rachel reached for Lola Jade's wrist, aware that she was holding her own breath. And there it was, the faintest thread.

'She's alive. Just.'

CHAPTER THIRTY-EIGHT

'So – what are your plans for Christmas? Doing anything nice?'

Rachel and Brickall were sitting in a transport café a few yards from West Middlesex University Hospital. Her second hospital of the day, Rachel thought. It would have been the third if she'd gone with Rajavi to the maternity unit. Except, technically, it wasn't the same day. It was now 4 a.m. of the next day, 21 December. She could barely keep her eyes open.

'I'm going to my gran's,' said Brickall.

'Your gran? I thought she was dead.'

He shook his head. 'That was my mum's mum. This is Dad's mum, Nana Brickall. She's not dead, she's in Worthing. Which pretty much amounts to the same thing.'

'What do you think will happen to Lola Jade now?'

'You mean if she survives?'

'The doctors seemed fairly confident.'

Brickall shrugged. 'Her dad's in clink and her mum's headed that way. For a long time.'

'And her aunt and uncle are likely to go down for assisting an offender.' Rachel sighed, and took a gulp of her tea. It was stewed, but hot at least. Brickall had ordered sausage, egg and tomato with two rounds of toast.

'What?' he said, catching Rachel's incredulous look. 'Rescuing damsels in distress in the middle of the night gives a man an appetite.'

She swatted the side of his arm. 'Don't you dare, you sexist wanker!'

He grinned, shoving buttered toast into his mouth.

'Seriously, though, thank you. I'm not sure I could have done this without you.'

He shrugged. 'You'd have got there in the end.'

'But probably too late.'

'Just don't tell anyone, okay? If it gets back to Patten that I helped you while I'm suspended, it's not going to do me any good at all. In fact, quite the opposite. Conducting enquiries on a case when you're officially removed from duty is another potential bloody disciplinary.'

'My lips are sealed. I never saw you.'

Brickall offered her a triangle of toast and she took it, suddenly starving.

'So, which of your many suitors – or stalkers – are you spending the Christmas break with?'

'None of them,' said Rachel firmly. 'And I couldn't be happier about it.'

'So a jolly family Christmas chez Prince in Purley?'

'Chez Reynolds actually.' She sighed. 'Mum and I are going to my sister's house.'

Brickall raised his mug of tea in a toast, waiting for Rachel to do the same with hers. 'Merry fucking Christmas to us.'

Christmas at Lindsay and Gordon Reynolds' house was all about perfection.

At least that was how Lindsay saw it. To Rachel, it was all about fussing. Every year her sister wrote a long list entitled 'Christmas: To Do' and pinned it to the fridge. This was an excessively long schedule of details to fret over and get annoyed about if they weren't exactly as ordained when the list was written. At 3 p.m.

on Christmas Eve, mince pies were served while they listened to *A Festival of Nine Lessons and Carols* from King's College, Cambridge. Woe betide you if you didn't actually feel like eating a mince pie at that time. Such subversion would send Lindsay off into a spiral of fury.

A ham with Cumberland sauce was served on the evening of Christmas Eve, followed by fruit salad, and at 11 p.m., once six stockings had been hung in the proper formation, and correctly labelled, a party set out to the local church in Oxted for midnight mass. Rachel usually swerved this part, having not a religious bone in her body.

News bulletins were to be watched at 6 and 10 p.m. without fail, and this year they were dominated by the story of Lola Jade's rescue. The same piece of footage, of Michelle Harper being arrested at Sydney airport, was played over and over again. Michelle glared at the camera, looking furious rather than cowed, before an Australian police officer raised his arm to shield her face from the flashbulbs. Journalists camped out in Eastwell, outside Willow Way and in front of West Middlesex University Hospital, speculating endlessly about what was being called 'the sensational twist in a story that's gripped the nation'.

On Christmas morning, it was compulsory to gather on Lindsay and Gordon's bed at 8.30 a.m. to open their stockings, with carols playing on the radio. Then Tom and Laura – Rachel's nephew and niece – were tasked with collecting, smoothing and folding all the discarded wrapping paper, and making orderly piles of everyone's presents.

After breakfast – smoked salmon and scrambled egg, whether you fancied it or not – there was veg prep and table-setting, which involved lining up knives, silverware, mats and crackers at regimented right angles. Then, once the Labrador had been walked, 'bubbly and nibbles' was served in the living room, with the adults watching the two children solemnly opening some of their presents. The turkey was carved at two on the dot, accompanied by the wearing of paper crowns, and underdone kale the texture of wet tarpaulin. Even sprouts would have been preferable. Rachel laid into the claret, checking her watch frequently to see if another half-hour had crawled by.

Then after force-feeding of Christmas cake and chocolates and a compulsory game of Trivial Pursuit, Lindsay pounced on the TV remote. 'What time's the news on? Isn't it normally early on Christmas Day?'

She switched it on. Another reporter earning double time on an outside broadcast, this time with the all-too-familiar backdrop of Eastwell police station.

'*... and inevitably the question is being asked: why did it take so long for Surrey Police to find Lola Jade Harper when she was right under their noses?*'

The feed cut to a live shot of the outside of 16 Osborne Terrace, complete with police cordon, then an image of Lola's sad face flashed up on the screen. It was taken from the studio portrait of her in her shiny princess dress. The police press office must have released it.

'*So, all of us are left wondering—*'

Rachel stood up and switched off the TV.

Lindsay stared at her, aghast. No one but her ever had remote-control privileges.

'Rae, we were watching that!'

Rachel threw down the remote and stormed into the kitchen. She made a point of not discussing cases with her family, so none of them knew about her involvement in the search for Lola Jade.

'Absolutely typical!' She could hear Lindsay's strident tones, getting louder, which meant she was heading for the kitchen. 'She contributes nothing to the Christmas preparations – nothing whatsoever – then she shows up here and starts throwing her weight around, playing the big I am…'

Sure enough, Lindsay strode into the kitchen. 'Family means nothing to you, as we all know only too well.' She loaded the words with meaning. 'But for the rest of us, this is supposed to be a special time. Can't you make just a bit of effort to fit in?'

Rachel didn't answer. She knew that whatever she said would just inflame her sister more.

Lindsay opened her mouth for another rant, but before she could speak, Eileen Prince came into the kitchen clutching a glass of sherry in one hand and a holly-strewn paper napkin in the other.

'You all right, love?' She addressed her younger daughter.

'Everyone always jumps to the defence of poor little Rachel. Never mind about me!' Lindsay turned on her heel and stormed out of the kitchen.

Rachel attempted a smile for her mother. 'I'm okay. Just really, really tired.'

Eileen gave her a shrewd look. 'You're upset about that little girl, aren't you? She one of yours?'

Rachel nodded again.

'What you need is a nice mug of Horlicks, a custard cream and a night in your own bed.' She patted Rachel's behind. 'Run upstairs and get your stuff. Gordon!' Her mother stuck her head out into the hall. 'Would you call me a taxi, dear?'

Rachel came downstairs with her bags to find Lindsay standing in the hall, arms crossed, face like thunder. She was still wearing a bright green paper hat, which undermined her hauteur.

'I'm surprised at you, Mum.'

This was undoubtedly true. Eileen Prince never made a decision without Lindsay's approval, and always did what she was told while under her eldest daughter's roof.

'Your sister needs to rest,' said Eileen with uncharacteristic defiance. 'She's not the sort to ever mention it, but she's been through a trauma.'

CHAPTER THIRTY-NINE

It was there in her inbox, and yet she couldn't quite bring herself to open it.

Subject: Arrest and interview/Michelle Harper (video attached)

Rachel had spent the remainder of Christmas Day and most of Boxing Day in her childhood home, cocooned in her mother's familiar routine. They had been for a gentle amble round their local park, then come back and drunk Advocaat, reminiscing about how Rachel's father – who had died fourteen years earlier from a heart attack – loved the syrupy yellow liqueur. Then, armed with foil parcels of sliced gammon and Dundee cake, she had driven back to Bermondsey, grateful to put everything to do with Christmas behind her. Not only was there too much buying of extraneous stuff: when it came down to it, festivities based on a virgin birth seemed far too much like believing in magic.

Waiting for her amongst the heap of mail neglected for the past week had been a stiff hand-written envelope. At first glance she'd assumed it was one of those custom-made Christmas cards featuring a saccharine snap of the sender's family. But the card inside was thick, ivory and engraved.

Professor Stuart Ritchie & Ms Claire Amory
request the pleasure of your company
at a celebration of their marriage
on 25th February 2017

Stuart had attached a Post-it note that read: *Rae, would love to see you here but understand if you don't fancy it. Decree nisi just issued and absolute should be through end of January.*

Her first thought had been that he didn't hang around. A wedding a mere three weeks after his first marriage ended. But then he'd waited so many years for this divorce, why delay getting on with the rest of his life?

In the same pile of post, she'd found an official manila envelope containing the decree nisi rubber-stamped by Central London County Court. It had been shuffled to the bottom of the pile like an ace in a card trick, and left with the unopened Christmas cards and bills on her desk.

First thing this morning, itching to get back to work, she had gone for a long run, then come straight to the office without changing. The place was largely empty, but it still felt like a return to the real world. The combination of the holiday shut-down and her boycott of the news had left her feeling strangely disconnected. The only person she had heard from was Howard Davison.

Looks like I'll soon be single. See you in the gym soon? x

It would be fun to box with him, if nothing else. And perhaps now there could be something else too. Her reply was brief, but left no room for doubt.

Just try and stop me.

Now her finger hovered again over the email from Sydney.

But first, she decided, she should speak to DC Coles. Lola Jade was the most important person in this, not Michelle.

'Have you heard?' he asked, without preamble.

Her stomach lurched. 'I've no idea what you're talking about, so no.'

'Lisa Urquhart died. Apparently, despite the attempt to save her in theatre, she went into multiple organ failure and died the next day.'

'Christ.' Rachel covered her face with her hand briefly, steeling herself to ask. 'But Lola's okay?'

'She's fine. Discharged from hospital after a couple of days, and social services have found a great foster placement for her.'

'That's a relief.' She exhaled the breath she'd been holding without realising.

'We're just getting ready to make a press statement. We'll combine the news about Lisa with the release about Lola being found safe. Obviously it was best to hold off saying anything until we were sure Lola was going to make it and social services had found somewhere suitable for her to go.'

'We've done extremely well to keep the story out of the media this time,' said Rachel. 'Maybe the tabloid editors have finally got the message.'

Coles made a snorting sound. 'Doubt it. But the Christmas shutdown was definitely in our favour on that front.'

'Anyway, I phoned to thank you for your help in finding Lola Jade,' said Rachel. 'I'm going to speak to your chief constable about a commendation.'

She could almost hear him blushing down the line. 'I just did my job, ma'am.'

'Well… good work, Coles. And give my best to DS Rajavi.'

She procrastinated a few minutes longer, first fetching coffee then checking the Interpol databases, all the while trying not to look at Brickall's empty desk. Then, with a deep breath, she clicked on the footage she had been sent.

The first file was from Sydney airport CCTV. A confident, almost relaxed Michelle strode up to the passport desk, huge sunglasses on her head and make-up freshly touched up. The border official asked her to wait to one side of the desk, and Michelle barely even had a chance to turn and take in the sight of two armed policemen before they had grabbed her and handcuffed her. There was no sound on the tape, but it was clear from the snarling, contorted face that she was screaming at them. As one of them grabbed her under the elbow to drag her away, she turned her face towards him, puckered her lips and spat directly into his face.

Oh Michelle, thought Rachel as she watched it. *You stupid woman. You have no idea what's coming.*

The next file was the recording of her initial arrest interview, this time with audio. The bluff Aussie Interpol officer introduced himself as Pat Farrelly.

'So, Ms Harper, can we start by clearing up why you're travelling on a false passport? I believe Lauren Marie Hutchins is not your real name?'

Michelle completely ignored this. 'You've got absolutely no right to arrest me. None whatsoever.' She turned to the female lawyer who had been appointed to represent her, as though expecting to be backed up.

'And who is Jasmine Gabrielle Hutchins?'

'I have no idea what you're talking about.'

'Okay, then how about a child called Harry Brown?'

Michelle gave her best stony stare, flicking her hair over her shoulders.

'Jasmine Hutchins is your daughter Lola Jade, isn't she? The child you claimed was missing. She was with you all along, only you were passing her off as a little boy.'

'Like I said, I don't know what you're talking about.'

'But you did report your daughter, Lola Jade Harper, missing to the police in the UK?'

Michelle narrowed her eyes, but otherwise made no response. The lawyer leaned in and whispered something to her, which earned her a contemptuous look.

'You must be aware,' Farrelly continued in an eminently reasonable tone, 'that perverting the course of justice carries a maximum penalty of life in prison. So, with that in mind, can we talk about your decision to pretend your daughter had been abducted, while pretending she was a boy called Harry.'

'I can do whatever I want with my daughter,' hissed Michelle. 'She's mine; it's completely up to me.'

Pat Farrelly raised his eyebrows and looked down at his notes. 'I see. I also need to ask you what you know about the death of a woman called Carly Wethers.'

Michelle's eyes flickered slightly, but she resumed her outraged look. 'I don't know anyone called Carly Wethers. Never heard of her.' She leaned forward, getting into her interrogator's personal space. 'This is all just a stupid misunderstanding. I'm here on holiday, with my sister. Lisa. She arrived last night.'

There was a heavy pause. Pat Farrelly glanced at the lawyer, who gave a faint nod and coughed to clear her throat before addressing her client directly. 'Michelle, I'm afraid I have some very bad news for you. Your sister passed away. A few hours ago.'

Michelle's hand flew to her mouth.

'What are you talking about?' she said eventually, in barely more than a whisper. 'You mean she died on the plane?'

'No,' said Farrelly bluntly. 'Her husband crashed the car. They were being chased by police, who were attempting to arrest them. For assisting you.' He gave her a 'see what you did' look.

'The police!' croaked Michelle. 'The bloody police did this! I'm going to sue. When I get back to the UK, I'm going to sue the bastards for killing my sister.'

Ignoring this, Farrelly raised an eyebrow. 'Though of course their chief concern at the time was the whereabouts of your daughter. I'd say you're very lucky they found her.'

'Where's Lola Jade now? Are they bringing her out here?'

Farrelly shook his head. 'No, that's not going to happen. Your daughter's in the care of social services, where she's safe.'

Only now did Michelle crumple. She buried her face in her hands and started to cry. She'll never get it, Rachel thought sadly.

Or if she does, she'll never admit it: that her sister's death is her fault, and that she endangered her daughter's life. And when she's charged with murdering Carly, she'll plead not guilty. She'll put everyone through a gruelling trial in the hope that the jury get it wrong. Her sort always do.

She consoled herself by preparing Michelle's formal extradition. The arrest at Sydney airport had been under a provisional warrant; an emergency measure available when an offender was a flight risk. Rachel now filed the paperwork for a formal extradition order, which required input from first the CPS and then the Home Office. Then it would be the job of the force requesting the warrant to arrange for the offender to be collected and returned to the UK.

After a volley of emails and form-filling, and a couple of long phone calls to Nigel Patten, Rachel shut down her monitor, and went downstairs to see if she could secure a free patrol car.

'Hello, stranger!'

She looked up from her conversation with the reception clerk to see Giles Denton standing there, wrapped in a greatcoat and huge scarf and looking for all the world like a Celtic Heathcliff. 'Happy New Year.'

'Almost,' Rachel corrected him, aware that she was blushing again.

He flapped a large manila envelope. 'Just dropping off some reports from the guys in Victim ID.'

Her mind raced back to the mistletoe incident. She felt a craven urge to justify her behaviour. 'Giles, that night in the pub. I…'

'Oh, go on with you. It was Christmas. What else were we going to do?'

'Only I don't normally go round kissing people.'

'Good God, Rachel, nor do I. But there's nothing random about you.'

There was an unmistakable wink this time. Rachel grabbed the car keys the receptionist was holding out and turned to go.

'See you soon, I hope, Detective Inspector Prince.'

Without turning back to expose her flushed face, Rachel gave a curt wave, then hurried down to the car park and programmed the satnav for HMP High Down for what she hoped would be the last time.

'I'm being transferred,' Gavin Harper said as soon as she sat down at the visitors' table. 'To Ford Open. So, lucky you caught me.' He attempted a smile. 'But you're not here about that, are you?'

Rachel smiled. 'I wanted to talk to you before the details hit the news… You know we've found Lola Jade?'

He nodded, but seemed afraid to speak.

'It's okay: she's fine. Michelle had been hiding her, but she's not been hurt.'

'*Michelle?*' He spat her name. 'I knew it. I fucking knew she was trying to set me up. This had her written all over it. Where was she? What did that bitch do with her?'

'She moved her to another house in Eastwell and made her look like a little boy.'

'What, why? The woman's insane.'

Rachel inclined her head without comment.

'And all this was to take her from me? How long was she going to keep that up?'

'She was planning to take Lola Jade to Australia and start a new life with her there. That's where Michelle is now: in custody.'

Gavin was shaking his head in disbelief.

'There's a lot more to the story, but I just wanted to tell you before you heard it from somewhere else.'

'So where's Lola now?'

'She's in foster care.'

'Can't she go to Andy and his wife? Surely she'd be better off with family?'

'I don't know. But I'll look into it, I promise.'

Gavin rubbed his fingers on his forehead. 'Will I get her back? When I'm out?'

Rachel sighed. 'It's too soon to say for sure. But there's a chance.' She leaned in and squeezed his arm briefly. 'Assuming you keep out of trouble.'

'Oh, I will,' he said earnestly. 'I've got something to aim for now.' As Rachel stood up to go, he added. 'There's something I've been wanting to show you. I don't have my phone with me, but look on my Instagram for the video I posted in September last year. That will help you understand.'

CHAPTER FORTY

Merry Christmas from Worthing! trumpeted the lights on the seafront.

The town did not feel merry in the slightest, with a gunmetal sky, clammy sea mist and streets devoid of any activity bar SALE signs in the shop windows. It was probably quite nice in high summer, Rachel thought, trudging from West Worthing station in the direction of Goring-by-Sea. She stopped at a neat semi-detached brick bungalow and rang the doorbell.

'What the fuck are you doing here?' Brickall stood on the doorstep wearing jeans and a sweater with a reindeer on the front.

'I thought we ought to have a proper chat.'

'How did you find me? Oh, wait, don't tell me you breached the Data Protection Act and found my grandmother's address on the PNC. Because that would be insanely fucking hypocritical, in the circumstances.'

'Actually, I looked in the phone directory.'

Brickall grinned. 'How very old-school of you, Prince.'

'For our elderly population, the phone book is still very much a thing. And there are only three Brickalls in the Worthing directory. I reckoned my best bet was Edna Brickall, rather than Percy or Arthur.'

'Hold on a sec.' Brickall threw on a ski jacket and stuck his head round one of the doors in the hallway. 'Just popping out, Nana.'

'Where are we going?' Rachel enquired.

'To get some sea air. That's just about all there is to do in Worthing.'

They walked together down to the Marine Parade, stopping to buy coffee, and a cake for Brickall, then found a bench on the seafront. Seagulls swooped around them in a circle, waiting for cake crumbs, and the sea fret made their faces damp.

'How was your Christmas?' Rachel asked.

He shrugged. 'Quiet. Yours?'

'Same. I'm not a big fan.'

Brickall stared out at the grey horizon. 'I fucking hate Christmas.'

There was something in his tone that made Rachel turn and look at him. 'Why's that?'

'Because that's when Paul died. My brother.' He blinked rapidly, and Rachel could tell from his expression that he was furious with himself for this lapse into emotion. She rested a gloved hand briefly on his wrist. 'What happened to him?'

'He was killed in a car crash. By a drunk driver.'

'Shit, Mark; I'm so sorry.'

He jutted his chin. 'That's what made me want a career in the police. So I could lock up scum like that.' He gave a bitter laugh. 'My career in the police... yeah, right. Look how that worked out.'

'Actually...' Rachel swatted away a seagull and turned to face him. 'That's one of the reasons I'm here. I spoke to Patten yesterday, and he told me he's heard back from the PCC. There's still going to be a disciplinary hearing, and it will go on your record, but he's had unofficial word that it's going to be a six-month suspension only. A chunk of which you've already served.'

'Thank fuck for that.'

Rachel's tone became stern. 'I hope you realise how lucky you've been. If things had gone badly, you could have been looking at a four-year stretch. Apparently Amber Crowley's second statement – saying it was all a misunderstanding, and that she'd encouraged you – had a lot to do with it.'

Brickall gave her shoulder a brief squeeze. 'And I have you to thank for that. You're not such a loser after all, Prince. Or should I say, Mrs Ritchie.'

She shook her head. 'Not any more. I'm divorced: it's official.'

'London's male population has got to be running scared at the news.'

She thumped his arm. 'Just hurry up and get back to work, because right now you're about as much use as a vibrator in a mortuary.'

Brickall threw the remains of his cake to the gulls, pulled out his phone and checked the screen. 'Speaking of locking up criminal scum: news update about Lola Jade also says Lisa Urquhart's carked it. Nice one, Michelle: you probably killed your son, almost killed your daughter and now you've indirectly killed your sister.' He looked up at Rachel. 'Any news on what will happen to the kid?'

'In foster care for now, but Gavin Harper could be released early on a supervision order, so all being well, she'll be able to live with her dad before too long.'

Brickall whistled, shaking his head. 'All that absolute shit Michelle put everyone through; all that deceit and destruction…'

'And death. Don't forget about poor TruthTella.'

'… and death: all to avoid Gavin taking their daughter. And it looks like he'll end up with her anyway.'

'Oh, that reminds me. I visited Gavin and he wanted me to look at something online…' Rachel pulled out her phone and scrolled through endless posts until she found the video clip for 13 September 2015. Lola's sixth birthday. She held it up so that Brickall could watch too, and pressed play.

Gavin was filming a party held by his own family: Terry Harper, the Ingrams and the Whittiers were visible, but no Michelle. A cake with six lit candles had pride of place, surrounded by swags of sugar-pink balloons. 'Where is she? Where's the birthday girl?' teased Gavin from behind the camera. Lola Jade came into shot, and Rachel and Brickall heard her speaking for the first time. After all these months, she finally had a voice.

'Daddeeeeee!' She launched herself into her father's arms, sending the phone flying from his hand, and capturing a few seconds of carpet. Gavin refocused it on her face, lit up with a joyous smile. She had never looked like that in any of Michelle's prized pictures. 'You having a nice party, sweetheart?'

Lola Jade nodded vigorously. 'It's the best. Cus you're the best daddy in the whole wide world!' She flung her arms out wide and the clip ended with a freeze frame of the little girl's beaming face.

'I think the kid's going to be all right, don't you?' asked Brickall.

Rachel nodded, standing up and extending her hand to pull Brickall to his feet. They walked arm in arm along West Parade, the icy drizzle at their backs.

'I'd better head back to London. Not long before I have to pack my bags and leave the country again.'

'Good old "Call me air miles" Prince… Where to this time?'

'Sydney.'

He stopped in his tracks. 'You're kidding.'

She shook her head. 'Nope. We've put in the extradition request for Michelle Harper, and Patten wants me to go.'

'That's one hell of a lot of air miles. But also twenty-plus hours on a plane handcuffed to the Mother of the Year. Or "the most hated woman in Britain", as the tabloids are calling her.'

She grimaced. 'I don't want to go. At all.'

'You could have got out of it. Found someone else.'

'Possibly. But I need to see it through. Find my way to the very end of the maze.'

'Belt and braces, DI Prince.'

She reached for his hand, and squeezed it. 'Exactly, Detective Sergeant.'

A LETTER FROM ALISON

I want to say a huge thank you for choosing to read *Lola is Missing*. If you enjoyed reading and would like to keep up-to-date with all my latest releases, just sign up at the following link. Your email address will never be shared and you can unsubscribe at any time.

www.bookouture.com/alison-james

I had enormous fun creating and writing the character of Detective Rachel Prince, I do hope you continue to follow her story. There is lots more in store for Rachel - and I want you to be gripped by her future investigations just as much as this one!

If you loved *Lola is Missing*, I would be very grateful if you could write a review. I'd love to hear what you liked most about the story, as it makes such a difference helping new readers to discover one of my books for the first time.

I'm always pleased to hear from readers – so do say hello on my Facebook page, through Twitter, Goodreads or my website.

Thanks,
Alison James

 @AlisonJbooks

ACKNOWLEDGEMENTS ·

With huge thanks to the wonderful Meg Sanders, whose advice and encouragement helped this book become a reality.